T0380244

BLOODTRAIL

BLOODTRAIL

BOOK ONE

JAN P LEONARDY

iUniverse®

BLOODTRAIL
BOOK ONE

iUniverse books may be ordered through booksellers or by contacting:

iUniverse
1663 Liberty Drive
Bloomington, IN 47403
www.iuniverse.com
844-349-9409

ISBN: 978-1-6632-6628-6 (sc)
ISBN: 978-1-6632-6629-3 (e)

Library of Congress Control Number: 2024917743

Print information available on the last page.

iUniverse rev. date: 09/09/2024

CHAPTER ONE

JAKOOL'S FIRST HUNT

Remember what you have learned Jakool! I thought as I tightened my grip on my spear in response to a signal from Kiraat the hunt leader. He turned and looked at us saying "Be very cautious! If I yell run! You run!" I watched with a sense of excitement tinged with fear as the lead hunters disappeared into the many trees working further up in search of deer or other game.

We had assumed the formation used to trap and kill game when we stopped at the beginning of the many tall trees. We formed into the shape of two fingers extended from a hand. My young brothers and I made the place where they came together, while the experienced hunters formed the fingers. A cold wind blew as the snow fell around us, adding to the layer on the bushes and trees. We could only see as far as Kiraat, positioned at the far end of the left finger waiting to give the signal that game was approaching. It was some time before he made a hand gesture to be ready. I could hear something coming and it was coming fast! Gripping my spear with both hands I made ready to make a killing thrust if one came within reach of me, but I was not prepared for what happened next! Suddenly a scream came from one of the hunters ahead followed by more screams and yells, causing Kiraat to run ahead to see why they were screaming!

A large black, Rough Fur appeared running straight at him with a bloody maw! He immediately yelled, "Run!" As he faced it with his spear ready! Surprise and fear kept me and many of my young brothers frozen! Suddenly another, followed by another, appeared with blood around their maws and we ran! We ran in every direction away from the charging Rough Furs as the adults attacked them to give us time to get away! The sounds of snarls and roars mixed with the sounds of our hunter's screams and yells, followed us as we fled.

I went to the side and up instead of down, my heart pounding in my chest, breathing hard and fast! I leaped over bushes, and ran around boulders dodging low-hanging tree branches as I ran! I heard a snarl to my right and dodged just in time as one leaped from a copse of small trees to attack! I managed to keep my feet as it missed its charge taking it past me! I ran as hard as I could looking for any kind of cover knowing I could not outrun it. I saw a small hole in a hillside as I passed a pile of boulders and turned quickly to go towards it and stumbled! Looking behind me I saw it approaching the pile of boulders as I regained my footing. As I thought *I was not going to make it!* the snow on top of the boulders exploded and something leaped high into the air landing on the back of the beast! I heard a snarling yell that sounded like 'Rrruun!', but I was already up and running!

I ran up the steep slope until I reached the hole and frantically clawed the dirt, snow, and rocks away then struggled in. I crawled back two man lengths then sat there curled up to fit in the small space. The smell told me it was probably a deserted red tail den. The sounds of the two creatures fighting were all I heard over the sound of my heart beating rapidly! I silently prayed *Oh Spirits of the Sky and the Rock Fingers! Keep me and my brothers safe!*

I stayed in the den until there were no sounds of fighting outside. Crawling to the opening, I quickly looked outside and then jerked back in case one of them was lying in wait to ambush me! When no attack came, I grabbed my spear and left the burrow quickly, ready for an attack. There was blood on the covering of snow under the trees and signs of a struggle! Shaking my head thinking *What was it? Did I hear it yell 'Rrruun!'? Probably my fear talking!* I went to look for anyone who survived the attack. I started down towards the place where we were attacked looking for signs of either Rough Furs, my brothers, or the strange creature I had only glimpsed as it leaped to attack the 'Rough Fur!

Why? I thought again as I followed a set of Rough Fur tracks down the side of the hill. I saw traces of blood and fur on the trail and the bushes as I followed them to a dip in the land. I reached a thicket of bushes and pushing them aside I saw young Rankoo's body, ripped by the Rough Furs claws and now dead. *I cannot save him, he is dead. But I can send him to the Sky Spirits!* I placed my hands over Rankoo's head and heart saying the ancient words *Mighty spirits that move the sun and light the pale Goddess of the night! Please accept the humble spirit of my brother Rankoo into your domain!* I stood up and left him in the bushes for the scavengers as we did not place any special significance on the bodies of our dead... then.

I had not gone far when I saw more of the tracks that I did not recognize! *Maybe they are from the strange creature! Since it attacked one of the Rough Fur maybe it came further down the trail to attack the others?* I thought following the tracks as they left the trail and went into a deep gully. Blood splatters on the ground and some bushes led the way as I climbed down. Broken branches and damaged ground ended in a two-man height drop into a hidden ravine you couldn't see because of the thick brush and trees hiding it.

A stream ran down the ravine with fresh tracks in the mud of the banks. I stopped and measured them *One hand high, two hands across, and very shallow.* The next set of tracks was Rough Fur! Its tracks were longer and deeper, but not wider, and walked over tracks I recognized as one of the young tribesmen!

Following the tracks upstream, I saw tracks of Deer, Red Tails, Rough Fur, and the strange creature on top of them! I soon saw a cave at the near end of the ravine and approached it sniffing the air, smelling the water, the trees, bushes, and….*Death! Something or someone was dead!* I hesitated as I didn't want to die trying to find one of my brethren in there! *If he is in there he is surely dead!* I thought debating what to do. A noise coming from the cave caused me to hide behind some thick berry bushes that grew close to the edge of the stream. I watched as a Rough Fur came out of the cave moving slowly towards the stream. Several spears were sticking out of its fur and I saw deep claw marks that had ripped through the fur to its flesh! *The strange creature attacked it too!* I realized as it limped over to the water and bent its head to drink. I saw streaks of red float away from its muzzle as it drank slowly. I thought about creeping up from behind and killing it for what it had done to my brothers! But even with its wounds, if I didn't kill it with one spear thrust, I would be dead! A wounded beast is the most dangerous animal you can face!

Suddenly it gave several loud coughs that spewed blood from its muzzle and slowly fell over! I waited to see if it got back up or moved, but it just lay there! I got up the courage to go into the cave and look. What I saw sent me reeling back out heaving up what was in my stomach! I stumbled to the stream and washed the foul taste out of my mouth. Nothing would remove the sight of Denack, torn apart and fed on in that cave! No matter how hard I tried, I could not make myself go back into that cave to say the prayer to the Sky Spirits for him! I felt hot tears from my grief and anger over finding two of my brothers dead! I had not thought about the others during my frantic run from the attack by the Rough Furs and hiding from them. Now I had found two of them dead!

Have any survived the Rough Furs hunting them in the many trees? I wondered as I looked for more tracks but only found more of the ones from the strange creature again! These led away from the cave towards the other end of the ravine, but I retraced my steps back to the site of the attack following my training to return. I climbed out of the ravine and was soon back on the game trail leading downhill. I walked slowly looking for any signs of my brethren, alive or dead. It was getting late by the time I reached the place.

I could see that the falling snow was quickly covering the tracks, bloodstains, and the bodies of two of the adult hunters and a Rough Fur carcass. *It has not been butchered!* I saw when I got closer. I assumed they were still out looking for us as the light started to fade. I turned to look around for any shelter from the snow and make camp for the night to wait for their return. I ended up back at the burrow I hid in earlier, after deciding it was the safest place. I ate some dried food and drank melted snow from my cupped hands. Tired and hurting with the pain of losing some of my tribe I wrapped in my furs and quickly fell asleep. But the mystery of a creature that attacked a Rough Fur for me returned to me in my dreams.

The next morning I returned to the spot of the attack and looked for tracks or any sign that the hunters had returned. The fresh snow had covered up everything! I hung my head in despair thinking *They must have believed us dead and left! What do I do? I am not sure I can find my way home. I don't remember the way.* Then I thought *Here is one set of tracks I can follow! The strange beast that attacked the rough fur and saved me!* I realized. I decided I was going to follow the creature's tracks and see if I could find it. I wanted to understand why it had helped me. Retracing my steps to the ravine I found fresh tracks. *It must have come back here.* I thought knowing that the tracks from yesterday were all buried under the new snow. Following the fresh tracks along the stream thinking as I walked about them. *I was taught that all hunters try to hide their tracks from their game and other hunters. Why is this one leaving tracks? it knows they be can followed.* I couldn't stop thinking about this, along with fighting the Rough Fur so I could escape! The tracks led up a steep slope that reached the ravine's end. A waterfall was the source of the stream in the ravine and looking up I saw a narrow trail leading beside it and out of the ravine. In the soft wet dirt, I saw a partial footprint. *The same* I thought. I followed the trail as it wound up and across until it reached the top of the waterfall.

The trail ran alongside the stream leading up into the Fingers Of Rock That Touched The Sky. I could feel the bitter wind blowing harder here than in the many trees as I climbed higher. A thick snow lay on top of everything with more falling making it difficult to follow the tracks as they filled with the fresh snow.

I was clutching my hide around me as the wind blew harder trying to blow me off the trail which was now a narrow path that wound its way across a rock face slowly going higher. Soon the trees and bushes ended as I passed too high for them to live. Dark gray rocks, boulders, blinding white snow, and glittering blue ice were everywhere now, as the climb got more difficult, I began to wonder if I was going to survive as I climbed. A particularly strong gust of wind caused me to lose my footing! I felt my foot slip and my body slide down, but I fell towards the rock face! I shuddered at the close call I'd had! I managed to continue until I was standing on a wider trail at the top of the rock face.

Looking down the path I'd taken, I could see the land spread out below me! The hills, the stream winding its way through them as it climbed down until it disappeared into the many tall trees. The many tall trees far below were now covered in a coat of white, looking peaceful somehow. I could even make out the far edge of it and some of the long, never-ending green grass. I thought I saw a dark smudge on the other side of them! *That might be the hills of my home* I thought as I looked for any signs of the hunting party in the tall, green grass, but it was too far away to make out details.

I went more slowly as I worked my way up, stopping occasionally to allow my breathing to catch up. The sun was just clearing the top of the Finger Tips, when I came to a bend in the trail. The clouds were flying from over the fingertips to hide the sun making it colder. I worried that soon I would be in the clouds following the tracks as they thickened and hid the fingertips! I was shivering from the cold and the strong gusts of wind that tried to throw me off of the rock and realized *I had to find shelter or die here!* as I could no longer feel my fingers or toes!

I followed the trail several man-lengths around a bend and noticed a small cave mouth behind some boulders that had fallen onto the trail. *Thank you Gods of the Sky and Fingers of Rock!* I cried out as I stooped down to enter it. I had to stay bent over to get inside and saw it only went back a few man-lengths. As I went forward I started to warm up, as I was no longer in the wind outside.

While crouching there in the cave trying to decide what to do a slight movement caught my eye. I whirled towards it with my spear ready to fend off an attack, only to see a Bharal jumping up from behind the boulders and leaping up the trail towards me! *Food! Warmth!* I thought as I quickly readied my spear.

I heard it approach the entrance, saw its head then its body appear. I sprang forward and struck! It fell over dead with my spear in its heart! I fell to my knees and gave thanks to the Sky Spirits for sending me the Bharal to save my life!

I dragged the heavy animal back into the cave to skin and butcher. I needed the hide to survive the cold of night this high up. I spent the next few hours scraping the flesh from the inside of the hide. Once I was finished, I wrapped the new hide around me and went to sleep.

Sunlight streaming into the cave entrance woke me. I got up and took the hide to make a holder to carry the meat I had butchered. I ran hide strips through the leg holes and tied them to my extra spear, to make a large hide holder to carry the meat. I swung it over my shoulder and followed the ledge up towards the fingertip. There was more snow and ice so I had to go carefully as the ledge slowly became a narrow trail. I wound my way up and across for several hours until I came to a place where large boulders completely blocked the now very narrow trail!

I looked but didn't find any way to get around them. I sighed as I went to where the largest boulder touched the rock face of the finger, to get some shelter from the wind and snow. I was not prepared to have my foot suddenly slip down a hole all the way up my leg! The sudden fall and pain to my man parts shocked me for a minute. When I could stand the pain I started digging out the snow around my leg and found that the hole was big enough for me to go through and carefully used my spear to probe it. The spear went down its entire length before touching the stone. I went down and landed on a pile of snow. Looking around I saw that I was in a large tunnel hidden by the boulders. I still had enough light coming in through the hole to see my way, so I followed it.

I soon felt warmer as I continued deeper into the tunnel until it opened up into a cave. The air was changing too as I could smell it getting wetter and much warmer! I could see strange rock fingers that reached down from the ceiling and up from the floor! I had never seen anything like them! I approached one and saw that it was much wider at the base and came to a point at the top. I realized there was a glow coming from some of these strange rock fingers, that gave enough light to see! I wondered what could make a blue or green light come from rock, or how they came to be as I stood and looked in wonder at them.

I shook my head and then focused on the shimmer of light reflected on the ceiling of the cave, showing water was further inside. I found a shallow trail worn into the stone floor of the cave which led me to a large 'Good Water'! The water had a blue glow to it also! *I have shelter, fresh water, and food!* I thought as I went to the water's edge. I put down my spear and hide carrier to take mouthfuls of the clear cold water! Once I had satisfied my thirst I searched for any wood to make a fire. Close to the shore of the Good Water, I found some wood piled by a ring of stones. *Someone has been here* I thought as I studied the remains of a fire in the ring. I held out my hands over the ashes and embers feeling warmth!.

Using my knife I cut a small pile of bark and wood shavings from a piece of wood. I carefully brushed away the ashes on top of the embers and put a small amount on them. I blew gently on the exposed embers and suddenly the shavings caught fire! I fed it the rest of the shavings then the branches careful to not smother it. Soon I had a small fire burning and slowly added more wood until it was a good size to cook the meat.

Cutting some thin strips from the larger piece I put them on the end of my spear and into the fire. Soon I was eating them while the large pieces of meat cooked slowly on the fire. My body felt the fatigue of the last few suns, so I rolled up in my new fur and went to sleep.

While asleep I had a very strange dream in this place. The lake was glowing with a blueish light while the strange rock pillars glowed with green. There was a shadowy figure of an animal pacing along the lake, occasionally stopping to drink. It slowly approached until I could see it in the blue and green light of the cave. It was like the magnificent creature we called the 'Great Striped One', but smaller and with spots and circles of colors on its white fur instead of stripes.

Its paws were wide, its ears close to its head, and had a smaller muzzle and nose than the great striped spirit. Its piercing blue eyes stared right at me, making me think *It can see me,* as it padded silently towards me. It stopped in front of me and sniffed. I stood still as it sniffed me again, then sat back on its hind legs and made a chuffing sound. I didn't know what it meant or what to do. It yawned showing its sharp, stained teeth, then stood back up and walked back the way it had come! *A Great Spirit of this place I* thought as it just vanished as I watched. I wondered what it meant as I heard the dripping of water in the cave, and the sounds of water running over rocks, somewhere deep in the cave.

Suddenly I was outside in the sunlight, standing on the trail at the boulders. I saw the Great Spirit again, but this time it was sunning itself on top of the large boulder. I turned at a sound and saw something far down the trail. I watched as it slowly climbed up the trail until the beast took notice of it, backed up against the rock face, and then lay down facing the trail watching! First, a Tahr, or mountain goat, came into view from around a bend, then the hunter! I watched as a man taller and heavier than me wrapped in many thick furs with a large spear followed the tracks of the Tahr.

As it reached the boulder it lightly leaped up the smaller boulders until it jumped up to the top. It jumped down so quickly it didn't see the beast; hidden by its marked fur, only a spear length away, lying down flat in the snow! I turned to watch the man slowly approach the spot and stop to try and figure out how to get around it. Just as I had found, he couldn't find any way to do this! He went to the edge looking for any way to get around, then turned back towards the rock face. It was then the beast decided to make its presence known! It jumped down onto the trail behind the man. The man spun around in surprise, stepped back then slipped on the snow and ice! He fell heavily and started to slip to the edge! He seemed unable to stop himself when the beast suddenly leaped forward, reached out with a paw, and snagged the man's furs!

The man yelled as it slowly pulled him back from the edge until he lay on the trail in front of its paws! Just as it had done to me in the cave earlier in my dream, it bent its head down and sniffed the man's face! The man yelled in surprise, then started making loud noises and faces at it! The beast stopped sniffing and looked at him seemingly puzzled by the sounds and the faces. The man tried to stand up but the animal put its large front paws on his chest and pushed him back down! I watched as it suddenly bent down and licked the man's face! He was as shocked as I was, and started to make the faces and noises again! The animal sat back and just watched his face until the man stopped and looked back at it. The animal suddenly bent down and rubbed its muzzle against his face! He stayed still and didn't move or make faces or noises while it did this afraid it would bite him! When it raised its head up and looked down at him, he slowly reached up with his hands and started rubbing the sides of its face!

I watched in fascination as it made low rumbling noises as it leaned into his hands, so he could reach its face more easily. Soon he was making noises and faces again while rubbing its face! After a few minutes, he slowly tried to get up and the animal stepped back to let him! The man spoke to the animal and it seemed to understand him! *It must be one of the Great Spirits of the Fingers of Rock that touch the Sky! That is what attacked the Rough Fur! It saved him and one saved me* I thought as the man turned and looked again at the boulder blocking the trail. As if it understood, the animal went over to where the boulder met the rock face.

The man watched as it dug some snow out of the way and then disappeared down a hole! With a grunt of surprise, the man came over and looked down to see the Great Rock Spirit looking up at him! He lowered himself down into the hole and disappeared with the animal. The dream ended with me wondering *what did it mean?*

When I woke up my fire had burned down to only a few embers. I coaxed them back to flames and fed all the wood to it. I ate some of the meat that had been cooked while I slept then wrapped the rest in the fur. I drank deeply from the water and left the fire pit to follow the faint shallow trail deep into the cave. It seemed impossible that such a large place existed here! Many of the rock fingers that held up the roof were twisted into strange shapes now as I drew closer to the very back of the cave. The sound of falling water had gotten louder as I went and now I could see the source of the sound. A river burst from the cave wall above the great water and fell several man lengths into it making the sound. As I drew near the end of the 'Good Water' the ceiling suddenly came to meet me and I found another small dark opening where the ceiling, wall, and floor met. I crawled through and was in another low tunnel that I had to stay bent over to go through. It was short and opened up into another cave! This one was much smaller and I stopped at the entrance as I could smell something familiar. It took a few seconds for me to recognize it.

When I did, I started looking around the inside of the cave for the creature I had followed here. There was a little light coming from a fire ring that had burned down to embers. In the dim light, I saw a figure curled up on a raised ledge of rock in front of me! As I stared; trying to make out its form, it stood up on two legs and slowly walked towards me! As it got closer I gasped in surprise! I thought I was following an animal but this was no animal I'd ever seen or heard described! It looked like me but had thick, white fur; with markings like the Great Rock Spirit, covering its body! Its blue eyes were further apart in its head than mine, had a muzzle and a long thick fluffy tail! I drew in a breath as I heard it make a rumbling sound then stretch its arms over its head and turn slowly in front of me showing that it was female! I felt a wave of arousal and desire as she walked over until she stood in front of me put her arms around my neck and said "Ooh-man?" Then pointed at my face with a hand that was wider with shorter fingers than mine. Her ears were very close to her skull and were covered in thick fur. Her face looked like both the Great Rock Spirit and my people.

She was taller than me by a hand's length I realized, as I looked at her body and saw breasts under her chest fur. I was feeling an intense desire to get closer to her and feel her fur when I realized I had not answered her question! I replied "Human named Jakool" and pointed at myself. She smiled and put her cheek against mine and said "Mearoo", as she pulled me close to her. I felt myself responding to the warmth of her fur and the contact with her body, as she continued to hold me close! She started to nuzzle my face and then my neck. I felt lightheaded and stirred in my male parts, and then she let go of my body.

She took my hand and led me to the raised rock ledge at the back of the cave where I saw a pile of furs before she pulled me down onto them. I was having trouble trying to ask her the questions that had caused me to track her here. "Did you attack the Rough Fur that was chasing me"? I managed to ask her as she started to pull my furs off of me! "Yess" she replied as she got my furs off leaving me in my loincloth! I was now feeling a great need to mate since she had gotten close to me! Suddenly I felt her fingers in my loincloth, undoing the knot that held it! "What? What are doing?" I managed to ask as she got it off! "I want to mate with you," She said as she pulled me tightly to her body making it impossible for me to think! My desire was so inflamed that I felt myself grabbing her breasts as she took me into her body before I could say or do anything else! I was panting with the excitement from the burning need in myself and her! I felt my seed rising up in me and knew I would spill it in her! I felt her body urging me on and I felt myself convulse and jerk as my seed shot deep into her waiting body! I must have lost consciousness for a short time! After all it was my first mating!

I woke to find myself still in Mearoo's embrace and connected to her body. "Awake mate?" She asked me as she lazily stroked the skin on my chest. "No fur. Feels so different, so smooth!" She said as she continued to play with my skin. I found that I enjoyed the feel of her furry hands and fingers rubbing me all over! Soon I was returning her rubs, rubbing her chest, her face, and her body with my hands feeling, the firmness of her breasts, the softness of her facial fur, and the feel of her body against mine. She smiled as I played with hers and she played with mine. We were getting to know each other's bodies and what we responded to. I soon felt my body ready to mate with her again! I started to try and enter her, but she stopped me and then quickly got up on all four of her limbs arching her rear up at me! I knew this was how many of our women preferred to be taken by a man, so I grabbed her by her hips and pushed into her body! She made meowing noises as we mated again and climaxed with each other!

I fell on top of her and she rolled me over pulling me close to her and we touched each other with gentle strokes for a while. I became aware I was hungry and thirsty, so I asked her "Are you hungry?" She growled out "Yes! Mating makes me hungry and thirsty!"

I laughed as I replied, "Me too!" I reached for the large fur carrier and pulled out a big piece of the cooked meat. I took my knife cut it in two and handed her half. We ate the meat and then I asked her "Do we have to go to the water in the cave to slake our thirst?" She made a chuffing sound and then got up and said "Come with me."

She went towards the outer cave but stopped at an opening in one wall that I had missed before. She reached into it and brought out a large container that was round in shape, wide at the bottom, and narrow at the open top. She held it to her mouth and drank from it. She handed it to me and I was surprised by its heavy weight! I looked at the shiny surface and knew it was not made of any stone or wood, but something I had never seen! I held it to my mouth and tasted cold water as I drank my fill, then handed it back to her. She placed it back in the opening and then turned to face me.

I asked, "Where do you leave your droppings?" She took my hand and led me back to the larger cave and pointed at something I had not noticed before. Where the end of the water met the back of the cave, there was a small stream that ran from it and then under the wall. "There". She went over and squatted; the same as I did when leaving droppings, and I understood. After we had both relieved ourselves we returned to the warmth of the inner cave and the furs.

I finally got answers to some of my many questions about her and her people! My first question was "Why? Why did you save me?" She looked at me with her beautiful blue eyes and said "You were in great danger. I could not stay hidden and watch you die." I wondered why and asked, "Why could you not let me die?" I watched as she slowly got up and then said "Come. I will show you." She took my hand as I stood up and led me over to the fire pit, where a small fire was burning. She took several pieces of wood and added them to the fire.

Soon the fire was burning brightly and she led me to the back wall of the cave. She pointed and said, "Here is why." I looked at the wall and saw figures and symbols. I was surprised to see images that looked like a man and the Great Rock Spirit. She pointed at the man and said: "He was the First!" I was puzzled and said "First? What do you mean First?" She then pointed at the figure of the great rock spirit and said "She was the other First. The first of my kind to mate with an Ooh-man!" I looked at her, then at the two images carved and painted on the cave wall. How? How can this be possible?" I asked her stunned that she was telling me that somehow a man mated with the animal I now called 'The Great Rock Spirit'! She pointed at the next group of pictures under the first two. I saw pictures that showed what looked like small rock spirits just below. The next looked a little different. I got closer to see it better, to try and figure out what looked different.

Mearoo pointed at the face with one paw and said "Look at the faces. The muzzle is smaller, the ears bigger and the eyes are closer." Looking very close I saw she was right. "But that doesn't explain how she became with cubs, or children, from mating with a man. "Mearoo smiled and said, "I will tell the story to you as it was told to me." I watched her face and saw the red flames of the fire mirrored by her eyes as she began to tell me the incredible story of how her people were created!

CHAPTER TWO

MEAROO'S STORY

She pointed at the first figure of the rock spirit and started the story. "We call ourselves Snow-Leapers. This is because we can make quick, high jumps from hiding to ambush our prey. We can also travel up and down these high places easily by jumping and leaping from one place to another." She showed me her paws and then unsheathed her claws. They stuck out at least half a finger length and were curved at the tip. "These allow me to grab not only my prey but to climb up trees, snow, ice, and rock. My fur and my tail help to keep me warm in the cold here. We don't mate like Ooh-mans do. The female Snow-Leaper only mates when she is in her heat."What does 'in her heat' mean?" I asked confused. "It means that they become able to have cubs. It only happens in the early cold season. During the time it takes the Pale Goddess to show her full face twice, she must mate to have cubs." Please keep telling your story and I will try to understand." I said hoping that my hearing the entire story would help me to understand it.

Mearoo continued "They go out and travel into territory claimed by a male snow-leaper. They will leave their water and droppings on a trail back to the edge of their territory. The male snow leapers will smell this and know it is a female ready to mate. He will follow her trail until he finds her and mates with her." While this was interesting, it didn't answer the first question of "how"? Instead of asking I looked at the incredible symbols and pictures on the cave walls. Everywhere I looked I saw images, symbols, and painted walls. I had not noticed it before when I first arrived because of the dim light and Mearoo having all of my attention! Now I realized I was looking at the history of Mearoo's people on the walls, just as my people had done!

"The First snow-leaper had mated with a male snow-leaper shortly before she met the first human. She had just returned from that mating; and was sunning herself in one of her favorite places, that looks over the trail to this cave. She saw the human tracking an animal and watched as he got to the great rock that blocked the path. He could not find a way around it but the animal simply jumped up and over it.

I suddenly remembered my dream in the large cavern! I gasped as I said, "I dreamed I saw them!" Mearoo stopped in surprise saying "Dream? You had a dream of the First?" I replied "I think so. It was when I first arrived in the large cave there", I said pointing at the tunnel that connected to it. "I was very tired after following your tracks and then killing the Tahr. I first saw her in the large cave with the large water. She was pacing back and forth. She came over to where I was still lying in my sleep fur and sniffed me! She acted as if she could see and smell me! Then I saw her on top of the great rock as you say! She was sunning herself when a man wearing heavy furs came up the trail. He looked bigger and heavier than me. More like some of the others we have in our tribe that were here before my people."

Mearoo looked puzzled as she asked "What does it mean when you say 'before'? I do not understand this word." I stopped to think of a different way to explain. Slowly I said "It is this way Mearoo. A long time ago my people were just one tribe made up of one kind of people. We looked the same for the most part. But as time passed other tribes came to our home that were different. From their stories, we knew if they were in the land before us, at the same time as us, or after us. Mearoo nodded and said, "Like how we know that snow-leapers were here before you Ooh-mans?"

I nodded saying "Yes! Just like that! They mated with each other and the children looked different. Mearoo nodded her understanding again and said "They looked like both the father and the mother." I agreed with her saying "Yes but also some parts like one tribe, other parts the other tribe. Mearoo nodded and said "It was the same for the first. She had already mated with a snow-leaper when she met the Ooh-man. He was trying to find a way around the great rock. She was watching him and decided to jump down from the rock and show herself to him. Here! Let me show you!"

Mearoo pointed at symbols below the pictures of the first and said "Here in the first's record, it says he came to believe that she liked his smell and the faces he made when she saved him from falling off the trail." I said excitedly "Just like my dream!" She stopped with a strange expression on her face as she looked at me. "Mearoo! Let me tell you my dream!" I said excitedly.

"According to the Elders of my tribe, when you have a dream or vision of something that you then find out to be true, it is a true seeing dream! My dream is a true dream!" I said to her, as I remembered my dream! I then realized there was more of it than I first remembered when I woke up from it.

Mearoo looked surprised after hearing my dream and said "This dream is what we know to be the meeting of the First. It is written here in this cave! The cave where they mated, raised cubs, and lived for her entire life. When she died, he stayed here and put their story on the walls, so no one would forget. No outsider has ever been here and no one outside of our tribe knows this story! You should not know this.

How is this possible? Have you been sent here to me by Yuma Samang?" She said softly as if to herself. "Yuma Samang?" I said repeating the strange name. She turned back towards the wall saying "I must show you the rest of our story for you to understand who that is!" I was eager to hear her tell it so I could understand my dream and her people! "See here? The faces and bodies change only a little at first. But both knew they were different. He says that even the first cubs were somehow smarter, and more willing to stay together after the time when the mother usually sends the cubs away. "When does this happen?" I asked. Mearoo pointed at strange symbols below the first pictures of cubs and said "Three seasons." I was startled and asked, "They could count seasons?" Mearoo said "He could. She didn't need to. She had the knowledge of her kind that the cubs received from her. He says they were smarter and able to learn things from him, not just from her."

I listened and watched as Mearoo told the story of not only the first but their cubs and their cubs, cubs! I learned that they stayed together mating each season in the same manner as the first time. "The female would go out in search of a male. Once she had mated with one she would return to him and they would mate. After her death, he spent all his time in the cave mourning her and making this record. Because the cubs had changed, they would sometimes come to visit him. One sun; in the cold season, one of the daughters of their last mating, came back not to visit; as she had done before, but to mate with and stay with him. She did not need to mate with another snow leaper first!

This was the first time this was possible. So from her came another group of cubs that had more features from his human side." Mearoo then pointed to the next group of symbols and figures. "The first made these symbols here, showing how many cubs were born from which mother and how many were male or female. He ended up mating with several of these until his death. We have counted these symbols that show the number of cubs and the mating's.

I stared at the symbols in disbelief that she pointed at while explaining the numbers. "Mearoo? The first could count large numbers? Higher than the fingers on his two hands?" It was Mearoo's turn to be surprised. "It is not hard. See let me show you!" I shook my head saying "I know how. But I also know that the ones that came before us could not! At least not the ones that our tribe describes in our stories!" Mearoo was surprised and said, "We thought all Ooh-mans could count!" I shook my head saying Yes but not all can count as many things as others. The ones that were older than us could only count what they understood. They understood the number of fingers and toes they had. So their way of counting was to use them. When the number needed more fingers or toes they would just say 'many fingers and toes!'

Mearoo seemed to be thinking about this as she went to the earliest part of the symbols looking again at them. "Jakool? You see the symbols that look like two fingers joined together on your hand?" I nodded at the marks she pointed out. "He made them using the fingers on his hand. I think this shows he was one of those you say came before, and was older than your tribe." I saw this and said "He used two fingers to show one? Why would he do that?" Mearoo said no. The mark means two hands or ten fingers. See how he joins two of them here? That means four hands or four times the number of fingers. He does this many times. He could count the number of suns between the different faces of the pale goddess in the night sky. Here it shows that number to usually be five hands and four fingers, followed by six hands. Here he shows the number of seasons he lived here." I looked and saw the two hands symbol carved in a row. I counted them and saw that it added up to six hands of seasons!

This was very surprising as here on this wall, was a knowledge of counting that exceeded that of many tribes we had met! My own tribe had learned to count higher than two hands and two feet, only after we had met humans that came after us!

"So how many matings did the first have?" I asked interested in how much it took to change from the way the first snow-leaper looked to Mearoo. Mearoo went further down the wall and pointed at different-looking symbols for the number of matings and cubs. She explained "One of the last female cubs that mated with him took over being the Keeper of the First Cave after he died. He taught her how to count, as he was very old and suffered from joint sickness. He couldn't hold things in his hands as they were swollen and wouldn't work well." I nodded saying "Yes. Some of our Elders have what you call 'joint sickness' too. We also would do this when one of our Elders became sick, so another could take their place." Mearoo counted up the two-finger marks and said "He mated with the first for three hands of seasons. She was very old when she died and he took care of her the last few seasons, as she didn't hunt or mate anymore." I said to her "This is how we care for our mates too!"

Mearoo smiled and hug me! "I am glad to hear that Jakool." After the hugging stopped I asked "How many cubs Mearoo? Three hands of seasons is too short a time for such changes to happen." Mearoo nodded in agreement then pointed out "Yes but each time she bore at least four cubs, sometimes as many as seven! Of those, the females always came back to mate with him! He was surprised by this at first; as he records back here", Mearoo said pausing to find the right symbols on the wall. "Here he says that he was afraid the First would be angry at the cubs returning to this place, but she never seemed to mind! She also didn't seem to mind him mating with the female cubs!" This was very different than my own people! "We do not mate with our own children." I finally said to Mearoo. "Our Elders say it is bad for the blood to always mate to itself. They have seen babies with very bad backs, legs, and other parts of their bodies badly formed from blood mating to blood that is too close to the parents or their children." Mearoo replied "We know this too but this was different. The changes happened over a very long time. His mating with his own cubs increased the blood of the Ooh-man over the Snow-Leaper. That is why the changes needed less time to happen."

So I said, "So you are saying because he was human and she was a snow-leaper, his seed was stronger than a male snow-leaper?" Mearoo replied "Yes. We know this to be true as we have changed so much since the first. All of us can mate and have children with an Ooh-man. We have babies that sometimes grow to be Ooh-man. Less often we have babies that look like the first snow leaper, but can think like Ooh-mans! Between those two are many others that can be like me or like the kind of Ooh-mans that came after the first."

I was surprised to hear that other Ooh-mans had also mated with her people. "How did other Humans find you and mate with you?" Wanting to hear about them!" "Oh! Well, some came to hunt as the first did. It is dangerous to be here if you are not aware of the dangers. If you make too much noise in some places, you can cause snow and rocks on steep rock faces to fall. Once it starts falling it does not stop until it reaches a large flat place, the edge of the Cloud Stabber, or hits a large enough rock face that can stand its power. We call it a 'Snow Slide'. Oohmans who did not know this were often buried under it.

We would try to help them, but some would be afraid and attack us when we dug them out! We didn't understand at first. But over time we learned that many Oohmans believed us to be just animals. Others believed us to be demons sent to devour them and their spirits! But a few would be like the First. Not afraid enough to attack us and smart enough to understand we were trying to help them." I said "I can see how they would believe this after being buried alive by this snow slide and losing their brothers. But what is a 'Cloud Stabber'?" Mearoo smiled and said "What you call 'A Finger Of Rock That Touches The Sky', we call a 'Cloud Stabber!'" I laughed at her smile then said "I like it! It is much easier to say! But can you tell me more about the humans that stayed?"

Mearoo smiled and said, "You remember how we first mated?" I felt myself blush and she looked closely at my face as I felt the heat rise in it as I 'remembered' our first time! "How did you do that?" She asked as she stepped closer and put a paw on my face. "Do what?" I said as I was distracted by her touch, her closeness, and her smell! "Make your skin change colors like that!" "Oh. When humans get certain feelings they can cause the blood to rise into their faces." I said in reply as I felt my 'need' for her increase making it hard to talk or to think! She stepped closer put her mouth next to my ear and purred. The feel of her lips there caused me to groan as I felt myself become very stiff! "Mearoo! You are making me want to do things with you!" I said as I put my hands on the fur covering her breasts. I felt her trace my ear with the tip of her tongue then she said in a voice that left no doubt "I know. So did the ones that were rescued." And that was all it took for her to lead me back to the furs to mate again!

Afterward, I said, "I need to drink and eat."She got up and went out then came back with the container holding the water. She gave it to me and helped me drink. Then she got some of the cooked meat and we ate. Once we were finished I was feeling better and asked her to continue telling me about the other men that mated with them. "What is there to tell? They came up either to hunt or because they were escaping troubles down below. We would usually stay hidden unless they set off a snow slide or we felt a compulsion to mate with them. Many of those couldn't learn to breathe well enough to survive and either died or went back down. "What do you mean couldn't learn to breathe?" I asked.

Mearoo explained "This cave is only halfway up. The first had trouble breathing here. He slowly changed so that his breathing became easier. But he also says that others came that could not learn to breathe and died." "I understand Mearoo. When we first left the lands below, many died unable to breathe high up. The people like me did not have any problems. But others who joined our tribe did! Some like the first got better over time but others couldn't and died." Mearoo smiled as she said "The first kept count of how many men came and survived. Those that did eventually either left to find others or stayed and mated many times with his female cubs that returned to the cave. But 'All' mated with them while here!"

Mearoo got up and went back to the wall and counted the symbols for the number of men and the number of their cubs "If I am doing this right, there were five hands and three fingers, of female cubs total that mated with the First and other Humans. The number of mating changes as some litters only had one female, others as many as three. So if each new one is counted as a new change, you are looking at five hundred and sixty new changes!" I asked, "Does it show how many seasons this took?" Mearoo nodded and answered "Eight hands and one finger of seasons". "After forty-one seasons did the cubs look like you?" I asked not believing such changes could occur in such a short time!" "No! Of course not!" Mearoo said sounding a little irritated at me. "I said it took a long time!" She turned to face the wall again and I watched as she fingered each of the symbols that showed two or four hands, counting them. She stopped under an image of a snow leaper that looked similar to her in shape. "Here! The first snow-leaper that had human form and snow-leaper features, was named Lieta. He was the son of Farso and Parma and was born.." she paused while she figured out how many seasons from the First until Lieta. Finally, she said "It was ten times ten seasons times ten hands. I do not know the words in your tongue to describe this number. In our language it is "Che-ti" "We do not have a word or symbol for such a large number" I said.

Suddenly I felt very strange and dizzy then I fell!" "Jakool!" I heard Mearoo yell as if from a great distance as I kept falling instead of hitting the cave floor! I fell through it over and over again until finally, I was lying on it staring at the ceiling! I tried to stand up but couldn't as everything was spinning around and I fell when I tried. The spinning slowly came to a stop and carefully sat up expecting to see Mearoo. I was surprised to see two others in the cave. A snow-leaper male and female watching over five cubs. They looked different than Mearoo; more snow-leaper than humans, but I could see how they could become like her. Then I looked at the cubs and saw one that did look more like her!

I heard them talking and the man said "Lieta? It was my fathers, fathers name." The woman looked at him lovingly as she said "Yes Parma. It is a good name to keep in the family." I then realized I was seeing Farso and Parma, the parents of Lieta just after he was born! I watched and listened as they named each of the cubs. Once finished they curled up with them to keep them warm. I heard Parma say "He is different. Will the others be too?" Farso nodded then said "Yes they will. But they will always be our cubs! More than our cubs. They will have the memories of our bloodlines from the very beginning."

The scene faded and I was back in the cave only now Mearoo was holding me in her arms shaking me! "Jakool! Come Back to me!" I made a noise then said, "I will if you stop shaking me!" She stopped and looked relieved as I sat up and put my arms around her. "I was there. I saw Parma and Farso naming the cubs. Lieta was the only one who looked human and snow-leaper, but Farso answered 'Yes' when Parma asked if all of them would be different. Mearoo said slowly "Farso and Parma were rather special. They were the first to master the Ooh-man tongue and to mate to strengthen the Ooh-man blood. But for you to see them here and now? I do not understand how this is possible! "

"I do not know Mearoo." This is all very strange to me." She looked deeply into my eyes holding my face in her hands then said "I think that you were led to this place for these 'true dreams' to be happening. Mearoo said after some time. I simply shrugged my shoulders thinking *I do not understand why I sought her out or why I am having these dreams."* Something else was bothering me about what Parma had said. "Mearoo? Do your people remember everything?" I pointed at the pictures and symbols on the wall as I asked her this. She slowly nodded and said "Yes. I am the "Keeper Of The Cave Of The First" because I am a direct descendant of them. Everything that he wrote down and she knew I also know as well as the knowledge of the ones between us." I sighed now understanding how Mearoo's people could have developed so quickly since they didn't have to learn everything as they grew up! I started to explain how you learn the skills and things you need to know to survive in my tribe when it hit me.

As soon as I said "My tribe" I stopped and looked dumbfounded then slapped my forehead! *My tribe! I forgot about them! I was ashamed of myself as I thought of them. I have forgotten about my brothers and sisters! Ever since the 'Great Smoke Years' we have grown smaller and weaker as a tribe! We lost half of our hunters when we were attacked by the Rough Furs! We will not survive the cold because of that loss! I have to try and find them! I could tell them I may have found another tribe that would allow us to join them! We would become strong again! I could help them!* I turned and said "I must leave Mearoo! I have to go and find my tribe! "What is wrong Mearoo?" I said seeing her staring at me with a very unpleasant look on her face! I went over to her but she quickly stood up and said "I thought you liked me! I thought you wanted to be my mate! I see now that I have made a mistake in choosing you!" I stared at her not recognizing the woman I had held in my arms a short time before as she was now hissing, spitting, and making other threatening sounds!

I tried to calm her and explain by saying "Mearoo Please! This is important! My tribe needs.." I felt a sharp pain on the side of my face; as my head snapped back from a blow, and then I was falling over backwards! She leaped on me and started clawing and biting me! I tried to fend her off but she was too strong! "Mearoo Stop! Your Hurting Me! Mearoo!" I cried out in pain and anguish; both from the wounds she was causing my body and the sudden pain of the thought that I had lost her! Mearoo gave my face a final slash with her claws which I was only able to partially block. I was crying from both the sting of the final blow and the sight of her leaping away and down the tunnel! I struggled to get up as I felt the pain of the wounds she had inflicted on me. "Mearoo?" I cried out in agony as I made my body stand up and slowly walk to the tunnel and then through it. I called her again and heard her name echo in the vast cavern.

My voice was the only one I heard answer me as I realized she had gone! I had lost my mate!" I now knew what she meant when she called me that! I went back to the furs and sat down overwhelmed with feelings I had not experienced in my young life! I cried. I was hurt and didn't know what to do. I decided to wait for her to return. I had to make her understand that I wanted to be her mate but my tribe needed my help! *She'll come back. She is just angry at me. Once she calms down she will come back!* I told myself as I examined my wounds and found that most were shallow. I sat and thought, slept, ate, and sat some more.

I went out into the outer cavern several times calling her name; believing I had heard someone, but she was not there. Finally, after what felt like several suns I realized that she was not coming back. I gathered up my spears, food, and furs. *I have to find her! I can look for her as I go down to look for my tribe.* I thought to myself as I made my way across the vast cavern.

. As I prepared to leave, I decided to leave her a message, in case she returned. I took burnt charcoal from the cold ashes of the fire and drew an image of her and then me. Then I drew one showing my tribe, the many trees, the endless grass, the hills, and where to find us. I hoped she understood and added two fingers connected together under us! I went to the entrance; turning once to look back, then I left the cave.

Once I was outside the sudden cold, gusty wind, cloud-covered sky, and snow seemed to awaken my senses. I went down the trail still looking for tracks or any signs of her. I called out her name many times only to hear it carried away in the wind. I thought about everything she had told me, everything we had done together. I relived all the feelings with those thoughts; and felt even worse, for making her think I cared more for my tribe than I did for her!

But I was supposed to care for my tribe above all else! That is what we were taught and we believed! I was arguing with myself all the way down the Rock Finger! By the time I had made it into the hills at the bottom of the rock finger, I was sure of two things. I wanted to find her and beg her forgiveness and I wanted to be her mate for the rest of my life! I found the river that fed the waterfall into the ravine and went around it this time looking for any traces of her or my brethren. *There were four hands of us* I thought as I made sweeps of the many trees looking for tracks or signs. *Two I found dead. Eight others fled into the many trees. Two of the Adults were killed* I thought looking for their tracks. I was now past where I had found Rankoo's body in the copse of bushes and was near where the attack had occurred. I was very tired after the long climb down with only a few rest stops and looked for somewhere safe to rest.

I settled on a group of trees with needle leaves, that grew close together with sticker bushes around them. I threw my furs over the bushes so I could climb through them safely then pulled my furs in behind me. I looked around and saw that the ground under me was carpeted by the needles that had dropped and turned brown, making a comfortable bed. I fell asleep quickly and had more dreams. Bad ones! I relived the attack on the hunting party, only now it was Mearoo and her tribe attacking! I watched in horror as they slashed and ripped our hunters apart saving me for last! I begged her to stop, to forgive me, but she was consumed by her animal side and only wanted to taste my blood! I cried out and woke up to find myself tossing from side to side and digging into the ground with my fingers! I cried and cried out my loss and her name several times before I finally fell asleep again.

I woke up suddenly as something prodded me awake! I opened my eyes to see several people like Mearoo only bigger and meaner looking! The tallest was the one that had prodded me with a foot to wake me. I stood up excited at seeing them and immediately said "Have you seen Mearoo? I must find her! I must tell her I am sorry!" I said to the tall, silent figure standing in front of me. I began to look among them for her but the tall one said "You are far from home Ooh-man. Why have you come here?"

I stopped looking for her as I realized I must sound sick in the head to him! I looked up at him and said "My name is Jakool. My tribe is called the 'Mihakoo'. We live across the never-ending green grass in the hills beyond the many trees. We were hunting here and were attacked by a large clan of Rough Furs! I am one of the young out on our first hunt! The hunt leader; Kiraat, told us to run when we were attacked so we did! I thought I would die when one followed me, but Mearoo saved me by attacking the Rough Fur, giving me time to hide! When it was safe I came out and couldn't find any of my tribe left alive, so I followed her tracks! That is how I climbed the Finger of Rock that Touches the Sky; that you call a 'Cloud Stabber', until I found the caves and her!" I fell to my knees in front of him, feeling the tears start again at the memories the telling brought back! "Please! Please tell her I am sorry! I didn't mean to anger her by saying I needed to find my tribe! I only wanted to help them! We need help!" I said to him as he stood silent staring at me. I felt so miserable, helpless, and all alone. Suddenly the silent one said "My name is Merkansoo. I am the Leader of the Snow-Leaper Tribe. I have listened to you young Jakool and am amazed by your story."

I was surprised when he turned his head slightly and called out "Mearoo! Come here now and face the one you accused of betraying you!" I stayed on my knees as the warriors parted and a smaller figure slowly came forward causing my heart to leap with joy! "Mearoo!" I cried out and would have stood up, but Merkansoo put a hand on my shoulder to prevent me from rising. "Mearoo? why does this Ooh-man have the marks of your claws and teeth? Did he attack you?"Merkansoo asked her sternly. She was unable to look up at his face and was hiding hers in her paws. "No Merkansoo. He did not attack me or hurt me in that way." "Oh? In what way did young Jakool hurt you then? It must have been very serious for you to treat him this way after you saved his life and took him as your mate!" Mearoo sobbed into her paws at this, as if he had struck her!

"No! Don't blame her! It is my fault!" I said quickly, as seeing her like this hurt me so much! "Mearoo took her hands away from her face and looked at me with surprise as I said this. Merkansoo nodded then turned to Mearoo and said "Do you wish me to kill him for you? You have foolishly told him too much to allow him to live or to leave! That is our way!" I stayed on my knees and hung my head awaiting the killing blow to fall. Suddenly I felt Mearoo's body against mine and her arms around my neck saying "No! Please! I was wrong!" She said sobbing as she held me tight against her! I was overjoyed with relief and said to her "Mearoo? Can you ever forgive me? I didn't mean to anger you! I would never do anything to hurt you!, I want to be your mate! For the rest of my life!" I said while I had the chance! Mearoo held my face at arm's length so she could look at me as she said "Really? You want to be my mate? You truly mean it?" In a hopeful voice.

"I shook my head up and down and said "I really do! I vow to never leave you until death takes my body from this place!" I made the sign of our tribe to the Sky Spirits while looking up at the sky. Merkansoo said, "I believe that you have done him grievous harm Mearoo, and must make it right!" Merkansoo said still sounding stern. I felt a pang of fear but Mearoo grabbed my face and kissed me soundly then said while crying "I want you Jakool I need you so much! I was angry! So angry when you said you had to find your tribe! I..I thought you were leaving me! I thought that you would never come back to me!" She said to me as I hugged her, kissed her, and reassured her. "It is okay Mearoo. I am okay. Now that you are with me." Merkansoo shook his head and said, "Now that you two young-lings have realized you have both been foolish in how you have behaved, I would like to hear more about your tribe Jakool."

I nodded and told him the story of my tribe. From our beginnings to the drying up of the lands, to the travels to find new lands. The many places we had stopped and stayed only to leave again. Of the Great Fire in the Sky and the Great Smoke Years! Of how we were reduced in numbers; and to a hand-to-mouth existence, while trying to survive! I told of how we climbed higher to escape the dangers of staying in the low-lying lands. I finished by explaining how few our numbers were and how we needed to find another tribe that would accept us, or we would simply be wiped out by other tribes! Merkansoo listened silently during the story never moving or indicating how he felt, by words, gestures, or the expression on his face. When I had finished telling him the whole story of the hunt, the attack, meeting Mearoo, mating, and the cave, he stopped me. "I have heard enough Jakool. Are you rested enough to travel?" I said "Yes. Are we going back to your tribe?" I asked feeling a little torn between Mearoo and my tribe's need! "No. We will go and see the truth of the story. If it is as you have said.." Merkansoo paused and had a strange look as he finished saying this, "Then there is more at work here than a chance meeting between you and Mearoo."

I didn't understand, but was happy to have them help me find my tribe! "One thing Jakool," Merkansoo said before we started out. "Can you swear by the Gods or Spirits you worship, that all in your tribe would greet us as friends and equals if we show ourselves to them? If we allow them to join us as you have suggested, will they all accept? Because if any do not wish to join with us they cannot be allowed to live to tell any of us!" I was shocked at hearing this condition but thought about it.

If we were the ones that had stayed hidden so long, would we be willing to risk that to help a strange tribe that looked as much like animals as men?

I shook my head realizing that it was a very difficult question to answer. But I knew the answer in my heart and looked up at Merkansoo and said firmly "I cannot swear as to how all of the tribe will greet you. I can swear that any who refuse your offer to join will die by my blade!" I put my hand on the hilt of my knife as I said this to him. He nodded and said, "So be it!" He turned and said, "Lead us to your tribe". I felt Mearoo's hand in mine as I walked passed the warriors who parted to let us through until we stood in front of the tribe. I scanned the many trees and found the trail I recognized and said "This way". The journey had begun, I was now mate to Mearoo and leading the Snow-Leaper tribe to meet mine. But what would my tribe decide? Would I have to honor my vow and kill my own brethren? I silently prayed to the Sky Spirits to send my thoughts to my brethren to warn them before we arrived!

CHAPTER THREE

THE SEARCH FOR BLOOD KIN

I was glad that Mearoo was with me as we followed the trail. I felt both fear and hope at the same time! Fear that my tribe would reject Merkansoo's offer; and terms, while hoping that they would! Remembering Mearoo's arrival with her tribe members I asked Mearoo "What did you do after you..left me in the cave?" Mearoo's face tightened betraying emotions that I could not yet read before she began to speak. "I was very angry with you. I thought you understood that I had picked you to be my mate! When you told me you needed to leave to find your tribe, I thought you were leaving me! I am sorry I got so angry that I hurt you!" I stopped and held her close as I was beginning to understand and saw her sadness. "It is alright Mearoo! I do not blame you. We are very different people and we come from different tribes. We are going to understand each other eventually, but until then, we have to listen to each other more carefully."

I didn't realize that Merkansoo and the scouts were watching and listening to us reach an understanding. I was startled when I felt a large hand on my shoulder and heard Merkansoo say "Well said Jakool. We will also try to 'listen carefully' when we meet your tribe." I swallowed and nodded as I was still holding Mearoo close to comfort her. She was the one that gently pushed me away saying "We will never meet them if we don't find them!" I laughed as we started waking and asked her "So what did you do when you left the cave?" Mearoo sighed and said "I went home to my tribe. I wanted to hurt you and your whole tribe! I know it was wrong of me but I couldn't help it! I am young and you were my first mating!" "I was your first? How did you know how to do all the things we did?" I asked her wondering how they learned about mating. She smiled and said "We are born with the knowledge" reminding me of her tribe's racial memory ability!

"I forgot you can remember everything that the humans that mated with snow

27

leopards as well as the snow leopards. That makes sense but it is still very strange to me!" Merkansoo and the others chuckled but didn't make any comments. When we stopped for the night Merkansoo came and took me a little way from the camp. He asked, "How many are in your tribe?" I sighed remembering how many we had lost during the hunting attack. "We were ten hands and four hands and four fingers in our tribe. I think that we had ten hands plus one finger of men, eight hands of women, and six hands and four fingers of children. Two hands plus two fingers of the men on the hunt were experienced hunters led by Kiraat. I was one of the two hands of young ones who were on their first hunt to make our first kill. We must make a kill to become full men of the tribe. Merkansoo asked, "Do you know how many survived the attack?" I shook my head saying "No. I know that two maybe three of the young ones were killed by the Rough Furs. When I went back to where they attacked us I found two bodies of the adults." Merkansoo asked, "Did you expect to?" "Yes, I did" I replied adding "We cannot carry our dead all the way back to our camp, so if any die on a hunt we leave them for the animals. We see it as a way to honor them."

Merkansoo said "A very strange belief, but I am glad your tribe believes that the animals that can kill you should be honored. But why do you believe that the hunting party returned to your camp?" My answer was "Because they didn't do what we are trained to do. The hunters should have all returned after the attack to search for any that were still missing. When I went back, no one was there. I looked but didn't see any signs of a search, so they must have returned to our camp." Merkansoo smiled showing his sharp front canine teeth and said "No. We looked and didn't find tracks going back down and out of the many trees to the endless grass. So they must still be in the many trees searching for you and the others." As soon as he said it I exclaimed "They are still in the many trees? How? Where?" Merkansoo shook his head and said "You are not thinking Jakool! Think! What were you trained to do? So what would 'they' do?"

My thoughts turned to the attack, *Kiraat yelling run! Most of us ran into the many trees away from the attack.* "Wait! I ran into the trees, but not the same way as the others! We split up so we would be harder to find! That is something we were taught!" Merkansoo nodded saying "Good! What else?" I was thinking and speaking my thoughts out loud saying "We would have hidden until the danger was over then try to rejoin the group." "What if you couldn't find them?" A memory of being with Kiraat, Bamal, and Merack with the rest of the young hunters learning what to do when on a hunt surfaced.

Remember if you are told to run do it! Don't stop to try and help! Run and do your best to hide. Once the danger is over come back to that place so we can find you! Rankoo asked, What if we get lost or no one is there? Merack replied You find as many as you can and you return! That way the rest of the tribe is told what has happened! That was my answer! "We would have tried to find the rest and then return home." "Excellent! So we will go and try to find them! I am sure that they followed the teachings as you did. So they will be easier to track now that they are in a group!" I saw the sense in this and said "Thank you Merkansoo! I believed them all to be dead!" He smiled and said "That is the problem with being young. You believe you already know more than you do!" I had to agree with his words as we returned to the camp and to Mearoo.

We spoke about what Merkansoo had said and the search in the morning for my missing brethren. "I am happy for you Jakool!" She said as she smiled then added "It would be good to find the young as they are the future of your tribe." She laughed at my expression as I had not thought of myself as the 'future' of my tribe! Mearoo was getting better at reading my face and added "You said that your tribe has gotten smaller than can survive by themselves. That means that the young will be the ones who have the best chance to help it survive." I thought about it and saw the sense in her words. "You are right Mearoo. I think that finding the other young hunters is very important!

Mearoo hugged me and nuzzled my neck as she said in my ear "They too will have mates from my tribe Jakool. It is the best way to make sure your tribe survives." I 'felt' the now familiar rise of my desire for her and knew she was right about that! She pulled me into the darkness away from the fire and took her time teasing me with her touches and kisses until I could take no more! She knew when I'd had enough as I pounced on her and mated until I gave her my seed! We rested and then mated again before she'd let us return to the fire to eat.

Later that night Merkansoo came over to where we sitting by the fire and said "We found tracks of both the young hunters and your adults. You said that a large group of what you name 'Rough Furs' attacked you?" I said "Yes! It was quick with no warning. We heard the scouts screaming and Kiraat ran forward to see what was happening. He gave the signal and yelled run as he ran forward to meet the attack." Merkansoo nodded saying "I remember. We found signs of the fight between them and two more Rough Furs were killed. We believe the tracks show the adults went to find the young hunters. You must have gone in a different direction than the rest." This gave me renewed hope that in the morning we would be able to follow their trail and find both the young ones and the hunters! I went to sleep with Mearoo feeling better about the fate of the other hunters.

We were up before the sun as Merkansoo's people could see well in the dark. Lasaa and Janai were the trackers leading us to where they had found tracks. They stopped not far from the camp so they could show us the tracks. Lasaa said "See? The young ones' prints are clear. First one, then slowly others joined up here. Then you see that a group of adults come from over there and found this large group of prints. After that, you see their prints over the young ones." I squatted down to see the marks clearly. "They all go deeper into the trees but away from the cloud stabbers." Janai said, "We followed them as far as the place where the many trees change faces." "What do you mean?" I asked not understanding.

Merkansoo explained "The many trees here keep going until the hills stop and the flat lands begin. It is much warmer there. The many trees change to ones that grow where there is no snow. There are more trees of different kinds, which are wetter, thicker, and more dangerous. We know because we remember it from a long time ago. I believe we will find them before we reach the other side of the many trees. We will track them to where they have taken shelter. There are caves in the area of the trees they could have used."

Changing subjects I asked Merkansoo "Is joining your tribe as easy as finding one to mate with?" I asked not sure I believed him. Merkansoo guffawed along with Janai and Lasaa. "Easy? Do you think being chosen by Mearoo and surviving mating with her was easy? Is your tribe that 'Hard' to join?" Merkansoo said grinning at my embarrassment at their humor. Wanting to surprise Merkansoo back, I said "You would have to ask Mearoo if it was "Hard" to join with her! My 'Tribe' will let anyone 'Join'!" Janai and Lasaa were now rolling with laughter at my jibe back at Merkansoo who was grinning from ear to ear! Just then Mearoo came up and wanted to know what was funny causing more laughter, as they explained to her they were joking with me. She smiled then gave Merkansoo a dig in his ribs with her claws causing him to yelp and jump away from her! "That's for teasing him! He doesn't know us well enough to know when we are joking! Yes, he was plenty hard enough to 'join' with me over and over again! So There!" She said as she took my arm and said "Since they need to lead us, they had better start!" I grinned as Merkansoo, Lasaa, and Janai made a big show of bowing to her, then leaped down the trail to follow the footprints.

The thought *How am I going to keep up with a tribe that could make jumps of over eight-man lengths'* was in my mind while running to stay up with Mearoo. It was easy at first because we were traveling downhill. Suddenly Merkansoo signaled back with a raised arm and Mearoo stopped and held me back! "Danger!" She whispered as several of the warriors slipped silently into the many trees on each side of the trail. Merkansoo stood very still as we watched to see what the 'Danger' would be! Merkansoo suddenly leaped high into the air and landed on a tree limb overhanging the trail. Something was moving from one side of the trail to the other and I strained my eyes to see it! It was a strange-looking creature with a large body; and a small head, that had large tusks sticking out of its jaws. It was rooting in the leaves and bushes with its tusks tearing it up in search of something. Everyone stayed silent as it crossed the trail; going deeper into the many trees, making noises as it went. Merkansoo stayed on the limb until he could no longer hear the creature, and then he lightly jumped down and waved us forward.

"What was that?" I asked Mearoo as we walked to where Merkansoo waited for us. "We call it a Two Tusk. It is a very mean and dangerous animal that eats anything! We avoid them as they are not worth getting injured or killed for their meat." As we reached Merkansoo he said "We will take a break here and rest. This will give the scouts time to go further down the trail." I thought *Good! I need it!* While we rested we ate some more of the cooked Bharal I'd brought. When we finished I sighed as Mearoo said "that was good!" licking her paws then her muzzle cleaned. I felt some envy at how long and flexible her tongue was to be able to do that! She saw me watching her and said "What?"

I just shrugged and said, "I wonder what it would be like to have a tongue like yours that you can clean your face with." Mearoo giggled and stuck her tongue out to its full length then pulled it back in to say "It has other uses too! I would show you but this is not a good place to mate!" I chuckled as I agreed with her and turned to walk a few steps into the bushes to relieve myself. Once I finished and returned, Mearoo said "We should rest while we can. I felt very tired and yawned in agreement. So we made a bed of soft leaves and lay down next to the trail and curled up with each other. Just holding her to me made me want to mate with her, but I was just too tired and soon had fallen asleep.

I woke up startled and had my knife out ready to strike, but it was Mearoo. "What? Is something wrong?" I asked looking around for any danger. "No silly! Merkansoo has heard from the scouts and the trail is clear for a long way. He wants to get moving again." "Oh!" I said as I sat up and stretched. I then got up and went to the bushes again to relieve myself. I was ready for another run now and joined Mearoo who was waiting for me. We made good time down the trail as it seemed to be smoother and not as steep here. Mearoo would run a short way then jump then run. I asked her why during a short break to catch my breath. She answered

"We can run on two legs, but most of us; built like me, find it much easier to run and jump. Much faster and less tiring."

Several hours later we stopped to rest, as the sun was now past halfway across the sky. Merkansoo came to us saying "If we can make it to the place of many streams by nightfall we will camp there." I asked, "Is this place far?" Merkansoo shrugged his shoulders and then answered "I do not know. I have never been here." I looked at him for a moment in confusion, then said "I thought your memory had all your ancestor's memories?" Merkansoo nodded but replied "This place is not one that 'my' ancestors knew. Others like Janai and Lasaa do have ancestors who knew it. We came from different tribes of Ooh-mans remember?" Merkansoo's answer gave me a better understanding of this racial memory Mearoo had told me about.

I nodded then grinned as I said "I suppose their ancestors had longer legs than mine! This seems far to me!" Merkansoo grinned and said "Quite likely. Many of the first Ooh-mans were much older than your people. We remember them from when my people first crossed from over the cloud stabbers." I was very interested in hearing more but Merkansoo added "Now is not the time. When we meet with your people, many stories will be told by both tribes. There is no need to tell them more than we need to." I had to admit he was right about the stories. When told too many times around the fire at night, they became too dull and it was easy to forget the lessons they taught.

Soon we were running again and I was breathing easier! *We have come down far from the cloud stabbers and the air was easier to breathe here* The thought occurred to me. I saw what Merkansoo and Janai meant by 'the face of the trees' changing. These trees were different than the ones on the higher cloud stabber slopes. There were trees with broad leaves that covered the sky during the middle part of our journey. These were disappearing and tall trees with cones and needles on the branches surrounded us. They were spaced further apart and underneath them, the land had fewer bushes as we went lower. Now I saw that the 'face' of the many trees was changing again, and it did it abruptly! The trees with needles now had thicker trees with large limbs appearing. Many of them had long rope-like plants growing up and around them that we called "Tree Stranglers". I remembered them from the stories of the Great Many Trees my tribe had crossed many seasons ago!

Merkansoo pointed to a hill in the trees ahead at something standing there. I looked up to see one of the Great Striped Ones standing on the other side watching us! I gasped as I saw an animal from our stories of long ago! He held his paws up to his mouth and called out to the animal with a roaring sound that went up and down in sound. The animal seemed to listen and then replied. Merkansoo nodded and turned to say "She says that she has seen the young Ooh-mans." I was shocked as I thought he was just making a noise not talking with it..her! Before I could ask how he could talk with the animal, he made more calls and then listened to the replies.

Finally, he gave a wave to the animal and it turned and left going back into the trees. Merkansoo turned smiling and said "The young are safe. Some are hurt but we will see how bad once we reach them. She will allow us to cross her territory to collect them!" I was a little puzzled so I asked "What does she mean collect them? Merkansoo smiled and said "They are safe in her den. She led them to it to keep them safe from the dangers in the many trees." I was speechless as I couldn't understand why such a large predator would 'help' young humans! I tried to ask Merkansoo but he just said "Patience! Your questions will be answered tomorrow when we meet with her! Now we make camp and rest. Her den is far from here."

The next day we started early on the journey to reach the Great Striped One's den.

The land was different as there was much more rocky ground hidden by the trees, causing me to trip several times. We came upon sudden drop-offs into gullies; hidden by the thick underbrush, many with small streams running downhill in them. The sounds of birds and animals in the trees; and on the ground, told me that it was full of life here.

We followed the winding trail until it came to an open spot in the many trees where a tall rock face seemed to rise out of the ground. Janai leaped up to a ledge that was only a little higher than the man's height and said "Here! I see tracks!" Everyone jumped up except me! Mearoo smiled before she suddenly grabbed me around the waist and jumped up then threw me! Before I could scream in fear, I felt someone grab me and pull me up onto the ledge. Mearoo landed lightly beside me as I tried to calm my fears. "Please warn me before doing that! I wet my loincloth!" That caused them all to laugh at my fear as it seemed silly to them. "I would never do something that would harm you Jakool!" Mearoo said as she lightly slapped my cheek. I grumbled but turned my attention to the tracks on the ledge.

I saw a mix of prints that were of the great animal's paws and humans. Hers were huge even compared to Merkansoo's. The human prints were those of the young hunters, some covered by the big animal prints. Lasaa and Janai went ahead as we followed the ledge around and up the rock face to a crevice. It was wide enough to climb through and soon we reached the other side. The rock face became part of a strange feature that formed part of a wall surrounding the land for many man lengths! I could see cracks and broken rock everywhere on the faces and wondered what had caused it. The ground was many man lengths below us so we continued on what looked like a worn trail that led up to the top of the rock face. We wound our way halfway around the irregularly shaped bowl made by the rock faces when we came to a drop-off in the trail. Looking down I saw that the trail had once been there but was now lying on the bottom as broken stone and rocks.

It looked as if we would have to jump over it, but Janai suddenly popped up from below us! I was surprised as she just appeared in the air in front of us! She fell back down and landed on a ledge we could not see just below us. We jumped down to the ledge and found it led to the rock face. There we found the cave that was the animal's den. She was outside sunning herself as we approached, Merkansoo said "Everyone except me and Mearoo stays here" as we got within ten man lengths. Looking at the size of the animal; its large head full of long sharp teeth and its huge paws, I was very glad to stay there!

They went forward and then dropped to all fours as they slowly approached the animal. It stood up and watched them stop and lower their heads and front legs as if bowing to her! She came over to them, stopped then sniffed them. She made some noises that Merkansoo and Mearoo returned. Soon Merkansoo stood up and waved us to join them. We walked forward as the animal turned and went back into the cave leading us to the young hunters! There I saw eight sitting and standing at the back of the cave! I ran forward shouting out to them causing them to yell in return as we greeted each other with joy!

"Jakool! We thought you were dead! Like Rankoo!" Kika said in a happy voice as we gripped each other's forearms. I nodded saying "I know. I found him and Denack dead in the many trees. Where are Kiraat and the rest?" I asked wanting to know what happened to them. Kika replied "We don't know. We went back to the place but no one was there. We saw many tracks that went different ways so we thought they were also hiding in the many trees. We tried to find them but couldn't. We went downhill looking for them and ended up here." "How did you end up with the great striped one? I am very interested to hear! But Merkansoo said "We must leave. Now that we are here she asks that we take them from her home."

Realizing I would have to wait to hear their story, we all thanked the animal! I was surprised when she came up to me and sniffed me then butted me with her head! "What do I do?" I said not sure as I was trying hard to not wet my loincloth again! "Mearoo said "She is very curious about you. I told her you were my mate!" I looked into her big yellow eyes with black pupils and saw something more than just an animal there! Slowly reaching out with one hand, I scratched her muzzle causing her to lean into it! I gave her a good scratching then said "Thank you for saving my brothers! We will always remember you and your kind! I promise we will never hurt you but will come to your aid if needed!" She seemed to understand me as she nodded her head up and down once as if she was saying "Yes!" We left her den following Janai and Lasaa as they led us down the rock face until we reached the ground it surrounded. They were following a path; she had told them about, that would lead us to the Ooh-mans camp.

I asked Merkansoo how they could speak with the animal. "We call her kind 'Tigre'. It means 'Hidden by Stripes' in our tongue." I replied "A very good description! Your kind has the same type of camouflage but for the hills, trees, snow, and rocks up high. I wonder if all hunters do?"

Merkansoo said "All of the ones we know of do. The Rough Fur, wolf, Tigre, Sahaat, and the Silent Black Killers of the jungle, all have coats of fur that help them hide. Ooh-mans do not but they have learned to hide themselves in the furs of the animals they hunt. I remember some that painted their bodies so they could hide in the many trees." I said "Two of our hunters are from a different kind of humans that do this! We have learned how to use burnt ashes and plants that provided different colors to disguise ourselves to be harder to see."

Merkansoo commented "That is what makes Ooh-mans so different from the animals. They see, they learn, they create and improve on what they learn or create." As we spoke about the differences between the different tribes of my people and his, we followed Janai and Lasaa around the edge of the rock face until we reached a spot where part of the face had fallen down. We stopped in front of a large pile of broken rocks and boulders at the base of the rock face. Janai jumped up to the top and looked, then suddenly said "Here! I have found a way out!" We climbed up carefully until we stood with her as she pointed at what the rock fall had hidden.

I saw a large depression in the wall near the ground that appeared to be where some of the broken rocks came from. I looked as Janai jumped down and stood in the depression then stepped into the side and disappeared! She came back out smiling and said "There is an opening that we can travel through." We all jumped down and saw that inside the depression the rock face was split apart from the ground halfway up the face. I grabbed Mearoo's hand as we stepped into the cracked rock, following Janai and Lasaa.

I knew that Mearoo and her people could see well in the dim light that came from the opening, but I wanted to hold onto her hand so I wouldn't trip! It also gave me a chance to ask her something! "Mearoo? The Tigre saved my brethren. I don't understand why she would do this. Did she tell you why?" Mearoo was quiet for several moments then answered me "She said that the spirit of the cloud stabber told her to". I was surprised and puzzled by this. "But I thought you and your tribe were the spirits of the cloud stabbers!" She said "No. The spirits were here long before we came to the cloud stabbers. How else could she know of them? As do we." I wanted to know all about these spirits but Mearoo said "Patience Jakool. It is something we will tell all of your tribe about if you join us. For now be satisfied that all that has happened to you; and us, was not just a chance meeting."

There was plenty of time during the journey through the rock, to think about the things Mearoo told me. *Is there a Great Spirit that is making this happen? The strange dreams showed me the true things that happened. The strange way in which the First Human and Snow-Leaper mated and had cubs, that slowly turned into Mearoo and her people. The amazing sights in the lake cavern and in her cave. How did the First know how to count such large numbers? Why did he stay with the snow leaper? Why didn't he go back down the cloud stabbers to find his tribe? So many strange things!* I thought as we walked through the narrow crevice in the rock and traveled some distance.

Suddenly Mearoo pulled my arm and whispered "Stop! Stay here!" She silently padded forward until I could no longer see her in the dim light. I strained my eyes and ears but didn't see or hear anything. I stood still trying to control my fears at what might be happening as I waited for Mearoo and the rest to return. Finally, after what felt like hours Mearoo returned alone and said "Come! Several are hurt!" She grabbed my hand pulling me forward out of the crevice into the daylight.

We came out of the rock onto a thick grassy slope that ran for a long way until it met with many trees. Merkansoo was squatting down beside a woman named Elasaa. I saw that she had several wounds in her side. Others were moaning in pain as Janai and Lasaa went from one to the other. "What happened?" I asked Mearoo as we ran up to help the wounded. "We surprised several of the Two Tusk as we came out of the crevice. They attacked us and their was a fight before we killed them." pointing at the now visible carcasses of the Two Tusks close by. Merkansoo was shaking his head as we reached him and said "I cannot heal this. The wounds are too deep and she is bleeding on the inside. The others are broken legs and ribs. Those we can fix."

I looked up thinking that if we could reach my tribe Paasi could heal her. I had seen her do so with others injured on the hunts. I could see far enough to notice the land was changing from many trees to more endless green grass. I*s it the same one we* *cross to hunt in the many trees? If it was then we were not too far from them!* I realized and excitedly said to Merkansoo "If we can reach my tribe, we have hide, medicines, and Healers. He stood up and looked in the direction of the grass. "How far are they?" He asked as he thought. "I am not sure. I know it takes us two suns to cross the endless green grass. It is one sun away from our camp in the hills on the other side of them. So from here? I think three to four suns?" was my reply. He was silent as he thought about the idea. I stayed quiet not wanting to interrupt.

Making a decision, he looked at Janai! Lasaa and said "Jakool believes his tribe is three suns from here about a day into the hills. You can make it there and back in that time, maybe sooner!" Janai and Lasaa both nodded then made jumps that landed them five man-lengths away and they were off to find my tribe! We watched as they continued making long jumps with short runs between them. It was the first time I watched the snow leapers do this and was in awe of how fast they were! We watched as they became smaller and smaller until they disappeared into the endless grass!

We worked on making splints for the ones with broken legs and cut strips of hide from the Two Tusks to wrap around them and the ones with broken ribs. Merkansoo checked on Elasaa once we were finished with the others. She was restless and had a fever, So Mearoo spent more time getting water into her to help her body fight the wound and heal. "Will she heal?" Merkansoo replied "I don't know. If the bleeding stops then she might. Otherwise.." He didn't have to say anymore as I had seen my own people die from such wounds."

It was now late and we took turns resting and watching over the wounded helping them to drink water or eat when thirsty or hungry. We spent two days doing this waiting for the scouts to return. On the morning of the third day I saw the scouts and someone else in the distance returning! I ran over to Mearoo to tell her the scouts were returning. Elasaa still looked weak, pale, and was muttering to herself, when she was conscious. I saw blood leaking out around the leaf! "Mearoo! She is bleeding!" I said dropping to my knees to examine her wound. Mearoo called out for Merkansoo who came over quickly and looked at the wound. "She is still bleeding from her wounds on the inside." He said as he carefully peeled the leaf off of the wound to see. The blood was seeping out of the wound which looked green around the edges. I had seen this before and knew it meant the flesh was sick. Merkansoo knew too and shook his head and said "The flesh around the wound is sick. She is dying from the inside and the inside." I became afraid she would die and was frantic trying to remember what to do to help her!

Suddenly the scouts came bounding up to us with someone held between them! "Paasi! They found you and the tribe!" I said excited and relieved to see her. She looked afraid until she saw me there! "Jakool? We thought you were dead! The hunters that made it back said all the rest were dead! We didn't believe these two when they told us that you and others were alive! The Elders decided to have me go with them because they said they had injured here!" I pointed at the woman saying "They do! She is bleeding from the inside and her wound is sick with the green color! I couldn't remember what to give her to help her body make new blood and fight to heal itself."

Paasi gave me a look that showed her disappointment in me! "Move! She said as she ran over to us and squatted by the woman. "What is your name?" She asked her as she studied the wound and the bleeding. "Elasaa," Mearoo answered for her as she was too weak and mumbling to herself. Paasi shook her head and turned to Jakool and said "I hope you remember what the plants and herbs we need look like!" I felt like I had let her, my tribe, and Elasaa down by not being able to remember! Elasaa said, "Does anyone here know anything about the plants and herbs in that many trees?" Merkansoo said "I do. I quickly said "Merkansoo is both the Leader and a healer. He and the rest of his people can remember everything that anyone of their blood knew." She looked confused and started to ask questions but stopped herself as she said "Get leaves of the Bhang. We will also need the leaves of the spike plant with yellow flowers. I brought Yellow Root Powder but if you find any bring them." Merkansoo listened carefully to her and she added several more plants, some fruits, nuts, and tree bark then he said "Jakool, Janai, Lasaa and Darshita, Farkis! You are with me!" I immediately turned to Paasi and said "We will get you everything you need!" She replied sternly "You had better or she dies!"

I ran to Merkansoo waiting for his orders. "We go together! Janai and Lasaa will be the lookouts. I want everyone to be within sight of each other! No one goes out of sight!" He didn't wait for our answers as he turned to me and said "You have been taught about these plants and I need you to recognize them!" He started towards the many trees and soon we were among them looking for each of the things Paasi had said she needed. Merkansoo pointed saying "The Bhang plants are this way. I think I saw the Gold Flowers near them." We followed him on the ground while Janai and Lasaa took to the trees to keep watch over us. I saw the Bhang plants and remembered we needed the leaves and the seeds. But then I thought *We can show them how to make strong rope with the stalks.*

"Merkansoo. We can use the whole plant." He nodded then said "You and the others with knives get it. Also the Gold Flowers over there. I will go to look for the spike plant and some of the others." I turned and said to Kika, Lavar, Timbu, and Garath "Let's pull up as many as we can first. Then we cut the rest. Paasi can use the roots too!" We went to work and soon had a large pile of the Bhang plants. We tied them into bundles we could carry using hide strips we'd brought with us. I heard Janai call me from the Trees! "Jakool! Bring everyone over here! We found the Ankol Tree!" We went to where she was perched on a fruit-heavy limb of the tree we needed! We soon had the bark, fruit, and leaves we needed and looked to see if anyone had found Yellow Root and Spike Plants.

We turned back and made our return to the camp. Once there, Paasi had us cut the fruit up and mash it in a stone bowl she had brought with her. Once that was done, we cut up the gold flowered plant and mixed it with the fruit. Paasi nodded when we showed it to her. "Now take the shells of the nuts, NOT the nuts! Just the shells and grind them up until they like powder. Mix that in then bring me it and the leaves." "Jakool! You and the rest cut the leaves from the spike plants. We will need the sap to treat and seal the blood vessels and the wound!" "I understand Paasi!" I replied as I dropped the bundle of Bhang and went to the pile of Spike Plants.

"How do we do this?" Kika asked me as I took one. "You carefully cut the sharp points off of the leaves first like this." I showed them how I slid my knife down from the tip of the pointed leaf to the bottom, cutting all the spikes off of that side then the other side. "Now you can hold the leaf and cut it from the plant. They all started working on them. Soon we had all the leaves and I brought them to Paasi. She'd been busy with the Bhang leaves and the mixture of fruit, nut powder, flowers, and Yellow Root Powder." Here! Take one of the Bhang leaves and coat one side with it. Then take one Spike leave and slice it down the middle to open it like so." I watched as she carefully slid her knife down the middle of a leaf and then carefully pulled the cut open to show the clear, sticky fluid inside.

"Now I will need you and Merkansoo to help!" She said as she went to the fire. "Yes, Paasi?" He asked as he joined her. "We need to find where she is bleeding. These kinds of injuries usually punch into one of the organs behind the ribs. Can you see if any were bleeding?" Merkansoo quickly answered "I cam see the ones closest to the broken ends of the ribs. They are not bleeding. But I cannot tell if the stomach or the guts were punctured." Paasi asked, "Has she passed water or waste since the injury?" Mearoo answered as she was taking care of her "No, she has not. I have been giving her water but she has not passed any yet."

"That is bad. Very Bad" Paasi said as she thought about the causes of such things. "My eyes are not good enough to see, so you will have to do this!" She said to Merkansoo. He nodded then said, "You want me to lift the other organs aside so I can see if she is bleeding from the stomach and guts?" "Yes! If she has a hole in the guts or the stomach, we have to fix it. If it is more blood vessels we have to fix them. I can fix the green flesh. This will help bring down the fever. The herbs will lessen the pain and help her body fight. "Merkansoo sighed and said "Very well. We need to do this while we still have sunlight. Paasi agreed and said, "Let me give her something to dull the pain first." She reached into her hide bag and brought out a small dried plant root. She carefully took a small piece off and said "Pound this into a power Jakool. A small amount will help with the pain and strengthen her body." I nodded and used the handle of my knife to pound the root into the stone bowl.

I soon made a fine powder and handed the bowl to her. "Take your knife and hold it in the fire until the blade is hot. Then bring it here." She said to me. I did this then returned to her handing her the knife. She turned to Merkansoo and said "I am going to cut off the sick, green flesh. We cannot save it and if we leave it, it will spread." Merkansoo nodded and she gave Mearoo the powder and said "Put it in her mouth with some water. It works quickly." Mearoo did this and Paasi said, "It is time." She quickly cut the green edges of the wound until the healthy pink, red flesh was left.

"Now Merkansoo and Jakool. Rub this Spike Leaves all over your hands first." We then waited for her to tell us what to do next. "Jakool and Mearoo. You will need to turn her so the wound is facing up. This will help Merkansoo move the organs so he can see." We did this carefully as Elasaa moaned, but that was her only response.

Merkansoo carefully reached in with one paw and lifted something aside then said "I can see no wound in the stomach. I am checking the guts. He stopped and said, "I see something but I am not sure." Describe it to me." Paasi said. "I see blood seeping from under the guts but I do not see a wound." Paasi looked down as she thought. I knew she was remembering what she had been taught and what she had learned since then, about such an injury. "She may be bleeding from the small organ next to the guts below the stomach." She said finally. Merkansoo tried to see it but no matter what he did he couldn't reach it! "My hand is too wide!" He said trying to stay calm. "Then let Jakool do it! He has small hands and a keen eye!" I was surprised but knew she was right. My hand was half the size of Merkansoo's hand.

I took his place and listened as Paasi told me what to move and where to look. I saw it as soon as I slowly moved a section of her gut out of the way. A small organ was bleeding! There was also bleeding from blood vessels that were next to it! "I see it. What do I do?" I said after I described the bleeding to her. "Do you see a hole in the organ?" She asked. I looked again more closely and said "No. It looks more like a gash from the broken rib. It is right next to it." I said. Paasi nodded and said "Good! Take your knife and carefully cut out the organ. Only cut it at the top where it gets thin and connects to the gut." I slowly reached in with my knife and cut the small organ out! "Good," Paasi said as I pulled it out. "Now take this leaf and stick it to the cut." I did this and saw the bleeding stop."Now do the same to the leaking blood vessels." I had a little more trouble reaching them, but finally got a piece of the leaf around each one. "Now see if any more blood is coming out anywhere!" Paasi said to me. I looked carefully but did not see any bleeding. "I don't see anymore Paasi." "Now cover the hole with these leaves!" She instructed me and I did!

"Very Good Jakool and you too Merkansoo! She has a chance now of surviving this!" Paasi said as we sat down and rested after working hard to heal Elasaa. "If her guts were not damaged then why has she not moved water and waste?" I asked Paasi still wondering about this. Paasi said "Sometimes when your body is badly hurt in the middle, it sends the blood that usually goes to the gut to move the waste to help heal the wound. Also, she was bleeding, so she lost a lot of blood. Now the bleeding is stopped we will give her the juice of the Ankol Fruit and other things to help her make new blood."

"It was the juice of the Ankol fruit? Is that what I forgot?" I asked her so I would never forget! "Yes Jakool! That mixed with some of the dried bark and root of the tree, the Gold flowers, and a pinch of the yellow root." I sighed as I hung my head but Paasi said "You did well Jakool. You may have saved her life. Now it is up to her and the spirit of the cloud stabber." I nodded as I was carefully putting leaves over the hole as she had instructed me to do. Once finished she said "Now comes the hard part. She must not be moved and needs someone with her at all times. She must drink plenty of the juice and water. She will not be hungry until her guts start working again, but she must drink!" Mearoo nodded and said, "I will make sure one of us does this."

"Paasi nodded then said "Jakool! You have much to tell about what happened after the Rough Furs attack." I answered "Yes and so do the others. Kika and the rest are over there with the other wounded." Paasi sighed as she stood up then said "Let us look at them too. Once that is done you are needed by your tribe."

Reminding me of my duty to my tribe. "I know. But they will need more than me and the other young ones to survive and you know it Paasi!" She looked at me in surprise as I continued "I have brought more than myself and the other young hunters. I have brought another tribe that saved me and others during the attack. I am now Mearoo's mate and a member of this tribe too! I have spoken to Merkansoo about us and he wants to meet with the Elders to see for himself if they are worthy and willing to join our tribe with his."

Paasi stopped and looked at me then at Mearoo. "You? Are mated? You are not an adult yet!" She said trying to object, but I stopped her "I killed a large Bharal on the cloud stabber by myself. Mearoo can say this is true! I brought the hide which I have here"; I paused and pointed at the hide lying next to Mearoo on the grass. "I took the meat that I cut from the animal and cooked it to feed Mearoo and myself to survive on the cloud stabber." Paasi gave me a searching look then turned her eyes to Mearoo and asked "Is this true? Did Jakool make a kill and mate with you in celebration?" Mearoo answered her with no hesitation. "Yes, he did! I saved him from a Rough Fur by attacking it to give him time to hide. I did not expect him to track me into the cloud stabbers, but when he did, I knew then that he would be my mate." Paasi smiled and said "I see. In that case, we had better return to them to tell this remarkable story!"

Paasi turned to Merkansoo and said "I am an Elder of my tribe. I cannot speak for all the Elders. I can say that returning with Jakool and the other young ones will mean that the others will greet you in peace and will listen to your words." Merkansoo replied, "I would expect nothing less from Jakool's people." I sighed in relief as it seemed that my 'hope' of saving my tribe by joining with Mearoo's may actually happen! I asked her "How far away is the tribe?" Feeling anxious now that I knew they were close by. Paasi replied, "Two suns when you don't fly through the air like these two!" She said as we reached the wounded and we saw Janai and Lasaa there helping them to eat and drink. Janai grinned and Lasaa chuckled as she gave them a glare. I grinned when Janai said, "You didn't seem to mind when we told you that you would feel like you weighed nothing?" I almost choked on my laughter at Paasi's expression of surprise then her shrug admitting her guilt. So who doesn't want to feel lighter? Especially when they get as old as me!" She said then giggled as Lasaa gave her a pinch on the skin over her ribs he said "You don't feel that old to me!" giving her a grin! "Did you feel this way about Mearoo?" She asked as she was obviously enjoying Lasaa's attention to her and the effect of his scent! "Yes, I did. Mearoo explained that we humans are affected that way by her people. The men and the women!" "Interesting. Well if we join then it will make things much easier!" She replied as she squatted to examine the first wounded hunter with the broken leg. Satisfied with the job we did of splinting and wrapping the leg, she moved on to the next one. She gave out herbs, hide for bindings, and instructions to each one to aid their healing.

She then met Kika and the other young ones with real joy! "You! I never thought I would be happy to see you again!" She said in mock anger! We could all tell she was happy to see him and the rest of the young hunters. She looked at each one and then asked " Where are Rankoo and Denack?" Kika answered "Dead. The Rough Furs got them." She looked up to the sky briefly, then nodded and turned to me and said "You have done well Jakool" I smiled back feeling good about myself for the first time in several suns! Mearoo smiled at me from where she was squatting next to Elasaa. After everyone had eaten, Merkansoo consulted with Paasi, Janai, and Lasaa about the way to my tribe. I didn't stay as they talked for a long time and I was tired from the hunt for the plants, the work on the herbs, and the healing on Elasaa. I joined Mearoo on our furs, while Farkis took over the duties of watching and caring for Elasaa. We curled up and after cuddling for a few minutes, we went to sleep both feeling better about our tribes' future.

The next morning we woke up and after tending to our body's needs, we broke fast and sought out Paasi and Merkansoo. "Ah! So you two are awake? Paasi said, then said, "Elasaa is much better this morning, so I think we should talk about how to approach the tribe." "What is there to decide?" I asked not understanding her words. Merkansoo explained "Paasi and I spent a long time talking about the tribes and their differences. While you told Mearoo and me some of the history of your tribe, Paasi answered many questions and gave me details about the other Elders of the tribe. You will need to convince them Jakool." "I thought that Paasi would be the one to speak with the other Elders!" I said surprised. Paasi said "You survived the Rough Fur attack, the harsh weather in the cloud stabbers, made your first kill, and found a mate! You convinced them to help you find the other young hunters, find our tribe, and allow them to join theirs! Your voice needs to speak to them, not mine!"

I couldn't argue with Paasi's words as I knew in my heart they were true. Merkansoo then said "Paasi told me that since the loss of so many hunters, they are hungry. I think that you, Paasi, Mearoo, Janai, Lasaa and myself should go to help them. This way we show them that we are willing to help them if they accept us." I thought about it and said "Yes. That is a good idea! The remaining hunters will be grateful and this will help in convincing the rest." Paasi said then added "I will stay here. Elasaa will need further healing. I think you should take the young hunters with you. It will help them become men. That is very important for both tribes." I didn't miss the emphasis she put on 'both tribes' and said "Yes. They need this to get over what happened to them." Mearoo said, "I think we should take as many females as the young Ooh man hunters."

Merkansoo looked surprised by this, and asked "Why?" Mearoo put an arm around me and explained "The hunters should be in the company of our females. That will do more to convince them to join us than any other reasons!" I chuckled as I realized she was right! None of the hunters would be able to resist mating with Janai or any of the other female snow leapers! Merkansoo smiled and said, "I think Jameeka, Sheena, and Darshita should go." I wondered why Darshita; as she was his mate, but didn't question him as I was eager to go and help my tribe and give them the hope of a future!

Mearoo said to me "Come! We should get the young hunters ready to travel while Merkansoo gets the rest ready." I agreed and we left Merkansoo to gather up our own things, then found Kika and the rest. I told them "You will be coming with us to go and help our tribe hunt! They do not have enough hunters and gatherers to feed them.

We do this to show them we are ready to be men and will bring home meat!" Kika and the rest were both excited to finally be going home and nervous to know they were now expected to become men on this hunt! Mearoo said "You have the honor of being the first of our two tribes to hunt together. Janai, Jameeka, Darshita, Samalaa, and Sheena will also be part of this hunt as well as Jakool, Merkansoo, and myself." That caused several smiles to appear on faces showing which ones Sheena had been 'practicing' mating with! Mearoo had told me that Sheena was only three years old and would be coming into her first mating heat in the coming winter. She loved the young Ooh men when she first saw them and decided to make them feel like members by practicing mating with several of them!

"We leave immediately so get your things, ready your spears and knives brothers!" I said and was rewarded by shouts and cheers from them! Merkansoo was waiting with the other snow-leaper hunters when we joined them and signaled to Lasaa and Janai to lead us. I thought *If there is a Great Spirit of the Sky Stabber, please help my tribe to understand the Snow-Leapers.*

THE HUNTERS

They went at a pace we could keep up with so we didn't become separated. We all ran hard to cover the distance between us and where the tribe was camped. Paasi had said it was two suns away but we were moving fast and I was hoping we could make it in one sun as Janai and Lasaa had done! On the first break, I asked Janai "How much farther?" She thought and said "we could make it by nightfall." "If what?" I asked hearing the doubt in her voice. Janai sighed and said "We did not wish to suggest it to you and the other young Ooh-mans, but we are very strong. We could get there before nightfall 'if' we carry you." I looked at her puzzled then remembered that Mearoo had shown me how strong she was! "Can you do this without harming yourselves?

Janai grinned and said "Kika! Come here!" Kika came over and without warning she grabbed him and leaped into the air with him and landed over six man lengths away! The look on Kika's face made me laugh! "You look like you wet yourself!" I said as they returned the same way! Kika looked a little dazed then looked down and gave an embarrassed laugh as he realized he had wet himself! Janai was laughing as she said, "So would that be faster?" I was also laughing as Mearoo came up and asked if we were ready to go. That started us all laughing again! Finally, I told her about carrying us so we could get to the tribe faster!

Mearoo looked at me then Janai and said "I thought if we suggested this you would think we were saying you were weak and needed our help." Reminding me of what I had said to her when I was feeling like that. I replied "I did feel that way! But now I 'feel' that I need to learn to rely on my new tribe and their strengths! So can you carry us?" I asked her. Mearoo smiled and said "Of course we can! Merkansoo! We will carry them so we can reach Jakool's people by nightfall!" I had to suppress another laugh at Merkansoo's expression when he came over to them. "Another sign you are learning young Jakool. You are willing to accept help when you need it. I will take one of the other young ones as Mearoo will carry you and Janai will carry Kika. Sheena! Pick one!" Merkansoo called out and soon all the snow leapers had riders on their backs as they crouched on all fours. Merkansoo nodded and Janai and Lasaa jumped forward on ground covering leaps followed by the rest of us!

Riding Mearoo was more difficult than I imagined as I almost fell off her back when she jumped and hit my head on hers when we landed! "Hold on to my sides tightly with your legs! Grab a hold of my fur behind my neck! Lean back when I go to land! Lean forward when I jump!" Mearoo said then she made another jump! It took me several jumps to put her advice into practice but finally, I was no longer having trouble staying on her. We started well before the sun had risen to its highest point and traveled this way until it went past and was starting its path down to the west. I expected Mearoo and the rest to need more frequent rest stops, but I was wrong as they continued until the sun was halfway to the western horizon.

We stopped and I could see we were over halfway across the endless green grass! I could make out the beginnings of the hills in the distance and knew we would reach them that sun! Mearoo was taking long drinks of water from the skin as were the rest of the snow-leaper people. I asked if she needed to eat but she shook her head. After she swallowed the water she replied "No. It is not a good idea to eat then travel this way! I understood as I was sure that it would be hard to keep food down while jumping with me on her back! Is *it possible to hunt while riding like this?* I didn't ask as she said "Let's go! We do not stop until we reach your tribe." I swung my leg over her back and set myself for her jump.

We took off and now that I was used to her jumps, I was able to watch the surrounding endless green grass and the hills. I started to see more details ahead as we drew closer to them. I saw the end of the endless green grass and the start of the needle trees, red berry trees, flowering plants, and other bushes and trees that grew there. A wide but shallow river fed by the glaciers in the cloud stabbers marked the end of the grass. I knew that the camp was not far now as we crossed it.

I discovered that riding Mearoo while she was jumping up and down hills was much different than on the endless green grass! The changing angles of her jumps made it more difficult to lean into the jumps and away from the landings! I managed to adjust as she reached the top of the first line of hills and descended into a valley that separated them from the next hills. We crossed two more lines of hills like this as the light slowly died because the sun was behind the hills now and dusk was starting. I looked for signs of my tribe and the camp; as we climbed a defile between two hills that I recognized! This was the path we used to reach the endless green grass! We were close and I was eager to reunite with my tribe and help them!

Suddenly I heard a familiar shout and knew it to be Kaga! I immediately told Mearoo to find him!" She listened then jumped in a new direction causing everyone else to change directions as I yelled out to get their attention! I could see a cleft that I knew led to a deep valley that ended in a narrow pass between two steep hills. On the other side of the pass was a low wetland that was home to a large herd of a type of deer with huge four-tinned horns! The males were as long as a man. They were heavy and dangerous with the many prongs on the four horns.

The females were smaller than the males but still bigger and heavier than any member of our tribe. We usually only hunted them with a large hunting party! *They must be desperate for food*! I thought as Mearoo headed for the other end of the valley and the pass! As we got closer I saw two hunters on each side of the narrow pass waiting with their spears ready! I didn't need to say anything as Mearoo was heading towards them. I started yelling as soon as I was close enough to be heard. Both hunters turned and I saw that it was Kaga and Chirac!

Mearoo made a final jump and landed right in front of Kaga; who was a solemn person normally, but now had his mouth wide open in surprise at seeing me riding a creature that looked the way Mearoo did! He was even more surprised when I jumped off of Mearoo and she stood up and spoke! "Where are the rest of your hunters! We bring all the young hunters back and they can help you!" "It is true Kaga, Chirac! This is Mearoo! She saved my life and is now my mate! We don't have time to explain everything now but you will hear the story later! Where are Kiraat, Bamal, Jarack, and Hanuman? Are there any others?" I asked as I knew that there were not enough hunters to hunt these large animals! Chirac answered, "They are in the thick part of the low wetlands, trying to separate some of the herd and drive them this way!"

I immediately said to Mearoo and Merkansoo, "You need to help them! I will stay here with Kaga, Chirac, and the young hunters!" Thinking this was best, but Merkansoo said "They will think we are attacking them for the animals". I realized he was right and said "Then I will go with you! Kika! You are in charge of the young hunters! Kaga! You and Chirac get them in position so they each have a chance to make the kill! Only if they get by them do you make the kill! Yes?" Kaga and Chirac immediately understood my plan and my intention of giving 'all' the young hunters a chance to become men! "It is a good plan! Now Go!" Chirac said as I climbed onto Mearoo and she took off again!

I clenched my teeth; to keep them from hitting each other hard, as she landed the first jump and then took off again! We were through the pass in four jumps and a short downhill jump took us to the endless green grass between the hills of the pass and the low wetlands. We couldn't jump because the ground was now very wet with different types of grasses, plants, and trees there. I looked to the right and saw the landmark I was searching for! "There! Where the large blooming plants are! Go there! I said pointing towards a spot between two large clumps of plants with large red, white, and orange flowers on them!

We went through the gap leading the rest of the snow-leaper scouts and hunters deeper into the low wetlands. I was carefully using my spear to check the ground in front of me, as I knew there were places where it was water and mud that you would sink into and not get out without help! We had seen deer step in them and just sink out of sight as they struggled uselessly!

Suddenly Lasaa and Janai jumped into the trees. Looking ahead Janai signaled ahead and to the left! We followed them as they led us deeper and deeper into the wet lowlands until we heard yelling and the sound of hide drums being pounded with spears! "That is them! I said. "Merkansoo! Mearoo! Come with me! The rest of you circle around as the main herd of deer must run here to get away from the hunters!" Merkansoo gave a signal and they all took to the flanks and disappeared quickly as they circled wide to not spook the deer! We ran straight ahead and risked spooking the deer.

I knew Kiraat was trying to scare the deer into leaving the low wetlands deep in the many trees, by making as much noise as they could! But it didn't work as they had gone deeper into the low wetlands! I finally saw the hunters ahead of us standing in a line stretched too far as they walked forward into the heart of the wetlands. This was very dangerous as it was also home to the many-toothed water lizard that could hide in shallow water waiting for anything to come along then leap up and kill it with its long teeth-filled jaws! I hoped we didn't have to fight any of these things as I ran towards Kiraat and Bamal shouting! They turned and then gave a shout of joy at seeing me! That turned to shock and surprise as they saw Merkansoo and Mearoo with me! Kiraat looked as if he might attack Mearoo when we approached, so I yelled "Friends Kiraat! Bamal! They are not enemies or creatures! This is Mearoo! My Mate! This is Merkansoo the Leader of their tribe! Listen to me!" I said while still a good two-man lengths away from them.

Kiraat slowly lowered his spear and stood waiting for us as we stopped our run and walked the last steps to stand in front of him. "I never thought I would ever see you again Jakool! The others? Did they survive too?" He asked looking eager to hear good news about them. "Yes! We only loss Rankoo and Denack. The rest are with Kaga and Chirac! I told them to form them up into hunting formation so 'All' of them have the chance at their first kill!" Bamal was surprised at hearing this and said "How? We failed when we tried to drive them towards the pass earlier! They were too smart! The large male that leads the herd immediately ran them deep into the many trees; where the low wetlands are, before we could strike any of them!" He said sounding both disgusted and frustrated! "I sent over two hands of hunters into the low wetlands around us to drive the deer out for you! We need to make sure when they come out we get them to go through the pass!" I explained to them.

Kiraat was too experienced a hunter to question this as he knew we had to keep the deer from scattering: as they would do when scared out of their hiding place! Merkansoo said "We are much faster than you, so we can keep up with the the herd. The best way to do this is to make the big leader go where we want them to go!" Kiraat said "Yes! What can we do?"Jakool thought for a moment then said "We will need to follow the herd to make sure they don't get the chance to turn back!" Remembering my hunting lessons! Kiraat smiled and then gave me a slap on the back that sent me stumbling forward! He laughed and said, "You did learn something!"

He chuckled when Merkansoo and Mearoo both grinned then turned and put the others; who had now arrived, into a long corridor leading to the pass! "Good! Now we go to scare that Leader your way!" Merkansoo said! He turned and made a huge jump and landed over ten man-lengths away!

"Show Off!" Mearoo said grinning then with a gleam in her eyes she turned and jumped even further! I laughed at the faces of Kiraat and Bamal as they looked stunned by this display of jumping! "Kiraat turned to me and asked, "Can we trust them?" I replied "She is my mate! She saved my life from a Rough Fur when I was about to die! Merkansoo has given me his word that as long as you greet them as friends and equals, he will speak with you about joining their tribe! Yes, I trust them with all of our lives!" Kiraat looked at me in surprise then a slow smile spread across his face. "You have grown up Jakool. You have spoken like a man of our tribe should!" I felt a huge lift in my spirits at his words as they meant he accepted me as an adult and an equal!

Suddenly we heard loud roars and the higher-pitched sounds of the deer responding terrified! I gripped my spear more tightly as I heard water splashing; the sound of animals in panic, and felt the rumbling of the ground! Suddenly the lead male burst from deep cover from among the trees in front and to the left of me! Bamal and Kiraat were ready and rushed at him making him veer back towards me! We jumped up yelling and waving our spears once he approached, turning him to go forward to avoid us! Larkar and Mahendra were there waiting on one side with Samalaa! She was almost as tall as Mahendra: and easily as strong, as she was the largest of the snow-leaper people there! The lead male didn't even try to veer when he saw them yelling and jumping up and down on each side, he just charged straight ahead!

"It's working! I yelled! As the rest of the herd burst from cover, we were too busy keeping them behind the leader to talk! We worked together to hold them between us as they ran out of hiding towards the pass! I counted over four hands of animals and realized it was too many for just the young hunters; and Chirac and Kaga, to kill! "Kiraat! Too many! I shouted as I gave Bamal a hand signal and we both jumped together in front of the next two deer and thrust our spears into them! I was lucky to hit mine in the chest dropping it without getting hit by its horns! Larkar only got grazed along one arm as he had a larger male and had to dodge sideways and thrust through the ribs! I yanked out my spear and started yelling and jumping up and down to turn the rest of the herd back!

Kiraat, Bamal, Samalaa, and Jarack were also doing this, so we soon scared them into turning back! I took a breath and saw that Bamal and Kiraat had both made kills, so we had four animals already! I yelled ahead to Mahendra who immediately stepped in front of the remaining deer still going his way and ran right at the front two animals!

Seeing this Samalaa made a leap and landed on the back of one of them, grabbed the antlers, and yanked hard on them causing the animal's head to pull back and up snapping it! Samalaa jumped off just as it tumbled head first causing the following animals to trip and fall! The rest stopped in confusion as Mahendra plowed through them shoving and stabbing as he went! Samalaa was right beside him making the deer turn! We ran up to them and helped them turn the rest of the herd back! Once we did this I yelled for Mearoo to come get us!

I turned to Bamal and the rest saying "We had to get through the pass and to the ambush, or the young hunters would be trampled to death by that many large animals!" I jumped on Mearoo, Bamal on Merkansoo, Mahendra on Samalaa, Larkar on Lasaa, and Kiraat on Janai! I yelled at them "Hold on tight with your legs, lean forward into the jump, and back away from the landing! Hold tight to the fur behind the neck!" That was all the time we had as Mearoo bunched up in a crouch and made the first leap! It was dangerous to do this in the low wetlands, but we had no choice! I prayed to the Sky Spirits to keep us all safe; as we jumped, leaped, bounded, and ran until we cleared the wetlands and made the pass! The last animal was just entering the pass so Mearoo timed her jump to land in front of it, but on the hillside not in the low spot between them!

She then leaped up higher so she would be able to make a much longer jump from there to the lower side of the hill! She repeated this until we cleared the pass, then the strip of grass that led to the defile they were now stampeding across! I gritted my teeth as Mearoo made a particularly daring jump onto a rocky ledge that overlooked the middle of the valley to get into position, then jumped down and to the right of the deer! She was now in a race with them as they running for their lives!

I could see the lead deer as we gained ground on him, with the rest right behind us! I was leaning so far forward with the speed of her jumps, that my head was next to hers! I saw the almost feral look on her face and eyes as she let her full snow-leaper self be in control so she could move as fast as possible! It took me a few seconds to even realize it when she beat the lead male deer to the narrow defile between the two hills! "Now! I yelled as I stood up and leaped from her back!

I landed and rolled on the ground then stood up right in front of the middle of the herd and thrust into the first animal within reach! Mearoo gave a loud cry and jumped up and bit the underside of the neck of one while sinking her claws into its shoulders! It couldn't shake her off as she ripped out its throat! She jumped off then onto another animal as Bamal gave a mighty yell and threw his spear at a male that had lowered its head to gore Kiraat while he was thrusting at the animal next to it! I watched as Bamal's throw caught the animal in the right front shoulder causing it to stumble and fall! He was on it with his knife slicing its throat then retrieving his spear, as Kiraat finished off his animal! Merkansoo, Janai, Lasaa, Denala, Farkis, and Samalaa were taking down animals quickly as I ran to help Larkar.

I saw him in trouble with three males going for him with their antlers! I yelled as I threw my spear and drew my knife! I was lucky as my spear hit one cleanly in the side of the throat taking it down! Before I could reach another! I saw Larkar swing his spear high over his head as he jumped high then landed the tip of his spear with his whole body behind it right on the back of the animal's neck! It gave a loud scream as it dropped hard to the ground! The third animal almost got him but Darshita suddenly landed on its back and snapped its neck like Samalaa had done with one animal earlier! Within the space of no more than a handful of heartbeats, we had killed over eight of the great beasts! I yelled, "Let's get to the other side!" Mearoo practically slid between my legs and jumped right at the cleft! We landed at the narrowest point with the next jump taking us through it!

I immediately saw dead animals blocking the way as Mearoo had to jump sideways to avoid landing on them! I looked around to see if the young hunters were okay and was proud to see Kika taking down one of the large males by himself! Kiraat came up just then on Merkansoo and gave a yell of approval as he watched Kika drop and roll to avoid the animal's horns then thrust up through the soft belly from underneath! I turned to see Hanuman make a killing thrust right through the chest! Then roll to the right to keep from being gored! I looked for Harit and saw him in a fight with the Leader! *Oh No!* I thought as I watched the animal make a run at him! Harit looked afraid standing there waiting with his spear ready! I knew we couldn't reach him in time and prayed for the spirit to help him! It did in the form of one of the younger snow-leaper females named Hardika!

She appeared from behind him, and at the right moment she jumped over him; as he was thrusting his spear into its chest, and grabbed the leader's large antlers as she sailed over its back! The force of her jump caused the animal's head to snap up keeping it from goring Harit as he thrust forward into its chest to its heart! "He did it! Harit killed the leader!" I yelled jumping up and down in excitement at his kill! The Deer's speed kept it moving forward; knocking him over but he rolled and was back up!

I looked around and saw that all the young hunters were standing by their kills with varying looks of surprise, happiness, shock, and triumph! The only ones that appeared solemn were Kaga and Chirac! I went over to them and asked if someone had been badly hurt or killed?. Kaga just shrugged and said "No. We only got to kill one each!" That made me, Kiraat, Bamal, and the rest laugh! Kiraat finally said "Jakool? Count up the kill as you are the Hunt Leader!" I was stunned as I looked at him and then at Bamal as they stood there with big smiles on their faces! I turned as I felt myself fill with pride and said "I see two hands and two fingers of deer here. Kiraat. How many did we kill on the other side?" As I wiped the sweat from my forehead with my arm. "A hand and three! We have Four Hands! This is a hunt that will be told about by our people, by the spirits they will!" he said showing his joy and relief at such a good hunt! "No one will go hungry tonight or for many more to come!" He said grinning as he signaled the young hunters!

They all stood up straight as they signaled back! Mearoo asked me "What did that signal mean?" I smiled as I waved at Kika and the rest then turned to her and said

"Kiraat gave them the 'Good Hunt Men!' Signal! Mearoo didn't understand at first so I said "He signaled Good Hunt Men to the young hunters! They were not men before! He is telling them they are now!" Mearoo smiled as she understood and replied "I still think it is a silly custom to have to kill on a hunt before you can mate! But at least they will now have that to look forward to tonight!" "Yes, they will!" I said excitedly for them as I watched them all go down on their knees with their knives and cut out the heart of their animal! They all lifted them up to the sky in thanks to the spirit of the cloud stabbers! Kika then took some of the heart's blood and smeared it on his face! This would mark him as a man with his first kill when we returned to the camp! Now the men would know they were now considered adults, and the women would know they could now mate! I knew they would be well-mated that night!

I suddenly felt a little uneasy as I watched Larkar not cut out the heart of the animal he'd killed on this side. He just stood there with his head down shaking. I asked Kiraat "He is not well?" Bamal also took note of Larkar as he watched him and answered before Kiraat.

"No. He is worse. We have tried to help him, but he is filled with bitterness and hate for those who murdered his family and his tribe." Merkansoo heard and came up to us and asked "Who is this you speak of? An enemy?" Kiraat spit on the ground and said words in a language that only one of his father's tribe would know! But I had heard this curse before during the telling of the story of the migration. I knew why, but it was not my story to tell! Kiraat said "We will talk of this later. You have proven yourselves true friends to our whole tribe today! I would like to hear this amazing story that young Jakool mentioned earlier, but not until we get all these deer butchered and brought back to camp!"

Kiraat was in for another surprise as he watched Samalaa and Mahendra simply pick up the entire animal and put it on their shoulders! "By the spirit!" Kiraat said as he saw Janai pair with Jarack and Kaga to pick up another! Chirac, Samalaa, and Larkar followed their example and soon all twelve animals were on their way to the camp No butchering was needed! Merkansoo turned to Kiraat and said, "The rest of us should return and bring the rest of the animals!" Kiraat laughed as Merkansoo dropped to all fours to let him mount as I mounted Mearoo then off we went! It was a little harder carrying the eight dead deer out of the wetlands, and we almost lost one to one of the 'sharp tooth snappers'! It lunged out of hiding in a pool of scum-covered water as Darshita and two of the young hunters went past! But Darshita was quick and landed on its snout and stuck her claws in its eyes causing it to hiss in pain and quickly let go of the deer leg it had bitten and sink back into the water!

We marched out of the wetlands, over the green grass, and through the hills, until we reached the endless green grass again. Here we saw the trail left by the first group of hunters carrying the deer to follow. It took a few hours to reach the camp. We crossed several streams; that were hidden by the tall grass it fed and the rich growth of other plants there. We climbed a small rise and saw two lookouts watching for us. As they waved us on I knew we were almost there! From the other side of the rise, we couldn't see the camp as it was cleverly hidden from view! Another dip and rise in the land did this. There were small areas of rocky land on some of the rises and dips. We had made our camp in a dip outside a medium-sized cave. It was not quite large enough for the whole tribe to live in, but it was large enough for our small tribe to hide in if attacked! We had the entrance trapped so a rock slide could be triggered from outside if those guarding the entrance believed we were losing during an attack!

That way the young and old inside would be safe with plenty of food and water stored, there so at least the tribe would survive. We entered the camp with wild cheers, back slaps, hugs of women and men, and astonishment at both the number of beasts killed and our new friends and allies!

I walked proudly with Mearoo by my side as we carried one end of one of our kills! Merkansoo and Kiraat were carrying the other end showing our people they had nothing to fear from the strange-looking snow-leaper people! Right up to the great fire ring in front of the cave entrance we went, where we were met by the remaining Elders of the tribe! There stood Merack, Nada, and Gaieaa in front of the rest of the Elderly and Elders. Gaieaa and Pathak stood; even though it caused them pain from their joint ail, because this was a special event! Not only had we returned from death, but we returned with the largest kill a hunt ever made and with new friends and allies!

CHAPTER FIVE

A JOINING OF BLOOD

The tribe already had a big fire going, and the men and women were busy skinning and butchering the deer that arrived first. I addressed the Elders; at Kiraat's insistence, as I was responsible for returning the young hunters, bringing the snow-leaper people to help us and the large kill. "Elders! I have returned from my death thanks to my new friends, tribesmen, and my mate!" Here I put an arm around Mearoo and introduced her. "This is Mearoo! She and her tribe are different than us, but no different than the many other tribes that came together to make our tribe!

I saw some of the Elders smile in acceptance of this truth while a few were still trying to understand who or what they were. "I have heard the amazing story of how they came to be, but it is not my story to tell. When we sit around the great fire tonight to feast, you can ask their Leader Merkansoo here," I paused and turned to Merkansoo who nodded and smiled. I almost laughed at the gasps of surprise by some of the young and the old at the sight of his sharp canine teeth!

"Will tell you their story! For now know that they saved my life, the life of the other young hunters, and came to help all of us because by being chosen by Mearoo as her mate, I became a member of their tribe too!" This gave the Elders and the rest something to think about as this was a different way than ours. But new ways are sometimes good, as they cause you to think about the old and the new and if both are equally as important or even needed.

At this point, Merack stepped forward and said "Jakool, son of Randu. We the elders have heard your words and will listen to what Merkansoo and his people have to say. For now, let us work together on the task at hand! Preparing For A FEAST!" He shouted the last part, so all would know that now was the time for celebrating not questions or stories! I grinned as Merack came up to me and gave me the greeting of equals! He smiled and said "You have shown great courage and wisdom. I want to hear what Merkansoo has to say as soon as possible." I heard something wrong in his voice and looked at him closely. I realized he looked older and tired! There were new lines on his face around his eyes and around his mouth. I said "Merack. They are offering to allow all of us to join their tribe. We can save our tribe in this way."

Merack looked at me in surprise at my words then asked "Is this true? What do they want from a poor tribe like ours?" He said not believing the good news I gave him. "They want our tribe to help them by mating with them!" That caused Merack to guffaw in laughter and he looked up quickly to see Mearoo helping Nada skin a deer, Samalaa and Mahendra another! "I see! Does Mearoo's choice of 'you' as a mate have something to do with this offer?" "No. They will explain their reasons tonight at the feast. I am not sure I understand them myself."

I took a deep breath and told Merack the condition they set for joining with them. "They will accept us 'Only' if all wish to join. That is the one condition! They are a very old people and have an enemy tribe that hunted them for their skins, until they moved high up into the cloud stabbers, I mean Fingers of Rock", Merack interrupted me with a grin saying "I like Cloud Stabbers better! Easier to say! But I cannot speak for all. You know this." "I know", I answered then told him the rest of the condition. "They will not allow anyone who refuses to join to live. They cannot as they can be made to tell others they exist and where they live. It is the only way they will accept us."

Merack frowned then asked "So if someone like Larkar", he turned and looked around for Larkar, finally seeing him working on a deer with Darshita helping him. He looked like he was gritting his teeth and his face showed anger! I felt a hand on my shoulder and looked to see Merkansoo watching us watching Larkar! "I sent Darshita to work with him. He was not pleased but allowed it only because she had saved him a great injury and maybe his life! Is he troubled in some way?" Merkansoo asked politely. Merack answered him as he knew the problems of Larkar better than I did.

"Larkar was in a tribe that were all killed by a very bad tribe! They waited until the hunters had gone to attack the Elders, Women, and Children! They killed them in slow horrible ways after taking the women repeatedly." When the hunting party returned to their camp, they were ambushed by the killers! Larkar was at the rear and saw everyone else get killed by the surprise attack! He turned and fled even though he was wounded. They tracked him for suns before he lost them in a very bad many trees. "Merkansoo showed more emotion than I had seen from him since our meeting. "We will do everything we can to help him overcome his loss, his grief and his anger. You said this other tribe were cruel killers? Did they have a name?"

He looked fierce when he asked Merack this question. Merrick nodded slowly and answered "They call themselves 'Krieg'. When they attack they come at you yelling this name!" Merkansoo said "I believe that this was no accident that led you to us Jakool!" He turned to face Merack and said "We will help your tribe to recover and to grow again. How you do this is up to you. I have made an offer to Jakool to allow your entire tribe to join ours. I only made one condition!" Merack nodded and said "Jakool told me the condition and the reason. I understand why you do this, but I do not speak for the whole tribe or even all the Elders. This must be discussed by all before any decision is reached." Merkansoo gave Merack a nod and replied "As you should do, as we would do. But understand that Jakool here has vowed that any who do not join with us, he will kill himself." Merack looked at me for a moment then back to Merkansoo and smiled as he said "He is young, and not so big, but I would not wish to tell him I refuse to join!"

Merkansoo said "Neither would I! I have seen him today in the hunt! For one so small he is very brave and wise!" I had heard enough as I felt my face and ears burning with the red flush of embarrassment at such praise! I turned and said to Mearoo. "Let us help with the deer, so we can eat! I am starving!" Causing her to laugh as I grabbed her hand and ran over to where the remaining deer were laid out. Even with so many working, it took hours to skin, butcher, and prepare so much meat! One group of men and women were working on the skins as they needed to clean them of all flesh before wetting them in a nearby stream. They would then start rubbing them with their stone scrapers to remove more of the flesh and fat. They would be repeating this several times over the next few suns.

Once only the skin and fur remained, they would rub them with oils made from the fat and brains of the animal. When the entire skin was treated, they would start stretching them on wood racks raised over the fire pits to cure them. Another group was already cooking the deer meat in different ways for the feast and for the suns to come. Mearoo and I worked on skinning the deer; as we both worked well together on this task.

Once all were skinned we started on the butchering. She would hold large pieces like the haunch, so I could cut it from the body with my knife. With so much to do, I was surprised when I saw the shadows on the ground and turned to see the sun slipping behind the hills! I looked around and saw that almost all the meat was cooked, the other dishes prepared and hides brought out to sit on around the great campfire.

We washed up in the stream and drank deeply as we were thirsty from the work, then joined the rest at the campfire. We sat with Merack, Kiraat, Bamal, Merkansoo, Pathak, Gaieaa, and Darshita in a group. Merack had requested we do this, so all could hear both the story of how I survived and met the snow-leaper people. Before they had heard my story; and Merkansoo's, Everyone concentrated on eating, drinking, and giving the snow leapers choice bits from every dish! Mearoo responded by making faces at some of them, 'Oohs' of surprise at others, and outright joy at some! We also shared touches, caresses, long kisses, and lots of joking and teasing! The rest of the tribe were also getting to know our new friends and it was easy to see they were being affected by their scent, just as I was by them.

I laughed at the sight of Pathak and Gaieaa enjoying the attentions of Darshita and Merkansoo while we ate. Gaieaa turned to me and said "Now I understand how you ended up becoming Mearoo's mate! I have not felt like this in a very long time!" A sudden pinch by Merkansoo on her right breast stopped her from saying anymore! Pathak was trying to keep from mauling Darshita's fur-covered breasts as she smiled and played with him, knowing he couldn't resist her!

Once we had satisfied our hunger for food, and the Elders had gotten to know both Merkansoo and Darshita better, Merkansoo said "It is time you hear of how my people came to be. Mearoo?" I gave her a look of surprise which she answered by saying "I am the Keeper of the First Cave. As a direct descendant of both of the First, I have the honor and duty to tell their story." I smiled as Mearoo took over and told them of her heritage directly back to that First pair! She told them of the cave where they lived; where she met and mated with me.

She explained this is where the records of this; and other stories of their tribe, were carved and painted on the walls. Once she finished Merack said, "I think this is a good time to hear Jakool's story!" All agreed and I was now going to tell my first story! It was as much a part of becoming an adult as making your first kill and mating with your first woman!

As the Elders listened to my story I found myself realizing just how incredible it sounded! It was one thing to experience such events, but quite another to tell them to a group! They were very quiet as I told of the Rough Fur attack, the run into the many trees, the Rough Fur chasing me, Mearoo exploding out of the snow to attack the Rough Fur so I could hide in a burrow! No one interrupted me until I told of the dream I had in the First Cave by the lake. Gaieaa stopped me and asked,

"You had this dream just as you have told us?" "Yes, Gaieaa. It was very strange, as I did not know of Mearoo's people then. It was not until after I found her waiting for me, and we mated, that I learned the story behind the dream." Gaieaa asked "This was a true dream? It was real?" I started to answer but Mearoo answered for me instead! "Yes, it was! Jakool dreamed of the First! The first Man and the First Female snow-leaper to mate, have cubs, and live together!"

Gaieaa turned to Pathak and asked him "Is it possible? Does he have the 'True Seeing'?" I did not know what they meant by this and asked. "What do you mean, True Seeing'. Pathak answered me by explaining "We call what you say happened a 'True Dream'. We say that the ones that have them have 'True Seeing'. We believe that some are given these dreams by the Sky Spirits or other Spirits for some reason. We do not know the reason. We only know that it does not happen very often." I asked, "Why have I not heard of this before now?" Gaieaa said "Because you, me, and Tivash are the only ones that have it. She only speaks to me about her dreams. This is so I can help her understand them. She is still young and the dreams sometimes make her very afraid. Was this your first True Dream?" "Yes, it was," I answered her. "Well then how were we to know?" She pointed out! I had to agree with her! "I think I understand now. I was very confused at first; until Mearoo told me the story of the First!" I said after a few moments.

"Go on with your story Jakool!" Merack said stopping the talk of 'True Seeing' for now. I told of my first meeting with Mearoo, and the effect she had on me and our mating! There was plenty of interest in this, as it was much different than how we usually mated. Merack said at the point where I had lost consciousness "I would have probably died! It is good that you were the first to mate with them Jakool!

I worry that some of 'us' may not survive their first mating with them!' He gave both Pathak and Gaieaa a stare so they knew he meant them! "I don't know, but I can't think of a better way to die!' Gaieaa said to many laughs and chuckles. Pathak looked more thoughtful then asked "Merkansoo? When we get old, we lose much of our strength. It is a real concern for some of us." Merkansoo replied "We know. We have many Elders that no longer mate. But they are honored, respected, and needed by their tribe!"

Darshita turned to Pathak and put her paw on his loincloth above his man-pole and said "We can be very gentle when mating with those with less strength. We consider it an honor to mate with our Elders." Pathak swallowed hard and we all saw the flush of blood rushing to his face as she gently rubbed him there. "I can see that you are still able. I will be very gentle with you 'If' you decide you wish to mate with me." Merack and Gaieaa both laughed at his face and his unusual silence! "What? No quick reply? No Story?" Bamal said teasing him a little. Pathak gave him a glare that caused more laughter!

Thinking I should continue, I told them of the symbols on the cave walls; and Mearoo explaining them to me, and of the First's ability to count large numbers of things! They were all surprised to hear of this and listened closely as I told of his using 'two fingers' joined together to show 'two hands' of things! "That is not something any of his kind have ever done! At least not the ones that have been in our tribe." Pathak said." Merkansoo replied "There is a reason he knew this. I will tell you only after you have joined with us. It is something not shared with others outside of our tribe." Pathak would have asked more but he was stopped by Gaieaa saying "Yes. We understand Merkansoo. Please continue Jakool" I told them how I had forgotten about them; until I was reminded when Mearoo and I were sharing stories. I became upset as I told of how Mearoo had not understood me, and attacked me when I said I had to return to my tribe. I told of how I waited for her to return but finally left realizing she was not coming back!

They were very surprised; and a little confused as to why I was upset while telling them! "I cannot explain to you what I do not understand myself! I felt as if I had just lost my brother, my father, and my mother at one time!" I said trying to find a way to describe my feeling when she attacked me then left me!

Mearoo put her arms around me as she spoke. "When an Oohman mates with one of us, it is different. We have seen this in our own tribe many times. They are so strongly affected by our scent and form a strong bond with the one they mate with. But once they mate with another of us, they usually no longer try to stay with the first one. Is this different with you?" she asked them. The best answer was given by Merack who said "Sometimes a young one will believe that they will not have as good an experience with someone else after their first mating. This is common and usually is 'cured' when he finds that any of the women will now mate with him! So in that we are the same. But it is rare for older adults to mate only with each other. It does happen, but not often."

Mearoo nodded and said "I think this is different somehow. I do not know how as Jakool was my first mating. So we do not understand yet why we feel as strongly about each other as we do! I somehow 'knew' when he appeared in the First Cave that he was supposed to be my mate! Not just for that first mating!" Merkansoo added "In our tribe, we mate with many to have as many young as possible. Do you also do this?" Merack said "Yes. As long as the land will support that many we wish to grow in numbers and strength." Merkansoo replied "So you see we are alike in this. But we also have those that prefer one mate over all others." He turned and looked at Darshita who said "I prefer Merkansoo as my mate. He also prefers me. But we both understand the need to mate with others and we do. A few will only mate with one mate. In this, we are the same."

I told the rest of the story finishing with arriving in time to help the tribe hunt the deer and our return to the camp. "It is a story that will be remembered by all". Pathak said to me. This was how I knew that he would make sure the story was added to the ones that were put on the cave walls and told to all the young around the fires at night. Merkansoo spoke next and told of the time between the First and now. We listened as he told of the times other Men had wandered into the cloud stabbers and became mates of the evolving snow-leaper people. He told of small families and tribes; that were fleeing from tribes like the Krieg, that attacked and killed for territory, belongings, food, and pleasure! I started to see the long amount of time between the First and them, as he told us stories of bravery, sacrifice, blood bonds, and bitter losses when they encountered the Krieg!

"They came from the Great Salt Water in the East. We know this as you do." Merkansoo said explaining how the killing started. "We had come down from the cloud stabbers as it got colder and colder there. To stay would have meant death to all of us! The great sheets of ice came further and further down the cloud stabbers until they reached the great flat lands beyond the hills! The many trees there died and the animals either died or fled here before us! We followed the streams and rivers until we reached a place of many tall trees, unlike any we have here now. It took a full season to cross it and ended in great low wetlands, that emptied into the Great Salt Water. It was filled with all the things we needed and settled there.

Merkansoo turned his head and spat on the ground then said something in his own tongue before continuing. "My ancestors were there so I speak this from their memories!" He had explained to the Elders about the racial memory they possessed, so they understood how they were able to remember all of their history. "We were out hunting the great one-horned beast that lived in the many trees and the long grass. It is a great, strong beast; and becomes very angry when attacked! Its hide is like stone and you have to attack it at the neck and underneath to kill it! We were tracking a small herd of them when we came across tracks of men. We didn't recognize them; as we were familiar with the tribes around us, but were not alarmed. That changed when we came to a great river that runs from the cloud stabbers to the Great Salt Water, right through the many trees. It was there that we were attacked with no challenge or warning. Several died before we even knew we were being attacked!

Our hunting party was large; as the one-horned beast is a dangerous prey, so we were able to fight back and kill some of their attackers! We had started to win the fight when the attackers ran! Like frightened long ears, they leaped into the thickest part of the many tall trees and disappeared! We lost eight that sun. We thought it was over and continued on the hunt, but that night they attacked us again! To shorten the story I will say they attacked us when we least expected it, then would disappear before we could kill more than a few! We didn't know why they kept attacking us until we left the hunt to retreat back to our village. It was then we came across some of the bodies of our dead brothers. Their hide was stripped from their flesh, their teeth and claws taken! These killers were hunting us like we hunted game! Only they didn't do it for food! They wanted our skins!" This caused a stir among the Elders! Pathak asked "They took the skins off of your dead? Or were they alive when they did this?"

Merkansoo gazed at Pathak with a piercing look that made me feel as if he was looking into his mind. "What do you know of this?" Merkansoo asked him. Pathak said in reply "The killers we told you about. They did this to all they tortured and killed! If they captured you, they would string you up between two trees and use you as a practice for their spears! They made sure they didn't hit anything that caused a quick death! Many times they would start cutting the skin off of them before they were dead! They wear the skin as a trophy!" Merkansoo replied "We know. Most of ours they trade, but some they keep along with the head, claws, and teeth! They believe it gives them our strength and cunning!" Pathak sighed and said "Many believe such things. But to take the skin from someone in that way? It shows a cruel people that enjoy torture and killing!"

I saw what they were trying to tell each other and spoke up "The Krieg and our killer tribe are the same?" It was Gaieaa that answered my question "We know they attacked us when we crossed over from where the sun goes to sleep, to the coast with the Great Salt Water where the sun wakes up. Not at first, but later when we moved up the coast to the mouth of that river! Could it be the same river that you told us your tribe settled near?" Merkansoo thought hard then asked, "Did yours have marshes and low wetlands that ran from the bottom of the hills to the Great Salt Water?" Pathak answered as he was the keeper of our records "Yes it did! We gathered the wild grain seeds that grew in abundance there!" Merkansoo said "Then it is the same tribe! We now have a common enemy as well as blood ties".

Bamal suddenly spoke "I have already decided. The tribe that treats us as you have and hates our enemy has me as a member!" I was surprised by his sudden decision but even more so when Pathak, Gaieaa, Merack, and Nada all said the same! Merkansoo looked at them and then asked, "So what happens now?" I looked around at the Elders wondering the same thing! Merack smiled and said "We will present your offer to the rest of the tribe tomorrow after the celebration feast tonight. Many will be in very good moods after this meal and the mating!" Merkansoo smiled at this clever idea and said "Good! I am hesitant to ask this.." He paused giving them the opening to ask him "What is it? You can ask us anything!" Merkansoo still looked hesitant but finally said "I wish to discuss Larkar."

That was a surprise to some of the Elders! "Larkar? What about Larkar?" Merack asked. But I knew, Bamal knew and Merack knew what worried Merkansoo. Darshita actually spoke "Larkar is different. I have spent time with him and I can tell you that he is hurting inside! He is filled with grief, anger, and rage! He is a danger to himself and to others!" This honesty about Larkar was needed and I knew it. Merack slowly nodded in agreement then said "We have tried everything we know!

We do not give up on one of our own because they are in trouble!" Darshita replied quickly to make herself clear "I am not saying you should! I am saying that we may be able to help him." She had everyone's attention as she spoke quickly and quietly so as not to be overheard. I snorted as the celebration was going well around us and no one was paying any attention to us!

I glanced around to be sure and saw several of the new adult hunters already paired off with either a snow-leaper female or one of our females! I turned back to the conversation to hear Darshita say "He wants to be alone yes? But why does he want to be alone? Because seeing this" She waved an arm around her at the tribe enjoying themselves "Makes his pain even greater! He will either go off one sun and not return until he finds his revenge, or is helped to lose the hate in his heart." "How?" I asked her directly feeling a fear in my own heart about Larkar! Darshita looked at me and said "The same way that Mearoo helped you. He needs someone as special as Mearoo to help him through this." Merack said "We have tried this. Unfortunately, none of our women could stand his constant anger." Darshita nodded and said "Yes. I understand as I have spent time with him. But there is someone that might be able to do this. She is not here now but if you decide to join us, then Larkar will meet her when we go to our home.

I wondered who this mystery person was, as I thought I had met all the snow-leaper tribe! I asked and was greeted with a chuckle from Merkansoo who said "This is just the scouting party that went to find you remember?" I slapped my forehead as I did remember Merkansoo telling me this before. Merack asked, "I did want to ask just how many are your tribe?" Merkansoo replied, "We are as many as the number of suns in ten hands of seasons." I was shocked as I had no idea that the tribe was so large! Merack stared at him as if he was not sure he heard him correctly! Pathak said, "I believe that means that your females still bear many young at once?" Darshita gave him a smile and said "You are very wise! That is correct. We usually have between two and five children at once. We do not have as much pain and problems as Ooh-mans do giving birth.

I suddenly realized what that meant! I turned to look at Mearoo who was grinning at me! "You didn't tell me!" I said in surprise at her keeping this from me!" Mearoo said with a laugh "I thought that I would surprise you when they were all born!" Everyone had a good laugh as I just stared at her not sure what to do! "Why does this trouble you Jakool? You will have plenty of help and by the looks of things you won't be the only father of many children!"

I gave Mearoo a sour look then looked around us again to see that Kika was just becoming a full man with Janai, Harit with Hardika, Lavar with Sheena, Garath with Cecina, and Timbu with Tivash! I had to grin then as I turned back to Mearoo and said "You will have to help me hunt for so many! I am but one poor man!" I had to duck her paw as she swung it playfully at my face! "I have enough scratches!" I said growling a little at her!

She looked at me in surprise and then realized from my face, I was only teasing her, so she just made some noises in her throat and I pretended to be frightened! Bamal laughed at our play and said "If this is how you act once mated, I need a mate too!" Merack gave a snort then said "You've already mated every female we have! Merkansoo! Beware of this one! He will wear your women out with his need to mate!" Merkansoo gave a laugh then said "I believe that Bamal will find our females quite able to keep up with him! Just ask Jakool!" I was busy with Mearoo just then and couldn't say anything as my lips were on hers! Pathak asked, "If your tribe is as large as you say, how do you keep from hunting and gathering an area until it can no longer support you?" It was a very good question! I realized that many would need a lot of food, hides, and all the things we made from our kills and the materials where we lived.

Merkansoo said "We do not all live in one place. We have many villages in valleys protected from the worst of the winter storms, camps in places we hunt, fish, and gather in and many caves in the cloud stabbers. They make very good places to stay and to store food." I wondered about this and almost asked him how many such caves, but a sudden move by Mearoo to capture my lips again kept me from asking this question. It was not until later when we were alone that she told me not to ask that question until everyone had agreed to join.

Merkansoo continued "We have always been careful in how we hunt. We only kill what we can from one area and then move to another to give it time to have more animals there. We do the same in the waters and rivers we fish, the many trees and long endless grass, where we gather plants, fruits, berries, and nuts." Pathak nodded and said "Very wise! We try to do the same but since we have become less in number, we do not have this problem." Merkansoo did bring up one more problem "Jakool and I discussed how some Ooh-mans have great trouble breathing high in the cloud stabbers. We recognized this problem as more Ooh-mans came into the cloud stabbers and joined our tribe. Some were able to adapt, but others couldn't.

Several died before we found that we needed to bring them up into the cloud stabbers slowly. This gives them time to adapt. This is one reason we have places in the deep valleys. Here they can breathe much easier."

Gaieaa and Nada were impressed with the explanation and the wisdom it showed. Nada asked, "Have you tried to use the breathing herbs to make the lungs and throat bigger?" Merkansoo looked surprised then said "No. We do not have this healing though we have many others.

Your Healer Paasi can do this?" Nada nodded and said "Yes. I can too and so can Gaieaa and several others in our tribe. Merkansoo smiled and said "This is very good news! When we reach one of the villages in a valley I will show you why this is important to us." It was now getting late and I wanted to go off with Mearoo and mate! I was young and had led a successful hunt that sun. So even if I was not interested in any of the other women who were available to mate with, I wanted Mearoo!

I turned and whispered to her "I want you." She smiled gave me a nibble on my ear and said "Me too." We left them still talking and went out of sight of the campfire. I knew that others would be in the cave, so I led Mearoo to the banks of the stream that was near. There were soft grasses on the banks so I knew we would be comfortable there. I wanted to kiss, touch, and please her as she pleased me! We spent some time pleasing each other; ending in another strenuous mating that left me spent, exhausted, and happy! We fell asleep nestled against each other's bodies; as was becoming our custom, while all thoughts of the problems discussed that sun disappeared in sleep.

The next morning we were up early and bathed in the stream. We had both worked hard in the sun before and wanted to get the blood, sweat, and dirt off of our bodies. "I am going to need new hides" I commented as I washed out my loincloth and my fur. Mearoo said "There is plenty of new hide now. We just need to finish curing it." This was true and it got me thinking about how long it would take us to get ready to leave. The same thought occupied the Elders of both tribes when we returned to the main camp sight. Merkansoo, Darshita, Denala, Farkis, and Janai were gathered together with Bamal, Merack, Pathak, Gaieaa, and Nada. "We should join them," I said sure they were discussing how long it would take to be ready. When we sat down I noticed that both Gaieaa and Pathak both looked better and were moving restlessly as if sore! I quickly realized that Merkansoo and Darshita had shown them that they were not to old to mate!

"I believe we can be ready more quickly If we make use of the new hide to make huts," Kiraat said. Merack disagreed saying "We will need that hide to make layers to wear in the cold of the cloud stabbers!" I looked at the faces of our Elders and realized it might take longer to decide how to prepare than to actually prepare! I looked at Merkansoo who stood with his arms crossed listening to them argue. I asked Mearoo quietly "We will need much heavier hides than the deer won't we?" Mearoo replied "Yes you will. Your people will not be ready for the cold. Rough Fur, Bharal and Masama would be best. Oh! Masama is what we call the very long-haired and long-necked grass eaters!" I remember my journey tracking her and how I came close to freezing to death! "Should we use the hide for huts?" I asked her. She replied, "What are huts?" I had to explain 'huts' to her. "When we journey long distances, we make a shelter from hides we have put together and tied to long poles. This gives us protection from the wind, rain, and snow. We can have fires in them to keep the people warm in the cloud stabbers." Mearoo thought about this and asked "Can you cut the wood poles in the many trees on the cloud stabber slopes? It would be easier than carrying them all the way from here."

I replied "A good suggestion! Now we just have to convince them" I said meaning the Elders who were still arguing over hides, how much food was needed, and what needed to be brought with us. I spoke up "Mearoo and I have talked about this. I have been in the cloud stabbers and can tell you that the deer hides are not thick enough to keep us warm. The wind is strong and the cold much worse than you know. I almost froze to death twice before I managed to find shelter in caves and make a fire. My furs were useless after a few hours. The huts make more sense as we can build fires in them to keep everyone warm." Merack looked at me and then said "That will not help us on the trail, only when we stop." Mearoo quickly said "We have much heavier furs from the cloud stabber animals we hunt and keep for food and other uses. Our tribe will meet us in the hills before we get high into the cloud stabbers with the furs." Merkansoo smiled when Merack turned to him and asked "Is this true? Why didn't you say something! We've been arguing over nothing!" In a voice filled with frustration.

Merkansoo said to him "No Merack. Not for nothing. This is how we learn about each other. I wanted to see if you would think to 'ask me' if I could help you with this decision. You didn't, but Jakool asked Mearoo!" Bamal looked puzzled then Merack made a comment "It seems we need to learn we now have friends and allies Merack. We are no longer alone." Merkansoo's smile turned into a grin as he said "Yes! Now you understand! Do you wish my advice?" Merack gave a grin then said, "Of course we do!"

Merkansoo then replied "Don't bring more than you actually need. There is plenty of food between here and the cloud stabbers we can hunt and gather. The huts are a good idea, but wait until we are in the many trees high in the hills to cut any wood you need. You do not need to bring much water as we will cross several rivers, and streams and pass some large waters and great waters."

I immediately thought of the large water in the cave and started to say something, but Mearoo gave me a look that I now knew meant to be silent. Darshita added "Bring all your healing herbs, potions, weapons, and tools. Remember that some of your people will need to be helped on the journey. Especially in the cloud stabbers!" Pathak asked "I would like to ask if we can find a way to use these preparations to mix our tribes together? While doing all that needs to be done? This will allow everyone to learn while working and playing together. This is the most important preparation we need to make!" Gaieaa agreed saying "We have so much to learn from each other we should start now!" Merkansoo smiled and said "This is very wise advice that we should follow. All of it." No one disagreed with him or the others so it was decided.

Merkansoo, Mearoo, Denala, and Janai started to work with Pathak, Gaieaa, Merack, and Bamal on putting together the two tribes into work groups and assigning them tasks that needed doing. I was tasked with rounding up all the hunters and finding out which ones had mated with snow-leaper females. Nada was finding out which of our females mated with snow-leaper males during the celebration. I said "Kika find out who mated with which snow-leaper females and bring that information to me. I will be with the Elders."

Kika nodded as I turned and went to where the Elders were now splitting up to oversee the work groups. Noticing Larkar standing off to one side watching the group working on the hides, Darshita cleverly mentioned that they were having trouble with the curing now they were to be used to make huts instead of hides for clothing. She spent some time drawing him into a conversation about the best way to cure and stretch the hides, then join them together so they would keep out the wind and snow. They would need to protect the people from them in the cloud stabbers. Larkar listened as she told him what Gaieaa had explained and what they remembered from the stories of the past. It had been many generations since they had used huts as we had been in our cave a long time.

Larkar listened carefully so he would understand her then nodded and said "Nada and Gaieaa have many ways of joining hide but not against cold and snow. The air is dryer in the cloud stabbers yes?" Darshita said "Yes it is! It blows hard then will change directions so quickly that it can uproot bushes, sending rocks and ice flying!" Larkar said "Ah! So the huts will need to be more than just able to stand up against cold and wind? They will need to be sturdy so that when the wind hits it like a solid blow.." He paused and demonstrated by smacking a fist into his hand", It will glance off instead of tearing through it." "Yes!! How do we do this?" Larkar's large brow furrowed as he thought about this problem.

Finally, he said, "Kaga would know how to do this. His people spent a long time during the worst of the cold surviving this way. Kaga!" He yelled and we saw him stop working on the hides and come over. When he explained about needing to build huts to withstand the cold, wind and snow of the cloud stabbers he said thoughtfully "When my tribe made the huts, we made the shape like this." He stooped down and picked up a dead branch, then used it to draw in the ground. We all stopped to watch him to see what he had in mind. "You take the hide and you use the sticky sap from trees that grow in the cold. You coat the end of each piece of hide at least a forearm's length, then you stick them to each other and stitch them together for strength. That way the two pieces can move but stay together. You do this at least three times on each seam where they meet. You then coat another piece of hide to fit over the place you put the stitches to make it not leak water or air."

We listened and watched as he then drew long lines that formed a strange round shape, that met at the top. "You run the poles like this bending them so they go around in a circle. You tie the poles together at the top. This will make them strong together! The round shape will keep the wind from hitting it hard as it will just blow around it." Larkar had been nodding and making suggestions as Kaga drew the shape of the hut. Merack looked at his drawing for a long time comparing it to what he remembered of their huts. Finally, he said "This is better. Much better! We can do this and they will be lighter and easier to put up and take down!" Larkar and Kaga actually smiled a little at Merack's praise! I had never seen Larkar smile since he came to our tribe! Bamal asked a few questions nodding at the answers Larkar gave then said, "Larkar! This is why we need you! You need to be in charge of the ones that make this!"

The change in Larkar's face makes me think *this was what he was like before his tribe was attacked! When he was a happy man with a mate, a son, and the respect of his tribe.*"His head rose up, his shoulders straightened as he stood up and his chest swelled with pride! He gravely said, "I will do what I can to help my tribe." Those simple words gave us all much relief when we heard them. I was very happy that I did not have to kill Larkar because he refused to join.

Gaieaa; and Nada, had Larkar and Kaga tell them their idea for the huts. They listened and watched as Kaga drew the strange round picture again. They nodded then asked him which trees he thought would be the best to gather the sap from to make the glue? Larkar thought then smiled as he turned to Darshita, who was making a point of being with him, and asked her "Which trees can we get sap from that won't turn brittle and crack in the cold?" Darshita thought for several moments then answered "The Elm trees would be best I think. They grow both in the hills and at the tree line. You can harvest the sap from the ones lower down and it should still work as the ones higher up do." Kaga agreed as Gaieaa said "The sap will work the same. We know this from our own history. We will send out a party to find the closet Elm trees and gather the sap." Larkar said "I will lead them. I know what we are looking for." Darshita said "I will go too. We will also need enough hands and containers to gather the sap." Nada looked thoughtful and then asked "Can you use the shells of the big nuts that grow in the lower many trees? The thick one that is wetter?" I knew immediately she meant the many trees we had traveled through when returning to my tribe! I remembered Lasaa easily jumping up and tossing down whole limbs full of these strange nuts! The shells were hard, but inside was a tasty meat and a nourishing liquid!

I didn't volunteer to go, as we wanted Larkar to choose his own party. This way Darshita would go with enough snow-leapers to carry them and to make the harvesting and carrying the nuts back much easier! Larkar spent the evening planning the journey and asking different members to join him. They left early the next morning with three hands each of men and women from both tribes. Merkansoo had worked with Darshita to match up snow-leaper and Ooh-mans so there would be an equal number of both tribes. Kaga had been chosen as he knew more about the size of wood they would need. Darshita asked Nada to help her decide which men and women would be compatible mates so the ones going would have a good chance of mating. I wondered about this and asked Merkansoo after they had left the next Sun. He looked at me calmly and said "You and your people are very important to us right now. We do not know if you will understand, but Mearoo told me she has tried to explain this to you."

I said, "Yes she told me about the need for new blood; and how your people helped yourselves to develop more quickly, by mating certain males and females together." Merkansoo replied "Yes. But there is more to this need than just continuing to develop our tribe physically. If you were to mate with say Janai." I must have looked surprised because he gave me a chuckle and then said "Didn't Mearoo tell you of the need to mate with many different partners?" I was confused; and unable to give him an answer quickly!

Merkansoo's chuckle stopped and he frowned. "Mearoo should have explained this since you are not familiar with our ways!" I struggled to remember what she had told me as Merkansoo waited patiently for my answer. "I think she did mention something when she was explaining about needing new mates with new blood. I guess I just thought since we declared each other mates..' I just stopped as I thought that explained my surprise and uneasiness. Merkansoo shook his head and then said "No it doesn't. Jakool you are young and full of seed. Yes, you will give Mearoo many children, but that is not enough! You will need to mate with others as will the rest of your tribe!"

I still didn't fully understand why this was so important to them and asked him "Why?" Merkansoo explained, "This is so that the blood of both males and females is mixed with ours and yours." Explained like this it made sense but didn't calm the feeling I now had that it was somehow wrong! Merkansoo was very keen and saw this then said to me "Mearoo was your first, but you heard us discuss our mating habits last night. " I gulped and said "Yes. But I thought I would at least be with Mearoo until another hunt and another celebration." Merkansoo replied "Yes. You told me of this custom. Are you unwilling because of your feelings for Mearoo?" I nodded unable to speak as my throat suddenly became tight with emotion. "I see. Mearoo will have to know this."

I sighed in relief when he said this! While I was just as affected by the other snow-leapers scent, I made sure I only mated with Mearoo, no matter how aroused I felt by Darshita Samalaa or Sheena! The thought of Sheena caused the blood to rise into my face! She had tried to mate with me when we were joined by them. She didn't understand why I wouldn't and seemed puzzled and a little hurt. I had told Mearoo about it but she just smiled and said "She has plenty of other young Ooh-mans to mate with!" I took that to mean that I was hers and she was mine!

Merkansoo changed the subject to "I watched how your people hunted the deer. I think we need to show all the hunters safer ways to do this. Several of your hunters would have been badly wounded or killed if we had not been there to save them." I knew this to be true as I remembered how close Larkar, Kika, and Harit came to being killed! I slowly said, "This would be something that the Elders should be told." "Oh! I agree! We already discussed it and they want this too. You have so few left they do not want to lose any more than they must!" I agreed with this as we needed every one of our tribe just to survive!

"Let us go see how Denala and Girivar are doing on this new tool to throw spears!" Merkansoo smiled and said "A good idea and a good place to start!" We went in search of Denala and found him with Girivar, Hanuman, and Mahendra by a pile of young trees stripped of their branches. Denala was showing how to shape a branch into his throwing tool. "You cut the wood just past where a branch grew out of it. He was using a stone hand ax to cut off the tree past a short piece of branch still sticking out of it. "Once you have cut it off, you cut off a small part of the branch that is facing the other end of the tree." He then used a stone chisel to cut off the round part of the branch as he had explained. "Now you make it deeper in the middle so the sides will hold the spear in place." He carefully cut out a little more of the branch wood. He then shaped it by rubbing it with a smooth stone." He did this until he was satisfied with the shape.

He stopped and picked up a spear that was longer and thinner than ours. He put the throwing end of the spear against the shaped branch end and we saw that it fit up against it tightly. "Then you chisel the face of the wood and sand it, so the spear lays flat against the wood!" He spent several minutes shaving the wood with a very sharp-edged ax-like tool we used to shape wood. "Once this is done, you make sure you shape all your spears so they fit. If they do not then the spear can slip off the thrower when you throw it." Denala then stood up with the wood thrower and spear held in one hand and said "I will demonstrate the way to throw your spear.

He brought his arm up behind his head then swung it forward letting the wood thrower stay in his hand while the spear flew off it at incredible speed! We heard a 'thud' and saw the spear buried in a side of deer that was hung up between two poles! We went to it to see how this smaller, thinner spear went into the meat.

"You see? The spear will go deep because it is going much faster." He worked the spear up and down slowly pulling it out of the wound. "If you fire harden the point of the spear, then you can just push the spear through the animal to remove it. Also sometimes the point will break off, but you can just shape the point back and harden it again. We do this instead of putting the stone spear tips on them."

"Jarack asked "Do you have to throw it over like you showed us? Or can you throw it from the side?" Denala smiled took another spear and put it on his thrower. "You mean like this?" This time he put his arm back behind his body a little lower than shoulder height, then threw it! The sound of the spear hitting the target gave Jarack his answer! "That could be very useful when throwing them from behind a tree or rock!" He said to Denala. "That is why you should learn to throw it from many places!" he replied. Soon he had everyone making their own throwing stick so they could practice with them! I turned to Merkansoo and asked him "So we will be able to throw our spears from much further away making it safer to hunt large animals?" Merkansoo replied "Yes. Does this make sense to you?" I said "Yes it does! How did Denala figure out how to do this?" Merkansoo chuckled and said "He told us that he learned it from a strange tribe that was very short. They came from somewhere far to the south and west." I nodded my understanding as many of us came from the lands there.

"Come! I want to speak with Mearoo." He said as he took my arm and pulled me with him! I was not sure I wanted to be part of this talk with Mearoo, but I had little choice, as Merkansoo was much bigger and stronger than me! We found Mearoo eating some different roots and plant leaves by Nada and Gaieaa. They were showing her what she should eat for her new children!" I realized then that even though she had told me we had mated and she would have children, it didn't seem real until I saw her with Nada and Gaieaa! I went and sat down next to her, so I could touch her body with mine at the hip, side, and shoulder.

Merkansoo said "Jakool does not understand why he will need to mate with others now that he is your mate. You were supposed to tell him." Mearoo suddenly looked a little frightened when he said this and I wondered if she had done this on purpose! Merkansoo continued "I realize you are young Mearoo, but we need him to mate with others. Just as all the other Ooh-man males and females will." Mearoo hid her face by putting her head down but Merkansoo was not fooled! "Mearoo! Look at me!" He said in a stern voice you could not ignore, making Mearoo look up at him.

"Do you want to be selfish and keep Jakool all to yourself? I felt Mearoo shaking a little as she finally said in a small voice "No Merkansoo. The tribe needs this." Merkansoo heard and saw everything that Mearoo was going through and said gently "Jakool will not have to mate with anyone else until after you have your first children from him. Does that help?"

Mearoo suddenly sobbed and grabbed me in a tight hug then said "I don't want to lose you! I feel so bad not telling you this! Please forgive me!" I held her tight and rocked back and forth with her giving her small kisses on her cheek as I replied "You are not the only one who feels this way!" This made her very happy and she suddenly embraced me and then kissed me with great enthusiasm!"

Merkansoo explained to Gaieaa and Nada while we were locked in an embrace "Our women's mood changes quickly when they are with children." Gaieaa said "We are the same. Sometimes the men go off for suns on hunts just to get away from us when we are with child!" Nada laughed at Merkansoo's expression then pointing said "Ah! Something else we have in common I see!" Merkansoo burst out laughing as the talk turned to 'men' and the ways they could find to avoid their mates when with children! Mearoo said to me "Do not think you will be able to get away so easy with me!" With a growl and a ferocious look, I quickly saw through this as I kissed her and said "You will have to kick me out to get rid of me!" Causing more laughter from everyone.

CHAPTER SIX

WE MAKE A NEW TRIBE

The talk turned to different healing plants and herbs we had here and if we could find them in the cloud stabbers. Merkansoo went through all the plants, herbs, and other healing things we would be able to find either in the cloud stabbers or in the many trees that started lower. At least we would be able to harvest more until we reached the high places, where no trees grew. I was interested in the talk about different ways to heal different injuries and learned many new things as well as remembering many old things *I should' have remembered! Remembering my failure to remember the plant that would help Elasaa! I will never forget such important names again!* I thought to myself as we listened to them.

Pathak came over saying "We need to find a way to carry the ones who can't walk." Gaieaa sighed saying "I am glad you finally thought of it!" Pathak smiled and said, "Did you think my old bones would let me forget?" Nada laughed then said, "Would you like to ride on Darshita?" Pathak looked at Nada and then said "If my bones are too old to walk, they are also too old to ride on someone who makes jumps and worse, landings!

Merkansoo kept a straight face as he turned to Gaieaa and said "I would be very careful to not jar your 'old bones!' But if you get aroused by my scent, I cannot promise I won't take you and mate again!" Pathak started laughing so hard he had to sit down as he lost his balance! Merkansoo lost his straight face and joined everyone else in laughing at the joke he had played on Gaieaa! Gaieaa just chuckled and said, "Old as I am I would jump at the chance! You proved that last night!" Causing even more laughter! Some things like making jokes and laughing were common with both tribes. It also helps to build trust and friendships between us.

Merkansoo did have a suggestion on how to help the old ones. "We have from a long time ago a way to carry large loads or injured or old ones. It is made with hide stretched tight between two wood poles. Four can hold the poles and carry two people. We attach hide to the ends of the poles and make a loop on each one. Then we can just slip into the loops and run on all fours. It is much smoother and faster that way." Gaieaa thought for a moment then said "Yes. But for how long before they tire?"Merkansoo said, "We are much stronger than you, but we would change out carriers often so no one is too tired." "We would need to make about ten of these carriers," Nada said counting up the ones needing them. Merkansoo said "Then let's make them now. Who is not working that can help?"

"We are!" I said as both Mearoo and I were not working on anything at the moment. Nada said, "I believe I can spare some time and so can Cecina, Kika and some of the other young ones that now 'think' they are men. This will be a good way to teach them there is more to being an adult than just making a kill and mating!" Gaieaa suddenly said "I will come as will Pathak. We need to know how to make these carriers and you can demonstrate one by carrying us back!" I chuckled at her clever way of involving herself and Pathak in the work and smiled when I saw Pathak and Gaieaa share a smile over the success of her words. I got up and led the group to a nearby stand of trees that I thought would be a good size as they were young. Merkansoo walked around marking trees he wanted to use by slashing the bark with his claws.

I took one tree and Kika another. It only took a few swings of my ax to fall into the small tree. Mearoo and Jarack started to strip off the branches of my tree while Nada and Cecina did Kika's. We soon had a pile of trees and I stopped to take a rest as I asked "Is anyone counting them?" Gaieaa and Pathak shouted, "We are!" From the boulder, they were sitting on watching. "So? How many more?" I asked as I wiped sweat from my forehead from the exertion of swinging the ax. "You have twelve. You need eight more!" Pathak said as he idly sat on the boulder enjoying the warm sun and the warmth the boulder gave off.

I started again and soon we had the last of the trees; stripped of all the limbs, ready to carry back. Merkansoo and Mearoo quickly took the hide Nada had brought with her and used thin leather strips cut from a longer piece. They used their claws to punch holes along the edge of the hide then put a thin leather strip through one hole, around a pole then back through the next hole. They continued doing this until both sides of the hide were now tied to the poles. They had Kaga and me hold the poles as if we were carrying them so they could pull the leather tight as they tied it to the two poles.

Once they were finished I grinned as I said "Okay Pathak, Gaieaa! You are to be the first to test it!" We took it over to them as they sat up and inspected the carrier. Looks tight enough" Pathak said testing it by pushing down on it in the middle. Merkansoo said, "Let me and Mearoo take the back, you and Kika the front." We changed the ends of the poles so they were now in the back. We put the carrier down on the grass so Pathak and Gaieaa could sit down on it. "Ready?" Merkansoo said then "Lift!" We almost spilled Pathak and Gaieaa off the carrier as Kika and I were a little slow lifting our end! "Hey! Pathak said as he grabbed onto Gaieaa. She let herself fall against him and then said in mock outrage! "Get your hands off me you! I am not going to mate with you!" Pathak made a gargled sound and then said "Merkansoo? "Is your offer to take her as a mate still good? I think I might need to find someone to fight this one off me!" We all laughed as we carried the two old ones as they made more jokes about each other and us.

By the time we returned to the camp, I felt the strain in my arms, back, and legs. Pathak and Gaieaa thanked us as we put them back in front of the campfire; so they could be available to help with some of the easier tasks. Just then I heard Bamal shout then call my name "Jakool? We need some help!" We all went to see what he needed and found ourselves helping with preparing meat for drying. This way it would keep for a long time but all the juices had to be dried out first.

Nada was seasoning the meat with salt, pepper and several herbs to give a different flavor to different pieces of meat. "We prefer the meat to not all taste the same" she explained to Mearoo and Merkansoo, answering their questions as they helped. I was helping Bamal and several others raise a drying rack over the big fire pit we used for smoking and drying the meat. Several of the young ones came from the stream where they had soaked the leafy branches from Oak, Poplar, and Cherry trees that grew close by.

We already had the fire burning as we put the meat across the thin branches that ran across the larger poles that made the top of the rack. Once it was full, we carried it by the four poles and placed it over the now-smoking fire. The young ones' job was to keep putting the branches on the fire to make smoke and to get them wet before they caught fire when they dried. With our part finished, Kiraat decided we would see if we could practice using the spear throwers that Denala and his group had made for all the adults.

Even the women would learn and practice using them, as they would need to defend the camp if most of the men were out hunting and gathering. I found the thrower to be quite easy to use and soon I was hitting a hide we set between two poles a good twenty man lengths away! Bamal and Kiraat could hit one even further away with their greater strength! Denala watched and made suggestions to each other until everyone felt confident using the thrower. The sun was setting when we finally stopped all work and took the time to inspect everything. Bamal, Merack, Pathak, and Gaieaa worked with Merkansoo to have each work group come and show them what they had finished and how much was left to do. Once this was done we sat down with them to eat and go over the remaining work and how long it would take.

"The meat will take another two suns," Bamal said as he was checking it every few hours. Nada said, "We will be finished preparing and packing all the herbs, plants, and dried vegetables by tomorrow." "Denala is finished with all the spear throwers and spears. Everyone has had some practice with them. Another two suns and they will be very comfortable using them" Kiraat said as he had checked with him and some of the other work teams. "We can easily finish the carriers tomorrow," Merkansoo said as he stretched his arms over his head. Pathak said I think we will be ready in three suns?" He turned to Gaieaa for her opinion and she agreed! "Three suns. That is good! Very Good! Merkansoo said thinking of the next step.

"What about Larkar and his group? Do we know when they will return?" Nada asked as they were the only work group not there. Merack said "I asked him before he left and thought it would only take two suns. So they should be back in no more than a sun maybe two. "I want to discuss the path we take," Merkansoo said as he finished his thinking. "We came by a difficult route to get here as quickly as possible. But I would not want to take that path back. I believe we should follow the stream here until it is past the hill. There we can turn towards the place where the many trees and the endless green grass meet. That is where we left Elasaa and Paasi." Merack said "it is a good path as it was the same one we used to cross the endless green grass into the hills, then the many trees on the other side at the foot of the cloud stabbers."

Everything seemed to be going well as we left to find our places to sleep. I was awakened by a blood-curdling scream and was up and running towards the sound before I knew I was doing it! Mearoo was beside me and I saw many others also running to where the sound came from! We went towards the narrow opening between the two hills that led to the many trees and the low wetlands until we found one of our lookouts! He was dead! He had a gash in his back from shoulder to hip! "Quickly! See if you can find any tracks!" I said as I bent over him to turn his face up!

"Chirac!" I said not believing he had been so cruelly ambushed by an unseen attacker. Bamal gave a cry of grief and anger when he saw it was him. "Chirac! Who did this to you! How did they sneak up on you! If only your spirit could tell us!" He sobbed as he fell to his knees as his friend and second in command was gone! I heard Merkansoo sending out Janai, Lasaa, and many other snow-leaper people as they saw better in the dark and could run down anyone trying to get away! I swore as I started to wonder who had done this and why? There were no unfriendly tribes nearby. "The nearest tribe is three suns away!" I heard Merack say.

Harit said "I don't think anyone from there did this. You see the way the cut is deep at the bottom and shallow at the top?" I looked again and saw that Harit was right. "Why?" I asked him. He swallowed and then said, "If they stabbed low and then pulled up their knife it would look like this." "I see. They were on the ground then stabbed from a crouch." I turned to Merack and asked, "Do you remember any other attacks like this?" Merack didn't have to think as he answered quickly "Yes. When we were on the great plans." "The great plains?" I said in surprise then shook my head as I realized what this meant.

Merkansoo had stayed behind and said "we were seen coming here". I slowly closed my eyes as I imagined a horde from the Krieg clan appearing from behind all the rocks and trees howling and attacking us! I sat there frantic to think of what we could do to fix this! Merkansoo stood silent with his arms crossed staring at the darkness looking all around us. I was very afraid now, as this was exactly what Merkansoo had warned us against! I expected him to turn on us and start killing us! But he just stood there in silence while we waited to hear from the scouts.

The great bright face of the pale goddess was now much lower in the sky when the scouts returned. Janai was carrying something. When she got close enough we could see it was a body! She dumped it down at Merkansoo's feet and made hissing and snarling sounds in her language. Merkansoo looked down then said "It is as I feared. This is a scout. Not from the Krieg themselves, but from one of the tribes that are like them. "Did you stop him before he reached the plain?" Merkansoo asked Janai. Janai spit out "Yes! We caught him before he made it through the hills on the other side of the low wetlands. He did not tell anyone of us!" I sighed in relief but Merkansoo still looked worried. "I am afraid we need to leave. Tomorrow. We will have to move quickly." Merack nodded and said "Yes. Even though we stopped this scout, there will be others." Merkansoo said "Yes. The Krieg will come eventually once they hear of us" He looked at Merack and said, "We need to be high in the cloud stabbers; where they will not dare to come, by the time they realize we were here."

I got up and went to Mearoo and she comforted me and said "It is not your fault Jakool. It is no one's fault". We need to focus on getting everything ready so we can leave this place. We lay down near the fire as everyone but the scouts on guard duty were gathered for safety.

The next morning everyone was up early and working hard to finish so we could leave. I heard the scouts on the other side of the camp give the call which meant Larkar was returning! I was glad to hear this but fearful of his anger when he was told about Chirac. We met him in the center of camp and praised him and his team for the amount of tree sap and nuts they carried with them. Larkar was in good spirits and when Darshita pulled Merkansoo aside she told him something privately which caused him to give Larkar a look and then shrug. I wondered what she said but now was not the time. Merack and the rest of the elders stood there to meet him.

He was surprised and seemed pleased until he saw their faces. He immediately changed from happy to closed and unhappy! "What has happened?" He asked knowing something was wrong! "Chirac is dead! He was ambushed from behind at the narrow trail to the low wetlands. He was on lookout duty last night." Larkar's face filled with blood causing the blood vessels to show as he took a deep breath. "It was not the Krieg Larkar. It was another tribe that did this! It was a scout from a tribe that will tell them we are here!" Larkar was ready to explode when he heard this but Merkansoo stood in front of him and said "Not Yet Larkar! We will once we have the old ones, the women and children safe! Hear me Larkar! We will wait and go to our villages where I will call out 'All' our warriors! We are very strong!" Merkansoo said trying to get through to Larkar so he would not make things worse by wanting to charge off and go after them.

Janai came up with the body and threw it at Larkar's feet making him look down. "This is what we do to our enemies!" She said showing Larkar the throat he had ripped open with his teeth! Larkar saw the gaping hole in the scout's neck and the deep claw marks on his back and front! Larkar looked up at Janai and asked her "You did this? You caught and killed him?" Janai said "Yes!" In a fierce voice, "He was a coward who attacked Chirac from behind instead of facing him!" Larkar stared at Janai for what felt like a long time before he smiled and said "Good! You have kept your promise to me! I am glad!"

He then turned to look at Bamal and Kiraat, and seeing the grief in their faces said "I will not rest until all of them are dead." He turned to Merack and said "We bring enough sap to make all the huts we need. Darshita gathered enough nuts to feed us and use the shells to carry water and other things." Darshita quickly added, "We also gathered several of the plants Gaieaa and Nada said we needed more of". Merack nodded and said "It is good you have done this. We must leave now!"

Everyone jumped in and helped to take the nuts and sap to store on some of the carriers we had made. Soon we were ready to leave. I took one final look around at the camp where I had been born and spent my entire life. I saw Gaieaa, Pathak, and the rest doing the same. We all turned away as Merkansoo said "We go!" We were now making a journey that would be long and dangerous! I just hoped that we didn't have to fight our way to our new home!

As we started our journey, I noticed that Larkar was silent. He was carrying his thrusting spear, a spear thrower, and enough spears to kill four hands of the enemy! His face was still red with blood and dark with anger and hate. *He has returned to the Larkar of before* I thought grimly as I took my place with Mearoo behind Merkansoo, Merack, Bamal, and Kaga at the front of our now united tribe!

The path was easy at first. Merkansoo insisted on sending out scouts to make sure no one could ambush us. It was a good idea! So good that when Merack said "We should have a group following us to erase our tracks. Merkansoo thought about it and smiled as he said "That 'Is' a good idea!" Why make it easy for them to follow us? Janai! Lasaa! We have a job for you!" I smiled and then thought of something. "Shouldn't some of our people also be with them? They know our ways and will be useful in making sure we leave no tracks to follow." Merack smiled as he said "Seems like good ideas are everywhere!" Causing a chuckle among us.

They decided that Bamal, Larkar, and Kaga should join Janai and Lasaa and the others who would be following the tribes making sure that nothing was left to show where they had gone! Merkansoo said to Larkar "I want you to be there in case we are attacked by these cowards that sneak up on you to kill you!" Larkar replied "None will sneak up on me! I thirst for their blood!" Janai quickly said, "I will make sure they do not sneak up on you or anyone else!" Lasaa snarled something in his language, then showed Larkar his claws! He was a fearsome sight and Larkar nodded his approval as they turned back to guard our backs!

Merkansoo sent Denali, Darshita, Samalaa Farkis Kaga, and Harit to scout ahead. Merack and Pathak led the tribes with me, Mearoo, and Merkansoo. The trail made it easy to carry the old ones as it was through the gentle rolling hills that ended with the endless green grass. I checked on them at each rest break and they were in good moods and enjoying the journey! Pathak was marking symbols on the hide of the different types of plants, trees, and such with Gaieaa! When I asked them why, Pathak answered "We have not been away from the camp in years! We want to have a record of where to find these plants when needed. Since we do not have these records; as we didn't need them, we had not done this before now." "I see," I said as I went back to Merack at the others and told them about them making this record.

Merkansoo said "It is a good idea. Many of these plants and trees do not grow any nearer to our homes than here." Merack said "It is more than that. It is something we should do for more than just the plants. We should make a record of our meeting, the members of both tribes! We should record everything we know, have seen, experienced! Once we leave here we will never come back! We need to know we were here!" I was not the only one surprised by Merack's sudden outburst!

Merkansoo was as surprised as the rest of us and said "How? Merack shook his head as he replied I am not sure. But I am sure that it needs to be done!" I suddenly remembered the incredible racial memory of the snow-leaper people and spoke up "Merkansoo? This journey is part of your memories right?" Merkansoo looked at me puzzled as he answered "Yes. I will remember what I see, hear, and do, but not everything that everyone experiences." "I understand, but every one of your people has this memory so we can make this record using everyone's memories. Your people will remember details that we may not, or get wrong. Once we have settled we can make a permanent record of these events in a cave. Like the ones I saw in Mearoo's cave. Like the ones we have left behind everywhere we have been!"

Mearoo spoke up "Yes! If we do it like that it will work. It will be a very long record but it will give all that follow everything we have known and experienced." I smiled and turned to Merack and said "I believe that takes care of needing a record!" Merack smiled and said "Yes it does! Now tell all of our people to look, listen, and smell everything!

They need to remember this!" Merkansoo said "Mearoo go with him make sure that they are paired! That will make sure that everything is remembered!" I smiled as we left them to tell everyone in the tribe what Merack and Merkansoo wanted them to do! When we reached the scouts in front of us Kaga was immediately concerned that something was wrong! "Jakool? Why are you here! Have we been attacked?" He said in a surprised voice. "No, no Kaga! We are fine! Merack and Merkansoo asked me to ask everyone to remember everything from this place!

He looked confused as I waited until Mearoo had called back the rest of the scouts. I explained Merack's words about wanting a permanent record made with these memories. "Every plant, herb, tree, bird, animal, the hills, the grass even the sky?" He asked grinning! It was so uncharacteristic of him to make a joke and smile! I laughed and said well maybe not the sky" Denala, Darshita, Farkis, and Samalaa looked at each other and then at Mearoo. Mearoo smiled as she said "Pair up with each other. One Oohman, One Snow-Leaper. That is what Merack and Merkansoo said to do. Samalaa looked thoughtful as Darshita nodded her head.

Denala grinned and said "This is good! Very good!" I was still not sure why Merack was insisting on this being done so I asked him "Why is this good Denala?" He replied "Because it gives you more than just the things you found here that you used for food, healing, making tools. This way; with our help, we will make a record that will tell our entire story! What you did, how you felt about yourselves and each other. Everything!" I thought I understood! They want everyone's memories recorded so we will always have them! I said believing this to be the reason. "Yes! But also by doing this, we all are working on something common to all of us! Who we are, where we came from!" I smiled and said "Thank you Denala! I was a little confused until you explained it this way!

Kaga nodded and said, "To do this will not slow us down?" I shook my head and replied "No. We just need to be aware of what is around us and anything that happens that should be remembered." Samalaa said quietly "I think this is a good way for our people to work together." She gave Farkis and Darshita a look; that they seemed to understand. Kaga looked at her for a long moment then nodded his head and said "This would be good for that reason alone." Good luck!" I said as we turned and headed back at an easy trot to the front of the main tribe.

I took notice of the needle trees blowing in a breeze, and the sounds of bird calls from the branches. The green grass felt good under my feet and the scents of flowering plants filled the air. I saw several of the plants and herbs we gathered to use then, smiled as I realized just what Merack meant by 'remember everything'! I was in a good mood when I finally reached Merack, Merkansoo, and Mearoo. They were speaking with Pathak and Gaieaa. I couldn't hear until I was closer but something had them looking worried?" I came up and asked, "Is something wrong?" As I went to Mearoo's side. Merkansoo said "I don't understand. What do you mean someone might be missing? Either they are or they are not." "Who?" I quickly asked wondering who would have wandered off!" Pathak said "Nada. She was gathering herbs and plants as we traveled so we would have a record of each one and where they grew, as Merack wanted. I turned away to say something to Gaieaa and when I turned back to see where she was, she was gone!"

Merkansoo quickly said, "Where did you last see her?" Gaieaa answered "Over there, where the tall ferns are growing. She went behind them to pick some herbs." Merkansoo said "Mearoo? You and I need to search now!' They both leaped and landed right at the tall ferns. They both looked around carefully around them as we ran over to also look. "Here. Her footprints go around the bush then off into the trees!" Pathak shook his head as he asked no one "Why?" "We need to find her to answer that question," Merack said as he called over several of the hunters to help with the search. Merkansoo called more of his people to help. Soon there were eight hands of people walking in among the trees calling out "Nada!" Merkansoo and Mearoo led their people in a search further ahead in case she was kidnapped. We continued the search on foot looking for any signs of her. "Here! More footprints!" I shouted as I stopped and dropped to the ground to look at them closely. Merack hurried over with Pathak to also look at them. "Only one set. Hers. But look at them! She is not walking straight! She is staggering!" I said pointing out the uneven spaces between the prints and the changes in the depth of them. Merack also got down to take a close look. Merack looked up and pointed saying "That way." We got up and signaled the others to close in on us and keep looking for more tracks or signs.

We had not gone far when we found more prints in the mud banks of a small stream. I immediately saw that she must be in some sort of trouble! "Look! She fell here! Then she crawled over to the stream and drank from it. Then she struggled to stand up here. Her tracks are getting worse!"

I said and got up quickly as I heard a call! "That is Merkansoo!" I said as we hurried towards where he was calling us from. We found Merkansoo and the rest of his people gathered around an oak tree. Sitting up against it was Nada! We ran up and tried to ask her what was wrong, but she was muttering and had a wild look in her eyes! She was covered with mud, ground, and leaves and had cuts and scratches on her arms and legs. I dropped down and held her face to look into her eyes.

I saw that they were wide open and the round centers were very large! The white parts were reddish and I could clearly see the blood vessels. "Nada! What did you eat?" I asked her sure that she had eaten from a plant that caused her to become this way! She kept muttering then laughing to herself and seemed to be unaware of us. I stood up and started looking all around at the plants to see if any might cause this effect on her. "Pathak? Do you know what she might have eaten that could cause her to be this way?"

Pathak looked at her carefully and then said "Gaieaa would know. I am not sure. It looks like what happens when you eat bad tree root plants." I looked around but didn't see any of them nearby. I started to follow her trail back as I saw nothing here and reasoned that it had to be near where she left the tribe. I stopped and said "We need to take her back to the tribe. Gaieaa will know what she ate and what to do to help her." Merkansoo simply picked her up in his arms and followed as I told Merack, Bamal, and the rest what I was looking for. We crossed the small stream and still, I didn't see anything that would cause this. We reached the place where we first saw her tracks and I asked everyone to spread out and look carefully from here to the trail.

Pathak was the first to find the plant. "Jakool! Here! I think I found the plant!" I ran over to him and saw a Bhangi plant that grew everywhere and was very useful! "What is it?" Merkansoo asked as we looked at the plant for signs that Nada had taken leaves or seeds from it. "We call it Bhangi. The leaves are very good eating as well as the seeds. The roots can be dried and then boiled in water to make a drink that helps stomach sickness, and bleeding and reduces pain. The seeds can be ground up to make different medicines. In fact, we can make rope from the stalks" I looked at the adult plant in front of me with seed pods growing from the stalk and long thin pointed leaves growing out from all around the stalk up to the top of the plant. "I don't see any leaves missing. Or the seed pods. We need to find the one she ate. We have to take it back for Gaieaa to see.

"Everyone did a slow careful search as we walked back out of the many trees to the trail. "Jakool! Here!" Merack called out. We ran over to him to see him bending over a much smaller Bhangi plant. I could see the leaves and seeds were still there! The plant had been pulled up some and I saw the roots. "The roots? Why did she eat the roots?" I asked out loud. "Mearoo asked, "Are they bad to eat?" I replied "Yes. But only if you eat too much. She didn't eat much from this plant. I looked at the roots more carefully and saw something growing on them! "We need to take this whole plant back to Gaieaa quickly!" I said as I started digging out the ground around the rest of the roots. Once I had them uncovered Merack pulled it up slowly so we got all of the plant.

"Let's go! I said as I took the plant and started back to find Gaieaa. Mearoo stopped me and said "I'll take it. Much faster!" She took the plant and immediately jumped away from us. I turned to Merkansoo and said "Follow her! Gaieaa needs to see her too!" Merkansoo just leaped right after Mearoo with Nada clutched to his chest. Merack asked "Why? What is it?" As I had not explained what I saw on the roots. I turned and faced him, Pathak, and the rest of the searchers and said "The roots had a strange-looking growth I didn't recognize. I think that is what is causing Nada to act so strange." We went back to the trail and caught up with the tribe to find Gaieaa and Nada. We found them with Pathak and several other of the Elders looking at the plant. Gaieaa had cut one of the growths from the root and turned it over and over as she looked at it.

Mearoo was standing next to her with her 'remembering look'. I then looked at Merkansoo, who was still holding Nada so Gaieaa could examine her without having to bend down. Merkansoo also had that look! I silently prayed to the Spirits of the many trees and the cloud stabber to let them find something that would help cure Nada! I was so worried about Nada, that I didn't hear the gasps of surprise from people that were standing much further away. It was not until I heard Janai say something in his own language that sounded familiar that I turned to see what was happening. I gasped as I saw Janai, Lasaa, Samalaa, and all of the snow-leaper people dropping to all fours and putting their heads down. I then watched as my people dropped to their knees and fell forward arms outstretched!

"What?" I started to ask then I saw something moving slowly towards us. As the people closest also dropped to the ground I saw the great striped beast from the many trees! She came right up to me and gave me a sniff. I dropped to my knees and gave her a hug around the neck and said "You have answered my prayers!" Believing her to be the spirit of the many trees! She walked over to Mearoo and then Merkansoo and butted both of them to get their attention. They both became aware of their surroundings and her, both showing their surprise at her being there!

"Yuma! What are you doing here?" At the sound of the name "Yuma, I watch something impossible happen! The great striped tiger stood up on its hind legs and transformed into a woman! A tall, beautiful woman with hair that was the darkest black color! Her skin was almost golden in color and her features were so different that any human I had ever seen or heard of, I truly believed her to be a spirit. She took a few steps over to Nada and then turned and said to Gaieaa "Show me this growth." Gaieaa handed it to her with trembling hands as she was as surprised as the rest of us! Yuma took the growth and sniffed it carefully. She made a face and then put it down. She then grabbed Nada and looked into her eyes then tapped her chest.

She turned and asked Gaieaa "Do you have any of the leaves of the plants that grow along the Great River, that flows east of here and then into the Great Salt Water?" Gaieaa replied "There are several large rivers that flowed into the Great Salt Water. When we moved from the shore of the Great Salt Water where the sun wakes up, we passed through a place with many such plants. The river is the one we followed to reach here. But which plant do you mean?" The hills and the valley had very thick trees and also small plants that grew well close to the river's banks. We would pick the leaves from several and make a drink from it that cured many sicknesses of the blood and stomach."

Yuma said "Yes! Bring them! I need them to cure her." Gaieaa shouted for Prinda and Tivash! They came running and stopped in front of her breathless. "We need all the leaves we dried from the plants we gathered in the great river valley and the surrounding hills. Also, any that we ground into powder!" "Yes, Gaieaa!" They both said as they turned and ran back to one of the carriers filled with supplies. It took them several minutes to find them, but they soon returned with a large hide bag full of the leaves and a smaller one of the ground-up powder! Gaieaa took it from Prinda and then asked "What do we do with them?" Yuma said "Nothing. I will do it."

She took the bag and emptied the dried leaves onto the ground. "Water!" She said. I took the water skin I kept with me and handed it to her. She took it and poured out all the water onto the leaves. "Now watch!

She said as she started to shine with a light all over and then bent down and touched the wet pile of tea leaves on the ground. We watched as the leaves turned from dried-up brown and black leaves, to tender young green ones! "How did she do that?" I heard Gaieaa and others whisper as she took a handful of the green leaves in one hand and then made a gesture over them with her other hand. She then turned to Nada and put the leaves in her mouth. Nada didn't move until Yuma touched her jaw with a glowing finger, then she started chewing the leaves!

Yuma then stepped away from the leaves on the ground and we watched as Nada struggled in Merkansoo's arms until Yuma said "Let her go!" She immediately dropped to her knees in front of the leaves and started scooping them up and stuffing them into her mouth! "She will need to eat all of the leaves. Then she will need to sleep. Make a drink using the powdered leaves. This will help her sleep. When she wakes she should be cured." I quickly said "Thank you Yuma! Thank you for answering my prayers!" She turned to give me a penetrating look that seemed to freeze me in place. Then she said "I did not do this to answer your prayers Jakool. I did this to answer mine!" She then changed back into the Great Striped animal; the snow-leaper people called a Tigre, and slowly went up the trail and soon disappeared. I did not realize until later that she went in the same direction as we were traveling!

We spent the rest of the sun stopped as Nada should not be moved until she was herself. So we gathered the Bhangi plants when Merkansoo asked about this 'rope' I said we made and Pathak decided we would need rope in the cloud stabbers. So I was gathering the plants with Merkansoo, Mearoo, Samalaa, Harit, Kika, Hardika, Kaga, and some of the others, so we could take them back to the temporary camp. Merkansoo asked me to explain the making of this rope from the plants. It made it easier to gather the plants so I told them the steps.

"We gather the entire plant including the roots. We take them back to the camp and once there we strip off the leaves and seeds for food. Then we cut the stalks in half and carefully slice through the skin on the stalk. What you see inside is what we use to make the rope." I paused as I showed him the many thin fibers inside. "We pull these apart so we end up with lots of thin fibers. We take those and dry them on the same drying racks we used for the meat. Once it dries out enough, we take them and start twisting them together. To make it longer, we tie another one onto this one here with loops and twist the ends together. We add more of the thin fibers together until we have the thickness we want, then we twist them all together."

Merkansoo, Mearoo, Samalaa, and Hardika paid close attention to the explanation but had so many questions that I said "I think seeing us make the rope will answer all of your questions better than more talking!" Merkansoo smiled and said "Yes. Seeing something made is much better than just hearing it told." Once we all had large bundles of the plants to carry we returned to camp. I had as many of the experienced rope makers help us so each snow-leaper person had an experienced teacher showing them how we made rope. This ended up taking all sun, but in the end, we had ten hands of man-lengths of strong rope, and Merkansoo and his people now knew how to use all the parts of the Bhangi plant!

While we were still working Nada woke up. She was weak but knew who they were and who she was. "I just remember taking a bite of the root. I walked further in as I saw more plants. Then nothing that made any sense!" Gaieaa nodded and asked her to try and tell them what she saw and heard. Nada replied "It was very strange! I was walking in the many trees but nothing was right! The trees were too big and all crooked and twisted! They kept changing colors and seemed to move! The ground seemed to move and I had trouble walking and just standing! I kept hearing strange noises from the branches that didn't sound like any birds I knew. I also saw things. I don't remember all of them but one stuck in my head! I saw the great striped beast walking towards me and talking to me! I could understand her words! She kept telling me that I was sick and needed to turn around and return to my tribe! It was silly as that is where I was going!" I knew from her tracks, that she had gone in the wrong direction! She had lost all sense of direction and she saw the Tigre named "Yuma", that is the spirit of the many trees! I returned to work while Pathak and Gaieaa continued to feed Nada and encourage her to rest.

When we stopped that evening and ate I noticed that some of the female snow-leapers had paired off with men of my tribe. Hardika was with Harit and they had gone off a ways from everyone else. Both preferred quiet solitude to being part of a large noisy group. Samalaa was with Jarack and it was plain to see that her scent was affecting him as he was smiling and talking more to her than he normally said to everyone in full sun! It was no surprise to see them go off together to find a mating place.

I grinned when I saw that Samalaa was with Mahendra! He was obviously paying attention to her and she was to him! Jameeka had Kaga off to one side and had her tail curled around him possessively, so I knew they would soon be mates! Sheena was too young to settle on just one mate, so I was not surprised to see her surrounded by Lavar, Timbu, and Garath sitting together eating, talking, and laughing. Sheena would probably mate with all three before the night was over!

Since we were sitting with Merkansoo, Pathak, Gaieaa, and Nada, I decided to ask about Yuma. "Merkansoo? What can you tell us about Yuma? We have never seen one of the spirits change from an animal into a human before." Merkansoo looked at Mearoo who sighed and nodded. I looked at her but she said "Listen to Merkansoo." I looked back at Merkansoo who stood up to tell us a story of the one called 'Yuma'.

"Long ago, even before the first, Yuma was here. She had no need to appear as 'Ooh-man' as the man had not come to this place yet. But the snow leopards knew her! The first man did not know her until his mate had left him to find a male snow-leaper to mate with. She did this every season and then returned to him to mate with him. He was alone in the first cave trying to record his experiences with the First and the first two sets of cubs. He was trying to figure out how to keep track and count the number of cubs.

He knew it was important to know which season each litter of cubs was born and which ones mated with which. But he couldn't figure out just how to do it. Suddenly Yuma appeared to him. First in her animal form; as she had watched him with the First, and was curious about him. He was surprised when a completely different large cat came into their cave. But he saw that she was not threatening him so he greeted her as he would the first! He chuckled and spoke to her and gave her scratches around her neck and her cheeks. She purred in satisfaction as he did this causing him to laugh at how like the First she was acting. He was more surprised when she started acting like the First and playing with him! Soon they were rolling around on the furs in the cave and before he realized it, he was mating with her! Only she had changed from an animal to the person you saw today!"

"What did he do?" I asked wondering what happened next! Merkansoo looked at me with a grin and said "What would you do if you found yourself mating with a woman that looked like her?" I blushed as I knew exactly what I would have done!

A sharp claw traced my neck and Mearoo whispered to me "You'd better be glad that it was not you" as I tried hard not to move away from the feeling of her running it down to my collarbone! I gave her a smile as I turned to face her and said "Are you going to be this way when I 'have' to mate with other women?" Mearoo gave me a surprised look then shook her head as she said "No. That is needed!"

I had no idea her words would also be spoken to me later by someone I would never have expected to hear them from! I turned my attention back to Merkansoo and he continued "Yuma showed the First how to count large numbers and create symbols for them to put on the cave walls.

She also showed him how to make a symbol for each cub from each litter. That when he mated with one of them, he would show the symbols for him and that cub. If it was another male cub, then their symbols together. This way the parents of every litter of cubs were shown on the cave walls. She left him after that one mating and the lessons in counting. He did see her again several times but those times are in other stories."

Pathak said "Long ago, when we first came to the lands south of here and beyond the Great Plains, we met a Tigre. We believed her to be a spirit of the land there. Were we wrong?" Merkansoo said "I don't know. There are many such Tigre both here and all through the lands from here to the Great Salt Water and back towards the place where the sun sleeps. It is possible that it was Yuma, but she usually only shows herself for some reason or purpose." I wondered something and then asked him "Did Yuma have young ones from her mating with the First?" Merkansoo's face showed surprise at my question and then said "She has never told us. She was asked by my ancestors, but simply ignored the question."

I would have asked more questions but Merkansoo said "One story is enough for now. You can hear all of them, but only one each night!" I smiled as I saw Darshita appear at his side and Merkansoo smiled then they left the campfire. I was feeling the hard work I had done that sun and was ready to sleep too! Mearoo sensed it in me and soon we were curled up in one of our favorite places! We had found a little hidden place within sight of the stream that was surrounded by thick bushes. We could jump in and be completely hidden from anyone coming to the stream. I was not as tired as I had thought as Mearoo started to nuzzle me with her lips and touch me in ways that meant she wanted to mate! I thought how I was so lucky to be her mate! She made me hot with desire and then I took her in the position she liked best! Me behind her, she on all fours!

I found myself giving her all of my seed, again and again, that night until we fell together exhausted. We slept entangled with each other until woke up hearing people coming to the stream for water and bathing. "When they leave let's bathe," I said to Mearoo quietly as we stretched and untangled ourselves from each other. It was not long before we heard the people leave the stream, so we got out of our hiding place and went to the stream to drink and then bathe.

I wondered how long it would take us to cross through the hills and the endless green grass and asked Mearoo. "I think it will take five suns. But that is only if we do not have any more reasons to stop," she replied as she rubbed my back. I grimaced knowing that when a large group like this travels, reasons always happen to cause you to stop! "So say ten suns with stops," I replied as she finished washing my back and turned so I could scrub her back for her. I was being careful not to rub her fur too hard when going up. I had learned this by rubbing too hard the first time we bathed each other! She had let out a yowl of protest jumped away from me and turned in a crouch with her claws out! I promised her I would never rub her fur that hard again before she would let me wash her back again! I also had to endure her efforts in bathing me as my skin was not as tough as her fur and she accidentally gave me bruises the first time we bathed each other! Once we were clean we went to the camp to eat and check on Nada.

We found her with Pathak and Gaieaa, eating and talking. "How are you today Nada?" I asked joining them. She smiled and said "Much better Jakool! Thank you for what you did to find me and the cause of my sickness." I smiled and said, "It is a good thing I remembered my lessons about tracking and the Bhangi plant!" Nada laughed and then turned to Mearoo and said "Jakool was always forgetting which plants were used for food, medicine, and materials for making the things we use. He couldn't understand why he needed to know these things as 'He' was going to be a hunter!" I laughed with the rest at my younger self's ideas on what I needed to know to be a good hunter! "I was only four years old Nada!" I said to defend myself from her accusations! Mearoo gave me a look and then said "By the time I was four years old, I had become the 'Keeper of the First Cave, made an Elder of my tribe, saved your life, and chose you as my mate!" This caused everyone to roar with laughter as I made a face at Mearoo and stuck out my tongue at her!

After the laughter died down I asked Nada "Can you travel?" Nada said firmly "Yes I can!" I looked at Gaieaa and saw her nod her agreement. "Good!" I said as we finished eating and went to find Merack, Kaga, Bamal, and Merkansoo to discuss continuing our journey. We found them up the trail discussing the best way to take to meet up with Paasi and the rest. Merkansoo turned at our approach pointed at me and said "He knows only a few of the dangers of taking that path! I know all of them! I say it would be foolish to go that way!"

I was surprised at Merkansoo's voice as he sounded almost angry! "What path?" I asked as we reached them. Merkansoo replied, "The one we took to get here!" I quickly said to them "No. That would put the entire tribe in danger! That is where Paasi and Elasaa were injured and four others! There are creatures called Two-Tusks in there that can rip you apart!" Merack looked doubtful, Kaga thoughtful and Bamal relieved! Merkansoo said "I understand that you are worried that the path through the endless green grass is easier to follow and you are right. But this is why we have our scouts following and erasing our trail! Kaga said "I want to try and find a quicker way. I am worried because we will be traveling too slow and will be easy to follow and catch!" Merkansoo turned his head to him and replied "The other trails are much longer. We would be adding at least four hands of suns by taking the shortest of them." Kaga shook his head as he replied "That would be bad!" Merack said "I would feel better if we could split up the tribe. Give anyone following two trails."

Merkansoo looked thoughtful as he looked at Merack. Finally, he said "Maybe. But what if something happens to one group? The other group will not know and have no way of finding out! They couldn't come to each other's aid." I agreed with Merkansoo on that, and then suddenly I had an idea. "What if we make it 'look' like we have split up. Not just two groups but many?" Merkansoo looked at Jakool and asked "Why? They will send scouts to follow all the trails. It is what I would do" Jakool said "Yes! It will cause them to split up their strength! Think about it. How many would you send?" I said to each one of them! Merkansoo slowly nodded then said I would send at least ten of my fastest on each trail!" Merack and Bamal agreed with him.

"So you just split up your hunting party into groups of ten. After seeing how they killed the deer and Mearoo fight a Rough Fur, I think it would be very easy to ambush and kill anyone trying to follow us!" Bamal gave a wicked grin and said "Larkar must be with one of the groups! This will give him something he needs to be whole again!"

I nodded in agreement as did Merack. Merkansoo smiled and said "We make up mixed groups to make each trail. Men, Women, Children. It must look like the entire tribe has split up. The snow leapers will go in front and up in the trees when they can. That way they will not leave any tracks, so anyone following will think they are only following your tribe. Our scouts that follow will drop back and wait to see anyone following and 'If' they follow every trail. This way we can know exactly how many we will be facing! Our scouts can easily reach us long before they can!"

I smiled remembering just how fast they could go even carrying us!" I could tell everyone liked this plan by the smiles, grins, and bright eyes. Kaga went ahead to where Larkar and his group were keeping watch, while Mearoo went back to the scouts behind us to tell them the new plan. Merkansoo, Me, Merack, and Bamal went back to the tribes to tell them and get them organized into ten groups. It took time to do but finally, we had ten groups, loaded with the amount of supplies and even some of the Elders!"

That night we discussed the plan with all the groups so everyone knew what to do. The next sun we started off together, and then the groups split off to take different trails one by one. The plan was to make it look like the tribe was in disagreement about the trail to take and where to go, making anyone following to be overconfident! Once they made a large path for each group, they made sure that only the human tracks were left. I had Mearoo, Samalaa, Sheena, Janai, Farkis, Jameeka, and Girivar of the snow leapers with Mahendra, Kaga, Nada, Tivash, and Cecina for the adults. Kika, Timbu, and Garath for the young new adults Farini, Birksa, Cara the girl children, and finally Bhani, Mobear, Zhana, and the boy children. We took enough of the other tribes people from both tribes so we had roughly the same as the other groups. We did speak of keeping the number from each tribe even, so if attacked, my people could ride out of danger on the snow leapers. But Merkansoo pointed out it was not necessary, as they could carry two children as easily as one adult. Even some of the young adults were still small enough to do this! So we just made sure we had enough snow leapers in each group.

My group was taking a game trail that led us north around the hills, and then into the endless green grass from that direction. Bamal and Darshita led their group close to the original trail that we used to cross the hills into the endless green grass, then to the many trees at the foot of the cloud stabbers.

Merkansoo and Merack led their group along the edge of the hidden ravine we had used on our journey to my tribe, and last Jarack and Lasaa led the group that would head directly over the hills and into the endless green grass avoiding all the other trails. There were some disagreements about who should be in which group. I let Merack and Merkansoo handle anyone who wanted to be with another group, as it was usually so they could be with a mate or child of theirs.

When Larkar heard the entire plan and the paths we would take he immediately became upset and furious! "I cannot be in four places at once! How am I to have my revenge if I am not with the group they follow?" Merack answered him quickly and sternly "Because we believe they will send scouting parties on 'each' trail. We want them to do this so we split them up. Larkar you will be in the rear group of scouts watching for them. If they do follow, all of you will follow until you are sure of which trails they follow and how many follow! Surely you see the need for this?" Larkar looked as if he would continue to argue until Merack said "All of you will return to me and Merkansoo so we can attack 'each' group with all of both tribes! You will lead one of the attacks! You will be responsible for killing all of them except the Leader! We want him alive!" Larkar had been too busy listening to Merack's words to question him until he said: "Alive". "Why? Why would you want to keep even one of those evil things alive?"

Merkansoo stepped right up to Larkar and put his face in his and answered "Because we want him to tell us exactly where the rest of the tribe is! So we can KILL THEM ALL!" He shouted the last three words at Larkar. Larkar looked as if he didn't believe Merkansoo then Merkansoo said "Larkar! You are not the only one who has suffered! I want one alive to make sure we end this now!" Larkar's face showed that he understood that Merkansoo wanted to do exactly what he wanted! Larkar gave Merkansoo a solemn nod and said "Then we will!" Merkansoo said "Good!" Then he said, "Now go and pick who will be the best to have with you!"

Larkar looked like he'd gotten the greatest gift with those words! I let out the breath I was holding as I expected Larkar to try and fight Merkansoo! Merack also let out a big sigh of relief and said "I almost feel sorry for the first member of that tribe he fights! Merkansoo turned and gave Merack the same look he'd given Larkar and Merack laughed and held up his hands saying "I said ALMOST!" I gave out a laugh at the snarl and growl that Merkansoo gave him before he smiled to show he was only joking. "I knew the only way to convince Larkar was to tell him exactly what he needed to hear. Besides it is the truth. We will never be safe until they are completely wiped out."

In the end, Larkar left with fifty of the best from both tribes. He had asked Merkansoo to pick the ones from his tribe so they could carry them back once they had scouted out the enemy! So now we were traveling on our different trails watching out in front and behind us!

CHAPTER SEVEN

A TRAIL OF BLOOD AND TEARS

I was nervous about being attacked until I realized that with Mearoo, Jameeka and Samalaa running ahead of us, no one would be able to ambush us that way! Girivar, Farkis, and Janai were behind us erasing our tracks and watching for anyone following. I led my group for several suns until we reached a place where the hills ended and the endless green grass began. We had stopped to camp there so Mearoo, Samalaa, and Jameeka could check further ahead into the endless green grass before we tried to cross. I spoke with Gaieaa who had traveled this path before. "It will take maybe a hand and three fingers, to cross until you reach the place where the ground rises up from the endless green grass. There is a river that runs down from the cloud stabbers that has carved a ravine down into the endless green grass. There is where we can climb up." I made sure that everyone knew what to look for and what we should gather while there. Gaieaa and Nada went over the different plants to look for that grew there, with the scouts and the group.

Our job would be to gather them so they could be dried and preserved. Gaieaa warned everyone of the dangers before we went. The Tigre kills silently! It can easily kill the largest grass eaters or Rough Fur with its powerful jaws and teeth! But worse are some of the snakes! Be always looking for them! Some are very hard to see in the grass as they also have skin that hides them! One bite from a Naga; or 'the Hooded One', will kill you! He is long and has silver-gray skin with a grainy look to it. The Daboia is smaller but just as deadly. It has Large black leaf pattern spots on its back as well as smaller circles and dots. The back is tan and changes to white on its belly. There is one that hunts in both the many trees and the many grass. It is huge and kills its prey by wrapping its body around it and squeezing it to death! Then it swallows them whole! The worst though is the one we call "Pretty Death!" It has bright blue scales on its back that turn to copper, bronze, and gold as you go to its belly. It has a small head and does not look dangerous! Its colors are so pretty that it makes people think it is safe to pick up! It is not! It has such bright colors because it is not afraid of any other living thing!" So we went carefully watching out for these dangerous snakes, Tigres, One Horns, and other smaller predators as we traveled the tall grass.

I would like to say we crossed them with no trouble but I cannot. On the second Sun, we ran into trouble of the worst kind! I heard screams coming from someone then yells! I turned and ran towards them with my new throwing spears ready. I found Kika and Nada holding Cara as Sheena spit and hissed at something in the grass! "No! Don't!" Nada screamed as Sheena suddenly pounced and fought with something hidden only a few feet from them! I ran up in time to see Sheena viciously strike the ground with her front paws then held one up with a struggling snake impaled on them! "Hold it! Do Not let it get loose!" I said as I drew my knife and with a quick stroke cut off its head! Nada was quick to try and treat Cara but as soon as I saw what kind of snake it was I felt tears in my eyes!

"It's a Naga!" Nada said as she held poor Cara in her arms and rocked her back and forth as the child screamed in pain! "Nothing?" I asked her hoping there was something we could do! Nada shook her head showing that she was crying too as Cara slowly stopped her screams then went rigid and died!

I turned and said to Kika "What happened?" Kika was in shock and just kept holding Cara's arm and looking at the now blackening skin where the Naga had bitten her! Sheena answered me instead. "We were looking for these plants"; She held one up from a small pile they had gathered, "Cara suddenly screamed when she bent down to pull one up! It happened so quickly Jakool! I wish I had checked all the plants first!" Sheena said sadly as she felt responsible as the only snow-leaper with them. I shook my head and said "It is not your fault Sheena. We were all told to 'look' for these snakes! Cara is" I paused then said "Was very young for an Ooh-man. She did not understand the danger."

Nada had stopped rocking Cara and carefully closed her eyelids over her staring eyes. "Jakool? What do we do? We can't just leave her here!" Nada said to me. We both knew our customs, but somehow with a child as young as Cara, whose parents were here with us, it didn't feel right! "We will bring her to her parents so they may decide," I said to Nada making her feel a little better as we were not leaving her where she had died. I knew as the leader it was my duty to do this, so I took little Cara's body from Nada and we went back to the main group. We found Prinda with Gaieaa helping her with plants they were drying. She saw me approach slowly carrying Cara and stood up silently and watched as I walked up to her and said "Cara was bitten by a Naga! It was hiding behind a plant she bent down to pick. Sheena killed it but it was too late."

Prinda nodded and slowly held out her arms to receive her child. Birksa was with her being too young to join the others in searching for plants. Timbu was her other child with us, and he was out with another group. I asked her "Is there anything you would like us to do for her?" Prinda was slowly stroking Cara's hair with one hand as she rocked her in her arms. "No. She is gone. I will take care of her body once I have finished saying goodbye." She turned and slowly walked away from us singly softly to Cara. Gaieaa kept Birksa busy helping her pull the leaves off the plants so she would not see what Prinda did with body.

I wept as I returned to the front. I had no idea how I could have prevented Cara's death but somehow felt that I should! I was feeling guilty and very sad as we continued forward. It was not until near sunset that I ordered a halt to make camp. I had no heart in me to return to the main group, so I waited there ahead of them for Mearoo and the rest of the forward scouts to return. I sat down in the tall grass and gave myself over to a grief I had never felt before. *Why did she have to pick that plant? Why didn't she look around it first? Why was one so young picking plants?* These and other questions kept running through my head; making it hurt, as I held my knees and rocked back and forth in my guilt and grief over losing someone I was responsible for!

Mearoo, Jameeka, and Samalaa found me like this when they returned from scouting. It was almost dark when I felt Mearoo gently take my face and pull it up to face hers. "What happened?" I felt the hot tears start again as I stammered out the details of Cara's death. Mearoo nodded but didn't say anything as she just held me. I never saw Samalaa leave and then return a few minutes later with Nada. I didn't hear what Nada said as I was too full of my own grief; and loud guilty thoughts, to hear her! Mearoo gave me a little shake and then said "Drink this!" Suddenly she held my mouth open and I tasted a bitter drink being poured into my open mouth! "Swallow!" Nada said in a commanding voice that habit caused me to do as she said. I swallowed the bitter drink and coughed at the taste. "Again!" Nada said as Mearoo gave me another drink of the foul-tasting brew. I did as I was told as I had no will to resist them.

After several such drinks Nada and Mearoo got me standing up and held me between them as we slowly went back to join the group. By the time we got there I felt very dizzy was having trouble walking straight and suddenly felt like I was losing all feeling in my arms and legs! Before I knew it I was lying down on furs and Mearoo was there with me by the fire. "Sleep Jakool. Just Sleep".

I couldn't do anything else as I felt my eyes close and fell into a deep sleep! When I woke Gaieaa was watching over me and gave me water to drink. I was very thirsty and drank several times from a water skin until I felt better.

"What is happening?" I asked but Gaieaa said "Listen Jakool. You are not responsible for Cara's death. I know you feel you are the leader, but you are not responsible! Nada gave you the sleeping drink; as Mearoo and she could see you were too full of your guilt and grief over Cara. I have already given new orders to all that 'No One' is to gather plants in an area until it has been cleared by two adults. One of us and one snow-leaper. That was Samalaa's idea. It is a good one. Mearoo told us the way is clear for a full sun ahead, so they are staying with the group so we have adults to do this. You should stay here today and let yourself recover. You are a good man Jakool, but you are young and have not learned what to be responsible for what you are not responsible for!"

I wanted to argue with her but I couldn't, not with Gaieaa! She was over six hands old and one of the oldest of our tribe. We all respected her wisdom, her skills in preparing so many different healings, and her knowledge of our people! She told me "You will feel this way until you learn to accept that you cannot be responsible for others that do not follow the instructions they are given. I know that Cara was told to look first; as I told all of them, that went out to harvest! So stop making yourself sick with guilt and grief. Yes, it is sad, but we must go on and you are our leader!" Gaieaa said no more about it and went about making a hot tea for me to drink with freshly cooked meat and some of the fruit we had gathered. Once I had eaten I asked her "Where is everyone else?" I had looked around the camp and only saw the Elders like her and the very young children. "Out. Now go and take care of yourself so I can get back to preparing something from the snake poison that 'might' help." I started asking her questions but she stopped me with a stare and then said "I cannot work with you here wanting to ask me such questions! Go!" I got up and left her as I knew she meant it, and if there was any chance of finding a way to heal the poison from a Nada bite, then Gaieaa would find it!

I wandered over to some of the other Elders and helped them with the simple chores they managed around the camp and with the young children. I began to understand the wisdom of Gaieaa's words; and having me stay in camp, to be with both groups, the Old and the Young. The Old gave me wisdom and advice that I needed! The Young gave me back some joy and happiness, watching them play games and invent new things to do in the way of all children! By the time everyone else started returning to the camp, I had come to terms with my guilt and most of my grief over Cara's death. Mearoo came to me and asked me if I was feeling any better. "Yes. Gaieaa helped me see that it was not my fault." Mearoo nodded then said "I wonder if we need to gather so many of these plants Gaieaa wants. "A good question! Let's go ask her."

So Mearoo and I went to see Gaieaa, who was with Nada looking over what plants were found that sun. "Gaieaa?" I said stopping and waiting for her to reply as a sign of respect to an Elder. "Yes, Jakool? Mearoo?" She said as soon as she finished counting the wild orange roots that were brought in. "We were wondering if we really need to be gathering so much food and plants for herbs and healings?" Gaieaa looked at me and then at Mearoo before answering our question. "Yes and No. Yes in that it is better to gather them when you find them than to find you don't have them when you need them!"

I grinned at the words as they were the same ones she and Nada had used to teach us as children about harvesting when you could, for use when you couldn't! "But do we have enough? Considering the dangers?" I asked pressing her. Gaieaa looked at Nada and asked her opinion "We have plenty of the ones for herbs, food, and most of the healing. The only ones we should still gather as we travel are, Amulthus, Ankol, Chickweed, Willow Bark." I nodded then said, "Willow trees grow by rivers, Chickweed under Oak Trees, Ankol and Amulthus grow in the many trees of the hills with the oaks." Gaieaa nodded in agreement and then said "We should then journey through the endless green grass, then into the many trees by the path I told you about. We will cross at least one river between here and the many trees." I agreed and we went around telling everyone to pack and be ready to continue tomorrow. Everyone was glad to hear this news and Mearoo and I gathered the scouts and told them the plan and the path we needed to find.

"How do we know which path to take over the endless green grass?" Mahendra asked me. I shook my head and said "I only know what Gaieaa has told us. Mearoo?" I turned to her hoping that one of her ancestors might have been this way. "No. My memories do not hold this place she spoke of". Mearoo answered my question. Finally, we decided to just have Gaieaa carried in the front so she could keep us going in the right direction! When I went back to tell her of this, she laughed and said "I will feel very useful there!"

I had to chuckle at her as she pretended to be the 'Great Hunt Leader Donaha', who once lost his entire hunt party! It took three suns for them to find him again!

"I know I left them here somewhere!" She said sounding confused and frustrated as she pretended to feel around her as if she could not see! I left her to organize herself, Nada, and Prinda for the journey as Mearoo and I ate and then lay down near the fire to rest. The next morning we started out in the direction that Mearoo and the scouts had traveled, knowing it was clear of human enemies. But we took care to be watching for snakes, Tigres, One Horns, and other dangers hidden in the tall grass.

We still made good progress and by mid-sun, we reached a small stream that Gaieaa recognized. "This runs from the high places I told you about. See how cold the water feels?" I tested it and found it to be cold and refreshing after walking in the sun with no shade. Although it was not hot, I was still sweating from the sun's warmth. Samalaa looked ahead and said "I think I see a rise in the land far ahead. Three? Maybe four suns." Gaieaa said "Yes! That would be where we need to go! Now just follow the stream but be wary! All animals need water!" With that warning, we checked the area around the stream before stopping to rest and eat. Once everyone had eaten and drank we continued along the stream course.

It wound its way slowly through the grass with plenty of flowering plants, berry bushes, and edible root plants growing along its banks. I urged Nada and the rest to be careful when picking them and watched carefully for any signs of snakes. What happened was something I did not expect as we came to a dip in the land that was hidden by the grass. Samalaa was ahead of us with Mahendra and they jumped back and yelled "Stop!" I immediately stopped the main group and went ahead with Mearoo to see what had stopped them. I saw as I got to the edge of the dip in the ground. A deer herd was there, or what was left of them! "What did this?" I said out loud as I squatted down to look at the dead animals to see the wounds. Samalaa and Mahendra were also looking and Samalaa said "I do not like this. See these gashes?" I nodded as she rolled a large male deer over to show its belly. "These were made from under it." I nodded as I thought about how we had taken down some of the deer from underneath, but this was an animal that did this!

"How?" I asked her. "I do not know. But they are dangerous!" was her answer! We spent time looking at each deer until Mahendra found something. "Here. Look at this" He held up a sharp, pointed horn or tusk that had broken off in the side of one deer. Mearoo immediately said "It is from a Two Tusk. But I have never seen one kill so many deer!

It doesn't make any sense! I agreed having seen the Two Tusks in the many trees. "Do they ever travel in packs? Like wolves?" I asked her. "No. Unless.." She stopped to think about this as Samalaa looked for tracks around the kill sight. "I think that if something surprised a group of them feeding they might have stampeded. But it would have to be something that they were afraid of!" "What are the Tusk Boars afraid of?" I asked them. Samalaa said "Those giant snakes!" Mearoo nodded then said "There is something else. "Hunters." I looked at her and said, "You said that your people don't hunt them!" Mearoo replied "We do not. Others do."

I asked "Are there any other tribes in this area? "Gaieaa would know better than us." When I reached Gaieaa, she was sitting on the carrier that Kaga and Tivash used to carry her. "Well? What is it?" I told her "We found a herd of deer slaughtered by what Mearoo calls Two Tusks." Gaieaa frowned and said "I think we know of them. We only hunted them when we couldn't find any other meat! They are dangerous animals!"

"That is why Merkansoo's people do not hunt them," I answered her. "Somehow they were herded into the endless green grass. Are there any other tribes either in the endless green grass or the highlands of many trees we are going to?" Gaieaa frowned and then thought hard. Finally, she said "I do remember one tribe that lived along the edge of the many trees where the river divides it from the endless green grass. But that was when I was a young child! I don't know what happened to them, but I remember my father coming back from a trading sun with them. He said they found them all gone! Just picked up and left!" I wondered where they had gone and why? I turned to Nada and asked her "Do you know anything of this tribe?" Nada nodded and said "When I was a child my father told me that 'Sekar' sent out several search parties to try and find them. The only traces they ever found went south and deep into the Great Many Trees there." "The Great Many Trees?" I repeated, trying to remember why that name sounded familiar, and gave me a shiver of fear at the saying of its name.

Gaieaa took up the story "The Great Many Trees south of the hills, covers a very great stretch of land! It goes from the great plains in the south to the saltwater in the west. It goes both North and South from there until it meets the foot of the great cloud stabbers in the North and a place where the salt water goes far into the land. We know this because it is written in our records by our ancestors. They spent many seasons traveling through it; before they finally found the way out into the hills, then the endless green grass. Once you are in it, it seems to go on forever and you cannot see the sun; or the blinking night spirits, to know which direction you are traveling. There are many snakes, Tigres, Wolves, One Horn, Two Tusks, Black Killers, and other dangerous animals. The six-legged crawlers are this big and poisonous!" She held out both hands with a space the size of four hands between them. "The biting fliers come in hoards at night, attracted by the fire and the scent of our blood! Many died after being bitten by them! More died from the Hooded One and other snakes, including the large one. Others hang from the trees and either kill you with their poisonous bite or wrap around your neck and pull you up to the branch strangling you."

I remembered the stories now. I was so scared by them as a young one, I had put them out of my mind until she told them again. I shuddered but asked her "If they went there, then how would any still be alive?" I asked her trying to make sense of this. "I don't know Jakool. I really do not know. Could the Two Tusks have been stampeded by something else?" I said "Yes they could have. It may have been a one-horn or one of the giant snakes. They are afraid of both of them." "They are also afraid of the Tigre. I remember now that they are easy prey to them." I realized that this would be true as the Tigre was an ambush hunter and the Two Tusk was noisy and much smaller than a Tigre. I nodded and said "Mahendra, Mearoo, and Samalaa have gone to follow their trail back to where they came from. We should wait until they return before we go any further."

Gaieaa agreed and I took Kaga, Kika, Tivash, Janai, Sheena, Timbu, and the rest of the adult hunters and set up a ring of scouts around the main group. I took Janai aside as the oldest of the snow-leaper people there and asked her "Are there any memories in your blood about this tribe the Gaieaa told us about?" Janai got that 'look' I came to know as 'looking inward' at the memories of her ancestors. I waited silently, as I did not want to disturb her while she did this. I did turn when I heard someone approaching, but saw that it was Sheena and nodded as I turned back to wait for Janai to finish. She looked at me as she finished and said "Maybe. I did find memories of a tribe that once lived here. We also remember them being in the jungle.

I believe they left because they were afraid of being caught between us and the Krieg. This was about the time we were trying to hunt them to make them leave us alone or to kill them all." I can see why they would risk the jungle to being caught between two warring tribes." Janai said "If they are still in that jungle then it was not them that stampeded those boars. It is too far away!"

I agreed with her and said "Please take Kika and go to where the deer were killed. We might as well take the hides and fresh meat." Janai smiled and said "That is a wise decision Jakool. You are learning." Then she said "Kika! Bring some of those other young hunters that 'think' they know how to mate with a snow-leaper woman and let's get that deer meat and hide! Sheena laughed at Kika's red face and then at the red faces of his three constant companions that Sheena had been practicing mating with! Janai gave Kika's hair a tousle and a smile to ease his embarrassment then they loped off together to skin and butcher the deer.

Gaieaa talking about the dangers of the great jungle made me think of the dangers ahead of us. "We will have to cross both the deep many trees and the hills and then climb cloud stabber trails. Most of our people will not be used to the cold the snow and the thin air as we climb higher." Gaieaa nodded and said "This is something we can help with. There are several things we use to improve the breathing of someone suffering from the effects of the breathing sickness." Gaieaa was talking about a sickness that some were born with that made it hard for them to breathe sometimes. Giving them a steady diet of Yellow Root, Sticker Bush Berries, and hot drinks made from the leaves of certain other plants, would help to open up their lungs, throat, and nose. "I think the same treatments would help us be able to breathe better in the thin cloud of stabber air." She finished saying to me.

"I remember times when the snow was so deep that I was wading through it!" I said knowing that the children and the Elders would not be able to do this! Nada nodded and said "I have been talking with Kaga and some of the others that once lived in such places. I also spoke with Darshita and they both told us of Ooh-mans who made a thing from wood and rope that allowed them to walk 'On' the snow instead of through it." I was taken with this idea and said "I will speak with Kaga and any others that might know about this snow foot. We will need them for all of our people."

Turning back to Mahendra and Samalaa I asked "What do you think we should do about the trail you found? I don't know if it is safe to say it isn't being used. We still do not know what frightened the Two Tusks." Mahendra frowned and said "The trail comes from the highlands but from a different place than the ravine Gaieaa spoke of. I saw this when we tracked them back towards the highlands." Samalaa slowly agreed saying "It looks to be true, but I don't know that it doesn't change. We would have to follow it to the source." I saw sense in her words and said "How long would it take you and a few other snow-leapers to go and come back?" Samalaa thought for a moment and said "No more than two suns. Maybe a sun and a half." I looked at Gaieaa who nodded and then at Mearoo who nodded, so I said "Samalaa, you are in charge. Do it! She got up and said "Then we leave now. We could be back by this time tomorrow." She disappeared calling out for Janai and Girivar as she left the fire. I said to Mearoo "Please get Farkis and Sheena. You need to be a lookouts until they return. Use Kaga and Mahendra too. Anyone else you need just do it!" I said sounding a little too harsh in my own ears but Mearoo just nodded and stood up as Kaga and Mahendra joined her to go setup lookouts around the camp."

Gaieaa said "Rest Jakool." I fell asleep and did not wake until mid-sun. I was surprised when after I finished the tea I saw Gaieaa standing over me. "Awake I see. How do you feel?" She asked as she leaned on the walking stick she used to get around. "I am feeling better." "Huh! Then you are a terrible liar! I can tell that you are still worn out by all that you have tried to do. So now is a good time for you to rest!" I protested "I have to check the camp and the lookouts!"

Gaieaa forbid it and that was that! I sighed as I lay back down and soon I was startled to wake up and find I had fallen asleep again! It was late in the afternoon and I felt better. I got up and went to relieve myself. When I returned I joined the rest in butchering and preparing the deer meat and skins to add to our supplies. Mearoo, Samalaa, Janai, and Girivar returned that night. I heard the lookouts challenge them and heard their reply. I knew something was wrong from the looks on Samalaa and the rest as they walked tiredly into camp.

They sat down and Samalaa told the story. "We followed the old trail all the way to a place where it crossed a river. It then ran along the river until we reached a place where it fell in falls from the highland. We searched for a way to climb up, but even if we could, we knew that the Ooh-mans could not. So we went south along the edge of the cliff that divides the never-ending grass from the highlands until we found this place that Gaieaa spoke of. It is blocked. A rockfall has happened and the ravine is now full. We spent the rest of the time looking for another way up but did not find one. So we returned to the ravine to see if a way could be cleared by removing some of the rocks. We think it might be possible, but will take many suns with everyone working to move them."

I knew why everyone had looked the way they did when they returned. "So we are cut off from the highlands on this trail," I said summarizing her words. "We will have to find another way. Maybe we need to go further north or south. We should send out scouting parties in both directions tomorrow."

I agreed and then was silent thinking. Soon I felt so tired that I lay down at the fire and fell asleep. I didn't realize I was moving in my sleep until I felt someone shaking me awake! "What? What is it?" I said sleepily as I opened my eyes. Nada, Gaieaa, and Mearoo were there by my side. "Jakool! You were talking and then yelling in your sleep! You became very agitated and were struggling as if you were fighting with someone!" I was surprised to hear of my behavior while asleep. I looked at Mearoo and saw that she had a scared expression on her face. I shook my head to try and clear it and try to remember what I was dreaming when they woke me up. Nada held a cup of something to my lips and said "Drink this! It will help clear your head." I took the warm tea and sipped it slowly as I tried to go through my memories. I finished the tea and said, "I remember being very tired."

I told them what I remembered. "I remember having some bad dreams. I do not remember them all, but I do remember one. I was following the trail of the Two Tusks. I found a secret place that we do not know about that leads from the highlands. It is hidden in a place very near the ravine that Gaieaa spoke of. I could see the blocked ravine as I approached the cliff. I looked closely at the ground and saw faint marks that showed me they had come from south of there. I followed them as they went along the cliff until they reached another sharp dip in the ground. I went down and found that the dip hid an overgrown red flower plant the size of a tree growing against the base of the cliff. I saw the trampled ground there and followed it to the place where the tree and the rock met. There I found a small opening in the rock where the tracks came from!

I was sure I had found the way they had used and started to climb into the opening. But I was suddenly attacked by a giant snake! Its head came out of the opening as I stooped down so I had no chance to defend myself as it quickly wrapped around my body! I struggled trying to keep it from wrapping around my neck as it tightened the coils around my body and squeezed me! I was yelling and fighting with all my life when you woke me!" I slumped back against Mearoo who was still holding me. Nada held a water skin up and said "Drink this Jakool. It will help. I was still shaking from the fear the retelling caused me. Mearoo said to Nada "Do you think what he saw had truth?" Nada looked very serious as she considered this. Gaieaa was humming something to herself as she prepared something. Finally, Nada said, "I think we should go and see."

Gaieaa stopped what she was doing and said "Yes we should. I don't think this dream was just a dream! Why would he dream of an opening hidden in the cliff? The snake? Yes! A hidden opening? We need to go see." I felt a sense of relief at this and said weakly "Not alone. Go with a full hunting party. Just in case." I knew I could not go in my condition but I knew we had plenty of strong hunters and warriors that could! "Gaieaa? Mearoo? Nada? I cannot go so you have to do this. Mearoo? I want you to stay but I need you to go!" Mearoo nodded and said "I will Jakool. We will be very careful!" I sighed as I felt the effects of the drink Nada had given me and knew I would be asleep very soon! "Take Samalaa, Janai, Mahendra, Farkis, and the best of our men. Leave enough to keep us safe."

I don't remember saying anything else as I felt my eyes close the last thing I felt was Mearoo holding me tightly to her body and whispering "We will find out Jakool! This I vow!"

CHAPTER EIGHT

THE BLOOD OF THE LOST

I slept into the next sun and woke up with the bright sun shining in my eyes. I walked a short way from camp to where we left our water and droppings. I finished and washed in the stream. By the time I returned, Gaieaa, Nada, Sheena, and others were gathered around the fire working on something. I reached them and then sat down on one of the rocks we had dragged there to sit on. Gaieaa handed me a plate of roasted deer, tubers, and greens. I ate slowly feeling the gnawing pains of hunger in my stomach. Nada gave me more of her tea to drink as I watched them working on shaping wood. Kaga had stayed behind so Mahendra could go with Mearoo and the rest. He also kept Farkis; as both of them knew the secrets of shaping wood, like we would need to make a snow foot.

Kaga was carefully holding a thin piece of wood he had cleaned of all bark and shaped with a stone scraper. It was now roughly flat on two wide sides and slightly rounded on the two narrow sides. Nada had a large pot of water on the fire boiling so that steam rose up. Kaga held the stick out over the steam and Farkis grabbed the other end. They laid it across the top of the pot and waited as the steam softened the wood. It took time but finally, Kaga said "Now we bend it like this!" He and Farkis picked it up then put it against the side of the pot and slowly pulled the ends causing the middle to bend around the pot! They stopped and put the wood back over the steam being careful to keep the now bent middle over the steam. I watched as they held the ends tightly against the inside of the pot causing the middle to bend slowly upwards as the steam made it soft. They repeated the steps, bending it around the pot, and then steaming it again. Once the ends were too short to press against the inside of the pot, Kaga took it and pushed the ends down towards the now curved middle as it rested on a stone. Finally, Kaga had the ends touching and a shape that was very curved in the middle and came to a narrower curve at the top and bottom. The ends were at the bottom.

He held it, looked at it carefully then handed it to me. "This is what we need to make. Once it dries we drill holes along the flat side to tie the rope through each side." I understood his idea now so I encouraged teams of workers to start bending the thin strips of wood that Nada and Sheena were helping the young hunters and children make. I was soon helping them by striping the bark off of the pile of branches they had gathered to use.

By night we had all the drying racks filled with the shaped wood pieces so they could dry overnight. Kaga had gathered all the stone drills we had with us to use the next sun to drill all the holes. He selected the ones that he felt would work best and gave them to Nada, who used them to figure out the size of the rope needed. I went to bed tired but pleased with our work that Sun. A sudden warning from a lookout woke us up! We heard the reply from Mahendra! Someone was hurt! I jumped up with Nada and we raced to see who was hurt and what needed to be done. We reached the scout in time to see Mahendra, Samalaa, Mearoo, and Janai carrying someone between them! As they got closer I saw that it was Nandu!

We ran to meet them and saw that he was pale with blood loss and had broken bones! "What happened?" I asked as we ran with them to the campfire. We needed its light to see his wounds clearly and to treat him. "We were attacked. He took the first blow and was thrown against the rock face." Samalaa said as we entered the camp. I saw that there were bad cuts and torn skin along one side of his body. He was breathing very shallow and I knew this was very bad. Gaieaa was ready when they stopped by the fire and lay him down carefully on the furs she placed there. Nada squatted down with me and we checked Nandu. I felt his fever as I touched his face and saw the color of his skin had turned a grayish color. Nada said "He has broken ribs, shoulder and arm. He's bleeding inside." I thought of Elasaa and asked, "Do we need to cut him open to let the blood drain out?" Gaieaa shook her head as she watched Nada's hands pushing gently on his stomach. "No. It is too late. He had lost too much blood and it was inside. See how swollen his stomach is?" I saw as Nada pressed the flesh and it didn't push in as it should. "We have to do something!" I said growing fearful that we would lose another. Nada sat back and said "We cannot do what you suggest Jakool. He is close to death. We can ease the pain and give him a sleep potion. He won't make it through the night."

I hung my head feeling useless at her words then looked in Nandu's face. "Nandu? Can you hear me? It is Jakool!" I saw a small nod from him but he was having too much difficulty breathing to speak. "You are dying Nandu. We cannot heal you. We can only help you with the pain and make you sleep. Is this what you want?" I was following our custom of asking someone who was dying how they wanted to die. As Nandu couldn't speak I was telling him what Nada had said and what would be the least painful way to die. Nandu didn't speak or nod or anything for some time.

Believing him to be unable to answer me I started to tell Nada to do it when he slowly raised up a hand from his other side. He pointed at me then at his chest. I felt the tears start as I knew what he meant. "So be it Nandu." I closed my eyes for a moment saying a prayer to the spirit then I drew my knife and plunged it straight into Nandu's heart! I only saw him jerk once then lay still now out of the reach of his pain. "Go with our ancestors Nandu," I said giving the traditional farewell to one who has fallen in death. I slowly walked away from them and sat down on a stone facing away from the fire. Mearoo came over and sat with me.

She respected my silence as I stared out into the darkness looking for any answer to my sorrow and grief at another loss of my people. Finally, I asked her "What happened Mearoo?" She then told me "Your dream saved us Jakool. We followed the Two Tusks trail right to the cliff and it went south as you said. When we found the large dip in the land we approached it very carefully. Nandu was center as we approached the large bush you described. Before we could react a large snake came out from the bush striking him with its body! He still managed to strike it through its head as it slammed him against the rock face. We leaped on it and finished it off, but it was too late for Nandu. I don't know how he managed to thrust his spear into it while being thrown against that rock but he did!" I nodded at this knowing that Nandu had acted bravely and fought well against a foe that had taken ten snow-leapers to kill.

"What do we do now?" I asked her. "Samalaa and Mahendra followed the tunnel and found that it opened into that ravine of Gaieaa's, past the rockfall. We can use it to reach the highlands." So some good had come from Nandu's death and we now had a way out of the endless green grass. I nodded then said "We need to pack up and go. I do not want to be out here any longer than necessary." She nodded then silently got up and left to tell everyone my decision. I don't know how long I sat there with my sight turned outward towards the darkness. I only remember Mearoo returning and urging me to rest with her. Sleep finally came along with bad dreams, but Mearoo was there to wake me and keep me safe all night long.

The next sun we got moving as we followed the trail to the cliff and the tunnel.

It took us until very late in the sun but we made it. Once there I sent a good-sized party through first to check the surrounding area for an ambush, traps, dangerous animals, and any more of those snakes! We butchered the dead snake while we waited and cooked the meat. We were taking a much-needed break to eat and drink while we waited. Finally, Janai returned and said "All is clear Jakool" "Good!" I said as I got up and led everyone through the tunnel, into the ravine, and up into the highlands.

It was very different up here as the air was colder and patches of snow appeared in places under the oak and elm trees there. It was not many trees but a mix of trees, rocks, bushes, and open areas of grasses. We traveled a winding path through the groups of trees; heading west and south now, so we knew we would eventually reach the place where Paasi, Elasaa, and the rest waited for us. This part of the journey was easy and gave us time to gather more of the plants Gaieaa, Nada, Pathak, and Janai said could be used to treat snake bites.

Late that afternoon we stopped to make camp early, as Gaieaa wanted to use the plants, fruits, and seeds gathered while they were fresh. "This makes them more powerful when used to make healings", she replied when Janai asked her why. I said to Janai "Now would be a good time to try and find any memories of healings from when your ancestors traveled through these lands." Janai had agreed to have all the snow leapers with us to search their memories for ways in which their ancestors treated them, as many had lived and traveled through these lands. Janai, Samalaa, Farkis, Jameeka, Girivar, and Sheena sat together with Gaieaa, Pathak, Nada, Mearoo, and me listening to them as they remembered everything having to do with healing and snake bites. Pathak and Gaieaa could tell when they described a certain plant or treatment if it was one we already knew and had tried. Nada had a trick memory that made her an excellent choice as a healer and as an Elder to teach our history to the young. She used it now to remember everything they remembered then helped Pathak, Gaieaa, and Prinda make records of this knowledge. "It is what Merack and Merkansoo wanted," I said when Prinda asked once why we were taking the time to do this. She nodded and said, "Like remembering how Cara and Nandu died?" I felt the tears and the tightening in my throat as I said "Yes Prinda. So Cara, Nandu, and Chirac are remembered. So others do not die of snake bites or the breathing sickness or other things that we can prevent or cure." Prinda smiled as I turned and left them to check with Kaga on the progress of the snow foot.

He was at the fire with Farkis, Timbu, and some of the others working by its light. I sat down and watched him as he carefully tested each rope. He would push it down until it wouldn't push any further to make sure both ends stayed tied to the wood. "Why are you doing this?" I asked as I sat down by him. Kaga didn't look up from the snow foot as he pushed on the next rope. Finally, he answered, "If a string is looser than the others, it will bend down further like this". He demonstrated one that he had already found while testing them. I watched as he pressed one string so far down it was at least a half finger below the rest.

"Now if you are wearing this as you try to walk on snow, the string will be pressed up against the bottom of your foot like this". He held his hand above the strings then pressed the loose string with the other hand. I watched carefully as the string made contact with his hand. "This string will rub against your foot hide until it causes a hot spot on your foot.

It is very uncomfortable but the real problem is that the string will break because of the constant rubbing. Once one string breaks, the rest will follow."

I nodded as he put the shoe needing to have that string replaced and tied tighter with the handful that were in a pile. Timbu was working with Sheena to cut off the loose string and replace it with a new one. Kaga did the actual tying saying "I don't want to have to do this on any that others tied wrong". It made sense so I got up and checked with the scouts then went in search of Mearoo.

When I found her she was with Janai, Samalaa, Farkis, and Jameeka discussing setting up guards. I nodded then said, "Will some of you be keeping watch?" Mearoo nodded answering me "From now on, every Sun. At least two of us need to be watching. We can see things that you cannot." I nodded trusting them then got up and went to find Gaieaa, Pathak, and Nada to tell them. After some talking they agreed that there was nothing we could do about it, so it was best to let Mearoo and her people keep watch. We all trusted them by now and were comfortable with this decision. I realized that in the time of one moon change, we had gone from strangers to allies, mates, and friends since our first meeting of the tribes. I went to sleep alone that night but woke up later to find myself curled up around Mearoo's warm, soft fur and sighed happily as I went back to a more peaceful sleep.

The next sun we made good progress through the highland hills and valleys crossing several streams that fed the river down below us. Gaieaa said it meant that we were nearing another place she remembered where we could cross over a ravine to get to the side where we left Paasi and the others. I kept watching the front scouts for any signs of trouble; as one was always in the trees, while the other stayed on the ground, watching for any danger. We only had to stop once while they checked out some strange tracks that turned out to be a 'One Horn'.

But they didn't see it anywhere when they followed them, so they assumed it had gone from the area. We reached the ravine by late afternoon and saw that it too had a stream in the bottom of it. This one was wider and deeper but still only came up to mid-thigh. I waited for Gaieaa to look around and then decide on the way to go as I enjoyed the refreshing cold water running over my legs as I took drinks of it. Gaieaa finally stopped looking up and down the stream and the ravine then pointed with her walking stick and said "Across the stream, then up where the sides are not as steep." I looked at where she pointed and saw that not far ahead, the side of the ravine had the looks of a rock fall or cave-in, as the edge had a more irregular shape and there were rocks and boulders down on the banks and in the stream.

Janai and Samalaa were already there looking at it and testing the climb. When we reached them Janai turned and said "We can climb this easily. Just be sure you check the rocks you grab!" She demonstrated by leaping up to a knob of rock that stuck out of the ravine side, which gave way under her weight. "How do we get Gaieaa, Pathak, and some of the others up it?" I asked her. "We carry them of course! She had Pathak stand up from the carrier and she helped him climb on her back. She then took three jumps and was at the top! Pathak was grinning as he was still holding on tightly to her neck fur and yelled "I beat you up here Jakool!"

I laughed as Samalaa took Gaieaa up as Janai returned and soon all the Elders were carried up as the rest of us climbed up. Janai, Samalaa, Farkis, and Girivar gave the children a treat by letting them ride instead of having to climb. Mobear, Farini, Birksa, Deena, Deran, and Zhana were happy and excited when they got to ride up to the top of the ravine. It gave me some temporary happiness too as I watched them jump up and down with joy as Samalaa, Mearoo, and Janai bucked up and down pretending to try and throw them off! Finally, Gaieaa said "All right, fun time is over. We need to leave. We are too exposed here."

"I agree. Let's move!" Mearoo said as we turned from the ravine and faced the first folds, valleys, and hills of the highlands. Gaieaa and Pathak were again leading' as they were the only ones with any knowledge of the area and its dangers! They had not led us far when we immediately ran into a herd of one-horned rhinos grazing in the thick, tall grass between the ravine in a dip in the land. Fortunately, Samalaa saw them and quietly stopped us before we ran right into them! Mearoo and Samalaa scouted around to find a safe path that was downwind of them then we continued.

I had to say that they were magnificent looking as they grazed peacefully on the grass. I could see groupings -of adult female Rhinos in loose circles with the young in the middle. "A good protective formation. Females around the young with the males in a circle further out." I said to Gaieaa and Pathak who were watching with me. Gaieaa said "I remember now. They are very nearsighted and depend on their herd to smell and hear any predators hunting them." "What predators hunt them?" I asked as I watched them grazing and just being themselves. I envied them in a way. "Tigre, other big predators like us but different that live down here. We call them the 'Sahaat'. In our language, it means 'Mighty Hunter'. They hunt everything from these Rhinos to those dangerous Two Tusks! This is why we name them such." I had to agree having seen the killing of the deer by the Two Tusks and imagining a fight between them and the Rhinos! If these Sahaat hunted them both then they were indeed mighty hunters. Just then I saw a rhino start pawing the ground and jerking its head up and down.

Then it turned it in several directions as if listening or smelling for something. "It hears or smells something it doesn't like," Mearoo said as we watched others of the Male Rhinos also doing this. It spread to the females who herded the young into the middle of them, as they tightened up their circle around them. The male Rhinos also backed up some but stayed a distance away from the females forming an outer ring around them.

I watched in fascination as the males all lifted up their great heads and horns and gave out a below-challenging something we could not see. I had very good eyesight and was watching but never saw the attack when it came! There was a sudden shift among the Rhinos as they moved to confront an enemy they only knew was there, but not exactly where. I heard a squeal of terror and then saw a large cat dragging one of the young out of the protective circle with its jaws clamped around its neck. The females snorted and stamped their hooves trying to strike it, but it dodged them easily and loped off between the males, who were spread out further apart. I was amazed at how much it looked like a snow leaper, except instead of its fur being mostly white, it was white on the belly with some tan and black designs. The rest was all tans with black and brown shapes that allowed it to blend into the grass, the hills, and the many trees.

Mearoo said "You see how he took a cub? He is too smart to try and fight and kill one of the adults, as they band together and would easily defeat him." I nodded as I watched the Rhinos continue being on guard for some time before they sensed the danger was over and went back to grazing. I noticed they stood closer together now, so they must have learned something from the attack. I pointed this out to Mearoo who said "Yes. But they will forget and then another will strike. There are many Sahaat in this land as it is rich with game."

Gaieaa asked her "Do you ever speak with them?" I saw a look of surprise on Mearoo that changed to one of interest as she replied "Why do you ask?" Gaieaa snorted then said "Because Mearoo! I can see that you are related just as you are to the Tigre! I am not stupid! You spoke with the Tigre so I assume you can also speak with the Sahaat! You could ask them about any dangers between here and where we are going! You could find out if they have seen any other tribes here!" I thought these were very good ideas and looked at Mearoo and said "Yes we can speak with them after a fashion. But it is not like having a conversation with you or even a Tigre. The Sahaat have not changed much since their beginning. They only know a small amount of things. They will not remember anything useful to us."

The endless green grass was easy to cross and we saw the first of the hills by late afternoon. After a brief rest stop, we continued on with our advance scouts ahead of us looking for any danger. Janai suddenly gave a warning and we stopped until we found out. Soon Janai came back to the main group and said "You remember the old hunting trail we found below? I just found it again! This time the tracks look fresh." We hurried forward to where she led us and soon were standing on a hunting trail made by men!

"I see many different tracks here," I said as I squatted next to the trail looking at the tracks. Pathak said "I see more than men's tracks. See there? Those are children and women. This was not a hunting party." "I agree Nada said as she walked up and down this side of the trail, then crossed over and did the same. She stopped suddenly and picked up something. "See this?" She was holding up a broken hide foot cover. She brought it over to us to look at. "It looks very worn. They walked a long way" Gaieaa said then handed it to Pathak. "Hmm...I have seen this kind of foot hide before. Let me think" He said turning it over and over in his hands. "I remember now. This is a hide cover that was used by some of the tribes from the great plains to the south. This could be the lost tribe or it could be an enemy!"

I chose to believe it to be an enemy and immediately said "Samalaa! Janai! Go find a safe campsite. We need to get out of sight!" Janai and Samalaa leaped away as I turned to Mearoo and said "Take the rest of the snow leapers and scout out the area. Everywhere around us! Look for any signs of humans. Watch out for a trap or ambush!" Mearoo whirled around with Sheena, Farkis, Girivar, and Jameeka and they jumped in different directions. "Mahendra, Kika, Timbu, Kaga! We need to make sure we are ready for an enemy! Get everyone their weapons!"

All of us hunters were already carrying our thrusting spears, but Mahendra and the rest knew I meant the new lighter spears and the throwing sticks. They went to the carrier that held them and returned. I help hand them out to everyone. Once that was done I said, "Let's get off this trail". I head towards the direction that went towards the nearest of the hills and away from the trail. The land had sudden dips, folds, and valleys so we didn't have to go far to be hidden from view. There was a small stream so we had water with bushes and trees to hide us. I stayed at the upper edge lying down so I would not be seen but could see anyone approaching. Mahendra, Kika, and the rest of the hunters were also there making sure no one could surprise us from any direction.

It felt like a long time before saw anyone returning. Samalaa and Janai were the first to return. I gave a quiet call to alert them to our hiding place. They jumped over to us and crouched down to tell me what they found. "No good Jakool. This spot you found is better than the open area ahead. You can see it clearly from those hills." Samalaa pointed ahead and to the left at the nearest hills. I could make out details of the types of trees, so I knew anyone there would see us out in the open.

"Go and scout this valley. We have not done this." I said to them. They left again going in opposite directions following the stream to each end of the valley. Before they returned I saw Mearoo appear then suddenly stop and turn then she dropped to all fours out of sight. "Watch her," I said quietly to Mahendra who passed it on until everyone was watching that place. Soon I heard the familiar sounds that meant she having a conversation with another animal and let out the breath I was holding. After a few minutes, Mearoo reappeared with a large Tigre! They both walked to where we were hiding and I stood to greet them. The Tigre was a male and he was huge! He looked regal as he surveyed us with his amber-colored eyes. I stood in front of him and barely came up to his head! I held out my arms wide showing I was not holding my weapons, having put them down first.

He watched me as Mearoo came over to me and said "He is suspicious but agreed to come and meet with us. He does not like Ooh-mans! He says whenever they come they kill too much of his prey and he is forced to hide or they hunt him too!" I said "I understand. Can he understand me?" Wondering how intelligent Tigre really was. "No. But I can speak and tell him your words." "Okay. Please tell him We are fleeing from humans that also are hunting us. They might be the same humans that come and invade his hunting ground." I stopped and Mearoo turned and spoke in the language that the Tigre understood. He showed more interest after she spoke and replied. Mearoo kept watching his face as she said "He says we may be right. He asks if they came from the great grass far below." I looked at Pathak and he nodded. I said "Yes. They came long ago and killed many animals and humans. Say that your people fought them and were forced to flee to the cloud stabbers." Mearoo repeated my words and the reaction from the Tigre was a fierce snarl and then he growled and hissed something. Mearoo said, "He says that he remembers!" Mearoo sounded surprised by this answer but didn't have time to explain as the Tigre was saying something else forcing her to listen. After several minutes the Tigre stopped then turned and slowly started to walk away.

Mearoo jumped up and said "I will tell you what he said later. Now we must follow him! Danger is hiding nearby!" "I knew it!" I said cursing the ancestors of the Krieg tribe as I ordered everyone out of the valley as we followed the Tigre. He led us across the trail going away from the hills for some time. Then he turned back towards them and traveled not quite towards them but close to them. By the time we saw the hills now, we were well past the two hills that were closest to the trail and in a grove of trees. The Tigre led us through it until we reached a stone outcrop that was at the bottom of a hill. He stopped and turned to face Mearoo. She made some noises, he replied and she nodded then turned and said "This rock marks the beginning of his territory. He says that two suns from here is a place where we can cross through a gap in the hills and climb up to the plateau where we left Paasi, Elasaa, and the rest. He knows our people are there. He spoke with the Tigre we met there. She has spoken with all the Tigre in the area and told them we would not harm them and need their help." I was surprised by this as Mearoo had said the Tigre was like they were a long time ago and only met at the boundary of their territories during mating season. If males meet it usually leads to a fight. But here was a male telling us that they were watching for us!

I asked Mearoo "Does he know how many of the enemy is here?" Mearoo shook her head and said "Tigre cannot count as we do. If he says he saw Ooh-mans then we have to assume it was a large party from those tracks!" "Yes, but those were not a hunting party" I pointed out to her. She nodded and asked the Tigre something. He replied and she turned and said "No it was a group like ours he says that made the tracks. But they are not the ones." "So we have two groups?" Mearoo nodded replying "Yes Jakool. The tracks are only of a large group also fleeing. Maybe the ones from down below. The other group? If it is the Krieg, how did they get past Larkar and the rest?"

I worried about this as we thanked the Tigre and left him to get as far away as we could before night. We only had a few hours of light left and when it started to fail, we found a small gully that had a stream coming from the hills. There were many of these streams coming down from the cloud stabbers and through the hills as the snow and ice melted. We made camp and after lookouts were posted we sat down to hear what Mearoo had to tell us about the Tigre's words. "I have met other Tigre. So believe me when I say that for this one to say 'He remembers us and the Krieg fighting! It must be the work of Yuma Samang or another such powerful being!

He said that his kind had been here long before the Ooh-mans and remembered when this was their land. They accept us and the other leopards and other cat-like hunters as we are kindred and serve the same purpose. I asked him what purpose and he replied "To make other animals better by killing and eating the ones that are sick, hurt, or do not learn!" I nodded as did Pathak, Gaieaa, and the rest. "Our people have known this for a long time. The big killers like the Tigre the Wolf and the Rough Fur keep the herd animals healthy by killing the weak, sick, or injured. This allows the strong, the smart, and the healthy to breed. They become stronger because of this." Mearoo nodded and said, "He said the same thing with fewer words." I chuckled as I replied, "Man's greatest skill is speaking." Samalaa said, "Also their greatest weakness!" Poking fun at us 'Ooh-mans'! I laughed with the rest as we needed a good laugh to relieve our fears. "What else did he say?" I asked her once the laughter died down. "He says that long ago these Ooh-mans came from where the sun wakes up. They were not like the Ooh-mans of the great grass! They killed everything, taking only the skins! He says that was enough to make them something to remember! That made them more dangerous than any one of them! He said that the strange snow leapers that sometimes looked like Ooh-mans, were the only ones to stand and fight them! This went on for several Tigre generations before we fled up into the cloud stabbers. By that time we had killed many of them and pushed them back towards the place where the sun wakes for a while. But now they are back and killing everything again. This was why the female Tigre we met came and told him we were also back to fight them! That is why all the Tigre have met and will watch out for us, help us when they can, and warn us if they can!" I was as shocked and amazed as everyone on hearing this! "To think that we now have the Tigre as our allies!" Pathak said with awe and reverence in his voice.

I agreed and then asked her the question that had worried me from the moment the Tigre told us of the Ooh-mans! "What has happened to the rest of our tribe? What has happened to Larkar and the party? They should have spotted anyone following us!" I asked her. Mearoo sighed and said "I don't know Jakool. We looked for any signs when we scouted the trail and the surrounding area. We saw nothing to show either them or the Krieg had come from behind us!" Samalaa said "Maybe, but they could have come using that old trail we crossed down below. Maybe they knew a way up that we didn't find." I looked at her then at Janai and then at Pathak.

They all thought about it until finally I sighed and said "It must be they did not come up the path we expected them to take. Many trails lead up from the Great Plains below." Mahendra said "I am worried Jakool. I think we should send someone to look for Larkar's party." "No. We may be the only ones they have found. If we send someone to find Larkar, they may also send someone to follow them!" I said knowing it was a bad idea! Mahendra replied, "I had not thought of this." He looked at me and said "You are a good leader Jakool. Keep us safe from ourselves." I gave him a look of surprise as I had not thought he thought of such things. I then smiled and nodded as I replied "As I expect you and the rest to keep me from my own stupidity!" Mahendra smiled and lost his worried look at my words and chuckled. Mearoo suddenly said "We need to get to Elasaa and the rest quickly!

I just realized that if the Krieg came by a different trail, they just might have used the one we used through the hills and up through the many trees!" I became alarmed at her words but then thought hard about them. I said, "If they came that way, I 'think' the female Tigre would have warned us." Mearoo knew that I believed her to be Yuma Samang so my words did much to calm her fear. "But we could send our forward scouts out tomorrow to see if they are safe?" Mearoo nodded vigorously at my suggestion along with Samalaa and Janai. "Tomorrow take three with you. Signal us once you reach them." Mearoo asked "How? It will be too far for you to see or hear us." I grinned and said "Make a fire and put wet branches with leaves on it. It will make it smoke and we will see the smoke!" Mearoo smiles at such a simple way to tell us. "If you put leaves and branches on then count to twenty and take them off, you make a large cloud of smoke. One cloud means 'Danger'. Two clouds mean 'Safe'. You count to thirty between the first and second cloud if you need the second cloud." Mearoo understood and after some other talk, we turned in to rest.

The next morning I woke to find Mearoo, Janai, Samalaa, and Farkis already gone. Jameeka, Girivar, and Sheena were organizing everyone to start moving again. I woke, relieved myself, and joined them. We set out immediately taking great care to not leave any traces and to scout ahead! I went ahead with Mahendra, Timbu, and Girivar as I wanted us working together; since Mearoo and the others had gone ahead, to make sure we kept everyone safe! So while they ranged ahead quickly, we scouted the area surrounding the trail the Tigre told us to use. Girivar and Sheena went ahead more slowly than usual so we could check the trail and the surrounding area together.

I sent Mahendra, Kika, and Timbu with Sheena and I took Kaga, Tivash, and Garath with Girivar. We took one side of the trail, they took the other and we spread out in our scouting formation. Everyone had everyone else within sight so if anyone saw anything they could stop all of us with a signal. This way we would not give away our positions by speaking or other noises. We made it a good hour down the trail before Garath stopped suddenly and held up his left arm with a closed fist! "That means stop," I whispered to Girivar. We were in a section of hills that had many trees and bushes with open spaces between them. I motioned and looked up at the trees so Girivar would know I wanted him up high to be able to see what Garath had found. Girivar easily jumped up to a low-hanging branch and then climbed higher until he could see around us clearly. I waited as he scanned the area around Garath and then the whole area.

He came down and said quietly "Garath sees a trail that leads off to the east. It winds through the trees into the hills that way." He pointed in the direction and I had to think to remember what might be there. I finally said "It could be a game trial. That would lead to where the streams feed the river wouldn't it?" I asked him. Girivar nodded and said, "I think we need to look closer and follow it." I gave a nod then we rose quietly and gave Garath the signal to 'follow', which is an open hand pointing towards them. Garath gave the understanding signal, then turned to his left and started following the path. "Girivar? Do you think you can follow him in the trees? Girivar looked at where Garath was moving along the trail and said "until I run out of trees, yes." He immediately jumped back up into the tree near us and started jumping from tree to tree as I made my way over to the trail and Garath.

We were joined by Kaga and Tivash as we looked for tracks or any other signs that humans had used them. I didn't see any tracks as we were walking on thick grass that sprang back behind us. The trail was narrow and only the slightly bent grass showed that something or someone had made it. We followed it for almost two hours, crossing two streams. There we looked for any footprints but found none. We did see deer, long ears and even Two Tusk tracks there. I asked Girivar, who had come down as it was a grassy meadow with no trees if he had seen anyone. He said "I didn't see anything from the trees. That means they are resting in hiding as it is almost mid-sun. I nodded as that made sense but I was still worried. No tracks at all? Something that could move through, grass, mud, and water and leave no tracks? I turned to Kaga and said "What could make such a trail? Deer single file? Wolf, Rough Fur, Sahaat?"

Kaga looked again at the banks of the stream and the grass. He pushed it down several times with his hands and watched it come back up. Finally, he turned to Girivar and said "I think this was done on purpose. Look at the grass." Girivar squatted down and looked at what Kaga did and then did it himself a few times. Finally, Girivar looked up and said "I think Kaga is right. We need to get back to the group as quickly as possible!" I almost panicked but instead, I said "Girivar! Go as fast as you can and get Sheena and the rest! We will go as fast as we can back!" Girivar took off in leaps and bounds as we ran! I knew we were several hours away but we had to try and reach them before danger found them. After an hour of running, we found ourselves over halfway back to the main trail and I took heart at our progress.

I kept looking for a quicker path to take but didn't want to take a chance on running into something that would slow us down. So I stayed on the trail we had followed. We finally reached the main trail and turned to run back to where the main group should be. I thought I heard yells and screams in the distance and gritted my teeth as I pushed myself to run as fast as I could to reach them. The yells and screams continued for some time, and then finally they stopped. I felt the grip of fear on my throat; threatening to cut off the air I needed to keep running, as it took hold of my mind. I imagined all of them dead, butchered, raped, and skinned! I vowed to not stop in pursuit of whoever harmed my tribe as I went around a slight curve in the trail and stopped at the sight in front of me. There scattered along the trail were not my tribe, but another one! One I did not recognize at all! I saw Girivar, Sheena, and Jameeka going from body to body making sure they were all dead. I saw Mahendra with some of the ones that had gone with Larkar and the rest of his group with several of the enemy tied up! I whooped with relief and joy at seeing this and ran to greet them and show them my gratitude!

It was short-lived as I saw Nada, Pathak, and Gaieaa huddled over someone lying on a carrier and knew someone was badly injured! I went over to see who and was shocked to see it was Larkar! I saw spear thrusts that opened several wounds in his shoulders and legs. His face was very pale and his breathing uneven and very shallow! He had long slashes on his chest that looked like they had been done by a Tigre or other large predator at first. But before I could ask one of the snow leapers that had gone with him came over and said to me "Jakool. Come over and see what we found on these Pataks!" I did not know the word then, but got up and went to where they had three of them tied up tightly.

All of them were dressed in hides that came from either the Tigre or the Sahaat! Two of them even had their paws of them attached to short spears, that they used to grab at their victims to hook them and drag them to them so they could finish them off with a spear!" I looked at their faces and saw a blazing hatred of the snow leaper people that made me want to know who they were! "Who are you? Why do you attack us? We do not even know you!" They just sneered at me and glared at the snow-leaper people. Finally, I said, "Take them and loosen their tongues for them!" Their faces showed me it was as if I had given them the greatest of gifts with my words!

The Girivar turned and put his face right up to the nearest one and opened his mouth showing all his sharp teeth then took his front paws and slowly sliced down the side of the man's body causing him to shriek in pain! "He has a voice." He said as he then took the man and picked him up easily and held him a foot off the ground! I saw his face change from his sneer to pain and real fear as he realized he was completely helpless in the hands of someone not afraid of him or of killing him! I let him demonstrate this; knowing the effect it would have on the remaining two and watched as he threw the man up high into the air then timed a leap that met him coming down! The thud of two bodies colliding was loud as they both came down together. The man was now gibbering with fear as he threw him to the ground and stood on all fours over him with his face only inches from his. "Please! Do not kill me! Do not let your beast kill me!"

I just shook my head and watched as Girivar reached down with his open mouth and ripped out the man's throat! I looked at the next man and saw the fear in his eyes as I said harshly "I said Who are you? Why have you attacked us? Do you want to be next?" Pointing at the now lifeless corpse of his companion. He seemed torn between two fears as I waited for an answer. He started speaking just as Jameeka and Mahendra started to untie him! Jameeka was using his claws to slice the ropes and sometimes his flesh, while Mahendra was using a knife and didn't care if he cut him!

"We are the Ones Who Are Lost! We came from down below a long time ago! We left as we didn't want to be between them and the ones who kill for fun!" I thought that was a good description of the Krieg tribe and said "You mean the Krieg?" He was surprised I knew the name but agreed. "Yes! You would do well to die before they find you with them!"

I nodded and said "They are part of our tribe now and we are part of theirs. You chose to leave so why have you attacked us?" He shook in fear as Saharit toyed with his man parts leaving pricks that bled slowly. "We tried to hide in the Great many trees! We almost didn't make it back out again! When we did, we ran right into the Krieg! They were hunting us and killed over half of my tribe! They said it was because we didn't stand and fight the snow leaper and kill them with them!" Saharit said "He speaks the truth. The Krieg did this many times in the past." I saw the surprised look in his eyes when he realized that Saharit could speak. "You can speak? But you are a vile beast! A killer that preys on humans! You killed many!" He said in both surprise and accusation. Saharit snarled at him and then said "I only kill other animals for food. I have never killed an "Ooh-man" until today. My people were hunted by the Krieg for their furs. Just as you are wearing the furs of the Tigre and the Sahaat. You learn this from them. You did not do this before you were taken by them." The man looked even more surprised to hear this from one he considered to be nothing more than a beast that only knew what its instincts told it. He said "It is true! We had no choice! They killed anyone who would not wear them! Many died in hunting these!"

He said indicating his fur and the remaining enemy. He had stayed silent during all of this and kept his eyes on me. I walked up to him and said "You have said nothing. I am the leader of this group, but not of my tribe. We are many in number and are strong. You dared to attack us while we were leaving this place to go to another, far away. Why?" I saw something in his face and eyes that made me suspicious of his silence and wondered what he was hiding. I suddenly wondered if they had all been caught and turned to Saharit and asked him. He said "We believe so. We saw them come up from the great plains seven suns ago. Larkar sent me and ten others to track them as they waited to see if others came. After two suns of tracking them, we knew they were following your trail, so I went back to tell Larkar. When I arrived they were in a great fight with a larger group of them! We lost several but they lost more! It was hard to tell if any escaped back down as we were all fighting to stay alive. It was very good that Larkar had put several of us in the trees; and hid some in the low wetlands, as they came up from behind them to cut them off that way. So I do not think any escaped back. They would have to go up into the hills.

There were Krieg among them. That is how Larkar became so badly injured. He became enraged when he saw them and charged into them heedless of the danger! He killed several of them but they were near the middle of the large group and he was cut off from us. I and several others jumped over them to reach him. He was still fighting with the wounds you see him with now." I now knew what the other was hiding! I turned to him and said "You have Krieg among you. We will find your tribe and them and kill all of you.

Do you understand? You chose death when you chose them!" I turned and said to Saharit "We want this one!" I drew my knife and turned quickly and sliced his man parts off of him! He screamed in agony as he crumpled to the ground trying to get away from me! I knelt on his back and sliced him from his shoulder down through his backside opening him up to the bone! "This is for the cowardly attack on Chirac!" I then let him die slowly as he lost his blood in the dead leaves and ground on the trail.

I turned to the one that had talked and said "The only reason I have to keep you alive is to show us where the vile creatures; that say they are men, but act worse than any men or animals! We do not kill anything for pleasure or just for their hide! You have the real beasts hiding among you. 'IF' any of you aid us and join our tribe, you will live. Any that choose to continue to be afraid of the Krieg and do their work for them will die."

I turned away not waiting for his answer as I went back to Larkar to see if I could help Nada and the others. He was unconscious now as they had given him a powerful sleep potion for the pain and were stuffing the wounds with various herbs that would help stop the loss of blood. I remembered what Merkansoo and Paasi had done for Elasaa and asked her "Do we need to check inside the wounds to see if his guts are torn?" Nada shook her head as her hands were busy putting leaves soaked in plant oils over the wounds that would help close them and keep out ground and bugs. "None were badly hit. He lost a lot of blood and is strong. If he lives through the next three suns he should live." Good! We need him now more than ever!" I said with an emotion I had never felt before. I was finally feeling what Larkar, Merkansoo, and his people felt about the Krieg. *Hate! I now know Hate!* I thought to myself as I went over to Saharit, Kaga, and Timbu. They were working with others to drag the bodies off the trail and hide them away. They spread them out so the scavengers could feed on them without fighting over them.

We worked for an hour on this task before returning to the main group and started the job of cleaning up the evidence of the battle and our tracks. Two hours later the sun was behind the hills behind us, and we had to camp there for the night.

I wondered how the rest of the groups were doing and said a prayer to Yuma Samang that they were safe and we were the only ones to have met the enemy!

The next sun I spoke with Pathak, Gaieaa, Nada, Kaga, and the rest about if we should continue following the path we were taking. Mearoo said, "Before we turned back the way was clear for a good sun and a half." We started off as usual with the snow-leaper scouts in the front and back with our hunters working with them to watch for signs and cover our tracks.

The journey had brought us together with each danger we faced and each new challenge we met. Garath was now greeted and befriended by many more of the snow-leaper; and our tribe, since his discovery of the trail we had followed. He was full of pride in his accomplishment and practically strutted around when in camp. He was out of camp more than in it, as we made sure he was always in one of the scouting groups having proven his keen eyes. While Janai and Mearoo were gone I spent time with Nada and Larkar as he was carried on one of the carriers with Gaieaa and Pathak beside him on another. Nada walked beside him so she could make sure the wounds didn't bleed from the movement of the carrier, and give him water and herbs to help him get stronger and fight the fever he now had. He felt very hot when I felt his face and he would groan and mutter, but nothing that we understood as we traveled. By the end of the sun, neither Mearoo nor Janai had returned but they had said it may take two or three suns, so I didn't worry any more than usual at their absence. The one good thing that happened that night was that Larkar became more aware of his surroundings. He knew that Nada was there, taking care of him as he mumbled her name once. This gave everyone some hope that he might live.

By morning they were still away, so we left. I could see a darkness in the distance that I did not like. "That looks like a big storm," I said to Pathak as we both looked at the dark mass that seemed to stretch across the whole horizon. He looked at it for a long time and then said "It is Jakool. We need to find shelter before it comes this far. We will not survive out in the open." I turned to Samalaa pointed saying "Have you seen such storms before?" Samalaa said "Yes! In the cloud stabbers in the east; where I have been, great storms like this come every year at this time. They have powerful rain, wind, thunder, and lightning. They can even rain down hard balls of ice that can damage and kill! They can last for weeks." I nodded and said "We have to reach shelter. A large cave or several caves." Mearoo said "The place the Tigre told us about. He said it was a place where the rock was split. So if there is rock there may be caves." Samalaa replied, "I will climb up and look."

She then climbed the nearest tree and took a long look. I knew she was one of the longest-seeing of her people so I hoped she could see shelter from that tree! She was up there a long time before coming down and said "I see the place. It is two suns away at the speed we are traveling. She then said "That storm may or may not come this far. It is difficult to tell this far away. I will be able to tell by tomorrow." I sighed then said, "We had better get moving then!" We got everyone moving while telling them about the storm and the possible shelter, encouraging them to move more quickly. We made good time with fewer stops because of the fear of being caught out in such a dangerous storm. But I said a prayer to Yuma-Samang to keep us safe and not run into the Krieg before we found shelter from the storm!

CHAPTER NINE

BLOOD OF THE LOST

I watched the progress of the storm all sun as we traveled through the remaining hills. We were still making good speed, despite rest stops to allow Nada to change the leaves on Larkar's wounds. He slowly became more alert as the healing herbs and drinks helped his body heal and replace the lost blood. By mid-sun, we could see the rock formation that Samalaa had described. It looked like something had slammed into the rock face and broken it. There was a deep gorge in the top half of the break with a large pile of boulders and rocks below it.

I couldn't tell if we could climb the boulders up to the bottom of the gorge, and I didn't see any caves. Samalaa looked and said we would be able to climb it without too much trouble, so we only had to find shelter once there. "I will go and scout the best path to take while you get everyone organized for the climb." "A good idea," I said thinking about how we would get the supplies, elders, children, and Larkar up to the top.

While doing this Larkar became clear-minded enough to speak. He asked for me and I came back to his carrier. "Larkar! You gave us a bad scare! Don't you even think of dying before we kill the Krieg!" I said sounding stern as I knew it might make him laugh, but also to realize he would not get his revenge if he was dead!

Larkar gave me a weak smile and said "If I had not been so badly hurt, we would not have arrived in time to save you!" I laughed at his reply and we spoke for a few minutes about the things that had happened while he was away. Nada gave him a potion to dull the pain and help him heal so I left him with a renewed promise and sense of purpose to live for. I returned to the front in time to see Samalaa returning from scouting ahead. She stopped and said "We are over halfway there. But I do not like that storm. It looks like it is moving faster and right for us!" I turned to look at the looming wall of dark clouds and frowned. I had not realized they had come that much closer until now. I looked around but only saw the hills, trees, and bushes. A few rock outcroppings but no signs of a cave.

I asked Samalaa "If all of the snow-leaper were to take the Elder and the children ahead, would you make it?" Samalaa looked at me for a moment then said "Yes, but that would leave you unprotected with no scouts and no way to quickly reach us." "I know, but it would be better than the weakest being caught in that storm!" Samalaa held up a paw to her eyes and gazed at the approaching storm for some time. She finally turned and said "We might be able to make it. I am not sure as it is hard to tell just how fast it is moving." I said as I turned "Let's talk with Pathak and Gaieaa, I think they should know." Samalaa nodded as I loped off to the center of the group where their carriers and Larkar were to protect them. "Pathak! Gaieaa!" I said getting their attention away from Larkar.

"We have a fast-approaching storm and will not make it to that gorge. I have asked Samalaa if they could carry all the Elders, Injured, and children there in time and she thinks they can. It will leave the rest of us to take shelter before it hits." Pathak spoke first saying "It is a good idea Jakool. But it leaves you and the rest in danger." Gaieaa took longer to reply and said "Jakool is making a decision to get the weakest to cover. Also, they can use the shelters that Larkar made." I had forgotten about them and felt better because we had them! Pathak still didn't like the idea but Kaga, Mahendra, Nada, and Cecina agreed with me.

I didn't waste any more time and told Samalaa "You get them to safety!" She put two snow leapers on each carrier and loaded two children and one Elder on each. That spread out the load evenly so that there were enough to carry all the ones that needed to go. I spent that time asking Larkar to explain how to set up the shelters to me, Kaga, Timbu, Mahendra, Garath, and Cecina. When they left we were sure we could set them up. We could see a place between the hills in front of us where there were no trees where we could wait out the fast-approaching storm.

When we arrived, I could see the first of the fast-moving clouds starting to fly over our heads as we started setting up the shelters. We each took a shelter and three of the young hunters to help us. This way we were able to quickly lay out the poles on the ground; as Larkar had explained, then spread out the hide over them. Then we tied off the hide to the tops of the poles. Once that was done, me and Kika went under the hide and picked up the pole ends tied to the hide, lifting them up. Then Timbu and Garath pushed up the same two poles from the other ends. This raised all the poles and the hide until it was as high as we could reach. We came out and grabbed the other two poles and did the same with them. Once all four were the same height we put the ends of the poles down and dug out holes for the ends. We buried the ends to make them secure then we helped put up the rest of the shelters. We got the supplies into the shelters just as the winds and rain hit! We had four in each shelter and were comfortable with the supplies and a fire in the center. The hole at the top let out the smoke and we hung up the meat from the poles to keep the insects out of it. We listened to the wind and rain outside and watched the hide move and stretch with the wind.

The poles stayed still and didn't move from the holes. "Larkar did a good job," I said in admiration as the shelters held through the long night. The rains did not stop the next Sun or the next. We were stuck in the shelters for four suns before there was a break in the rains. The trail was now a fast-moving river of water, mud, limbs, and even trees that the storm had washed down from the hills. We managed to get the shelters down and packed then looked for any dry path we could follow. There were none as the four suns of rain were more than the land could absorb, so it was in streams, pools, and puddles everywhere. Trees had fallen as their roots became exposed and bloated while trying to absorb the water.

We had to go around them. We tried to stay clear of the trees but the areas with no trees were flooded. The worst mistake we made was to try and climb higher to get above the water and found that the hills were slick with mud and wet clay. We were unable to climb as we kept slipping and falling down! We kept going despite the difficulties and made camp that night after a frustrating sun.

I was sitting outside as none of us wanted to be in the shelters unless necessary after being in them for four suns! "It was a strange thing that we lived in caves to not like being close together for shelter," I said in the silence. Kaga nodded and said something very wise "We have become used to the freedom of moving around. We've been moving for a long time. Yes, we stay in one place for a time, but we are not penned in together like sheep!" I nodded and saw Cecina, Timbu, Garath, and Kika agree. "I wonder if there is a way to make them bigger?" Mahendra asked as we all started to talk about what we could do to improve them. I smiled and said, "If we make them bigger the poles will be too big and heavy to carry and put up." Mahendra grimaced and said "True if we use only four poles. Kaga looked interested and said, "Could we use more smaller poles?" "Would that weigh less?" Mahendra asked. Cecina said, "Yes if you use the right kind of wood." I looked at her as I asked "What trees would weigh less?" Cecina replied, "Remember the tall, thin, hollow plants that grew everywhere in the jungles and many trees of the south?" Mahendra gave a grunt of surprise and then looked thoughtful. Kaga pulled out his knife and started to draw something on the ground next to the fire ring. We watched as he drew a different shelter with many poles instead of four. We made suggestions to make it stronger and larger until he had something we thought might work. "Now where do we find them?" I said knowing there were none in this area.

Then I remembered seeing them both in the low wetland areas of the many trees and the great many trees on the plateau. But that was still several suns away!

The next day we had to detour around fewer fallen trees, but it was still slow going because of the water and the mud. By that night we could see the dark wall of rock that was the beginning of the plateau and the place where the gorge was located. I believed we would make it there by mid-sun and set about the camp making sure that everyone and everything was ready. We would either have to climb up or ride up to the plateau. I stopped to speak with Nada and Larkar. He was showing some color on his face. Nada was feeding him as he was still very weak and needed to stay lying down for the deep wounds to heal. "Larkar. I want to show you what Kaga and I did with your shelter design." I realized that we had not had the chance to test the new design yet as we had not found any of the hollow plants yet. So showing it to Larkar was a good way to see if he thought it would work. I drew it on a hide with a burnt stick from the fire so he could watch me. Once I finished it he asked some questions then nodded and said "Good Jakool. This is good. But where will we get those hollow trees?" I quickly said, "In the many trees between the plateau and the hills we traveled through on my way here." I said with confidence. Larkar was tired out by our talk closed his eyes and was soon asleep.

I asked Nada "How long do you think he will need to fully heal? Nada said "He is healing but slowly. He will need at least two moons for those wounds to close and for him to be strong enough to be of use. *Two moons!* I thought with a groan. I thanked them and went to find Kaga and Mahendra. Once I found them we went to find Mearoo and the rest of the snow-leapers. Once we were gathered I showed them the hide with the shelter drawn on it and told them we needed to find the thin, hollow trees that grew in many trees and wet places. Janai and Samalaa both said "You will find many up on the Plateau. Both in the thick trees and in the wet parts of the many trees we traveled through. "So I did see them!" I said with some relief as we had seen another storm in the distance and I knew we would want them before it hit us.

Mearoo and I turned in and talked for some time before falling asleep. She told me about how snow-leaper women give birth and what I should do and expect to happen. It was very unsettling to hear her tell me that I would be expected to be with her when the cubs came out of her body. I explained that when our women gave birth, the healers and other women took them away from the men. So I had no knowledge of what to do.

Mearoo said "I know. I asked Gaieaa and she explained how your females give birth. We do it a little differently. The babies come out the same way but we prefer to be on all fours when we give birth. You will be behind me holding your hands under me to catch them. They will be small and will fit in your hands.

Janai, Samalaa, Sheena, and Jameeka will be there to help take the babies from you and keep them warm. The babies will not come out all at once, but one or two at a time. Once I know all of them are born I will lay down and you will put them at my breasts to feed. We need to keep them warm and fed so they will sleep. You will be spending a lot of time cuddled with me and our babies!" I smiled and said, "As long as you are with me I will be with you." We went to sleep as we were climbing tomorrow.

The next morning dawned with the wind blowing harder and more of the dark clouds much closer. I didn't like the looks of it so we hurried to make it to the gorge. Fortunately, the ground had dried up some and we made better speed. We reached the gorge and the tumble of boulders at the bottom around mid-sun The winds had picked up and were changing directions as it hit the plateau wall and bounced back at us. It would make the climbing more difficult but we had no choice. We did not want to be at the bottom of that gorge once the rains started! It would turn into a river that would drown us!

Samalaa, Farkis, Jameeka, and the rest of the snow-leapers that had taken the Elders and Children ahead, were waiting for us. They had run ropes from the top of the Gorge down to the bottom. This saved us time and effort as they started hauling up the supply carriers then Larkar! Mearoo and Janai went up to help so we had five teams of snow leapers pulling everything and everyone up into the Gorge then out onto the Plateau! Things went smoothly as they hauled up all the supplies and then started to haul up people. It would be safer; as the boulders were wet and slippery, and we could easily fall and be injured.

Over half my group was up in the gorge we saw the first of the lightning and heard the mighty crack of the thunder very close! A wall of rain hit us with howling winds! We got everyone up as fast as possible in the storm. Finally, we were all up and safe, but getting soaked as we were now fighting a stream of water coming down the gorge as we climbed up! We slipped and slid in the rushing water, slick rocks and mud! Some fell, but no one was badly hurt; as they were holding onto the ropes, so we kept going up until we made it to the end of the gorge. There was a short climb out then we were up on the Plateau! We had no time to celebrate as Mearoo took all of the snow leaper and took off to find the plants we needed to erect the new shelters.

In the meantime, we put up several using the four poles to get Larkar, the Elders, and the children out of the rain. Mearoo and the rest returned quickly with armloads of the green, springy hollow trees, which we stripped of the leaves and thin branches that grew from them. We soon had the first larger shelter up after some mistakes. After that, it went faster as we now knew how to do it. Soon we had the three shelters with the four poles and nine with the new poles. We were all inside and finally could start fires and get dry and warm!

It took some time for the snow-leaper's fur to dry but it didn't seem to bother them. They did look funny with their fur all soaked and hanging down around them! Mearoo dropped to all fours when I chuckled then she shook herself, showering us all with the water from her fur! "Hey! Stop that!" I said as the cold water hit me making me shiver again. "You deserve it for laughing at me!" Mearoo said as she did it again until she had most of the water out of her fur. Then she sat down with me next to the fire and had me rub my hands over her fur to help dry it. Soon Janai had Kika and Timbu doing hers and Sheena had Garath and Farini doing hers. We all felt better dry and warm as we took out food and warmed it in the fire.

Once we had eaten we went to sleep as no one would attack during such a storm! The shelter held up well against the wind and rain all night as we slept in watches. That morning we woke up and heard the still raging storm outside. We had more room too, so we were able to stand up and stretch! I walked around the inside as we had changed the shape to a circle with high sides. Using the thin hollow trees allowed us to run them up and then connect those with ones that ran around the sides. It made the walls higher and stronger! This gave us much more room than ones with four poles!

During a lull in the heavy rain, I dashed out and went into the first one to find everyone okay and enjoying the space and shelter it provided. The same was true of all of the shelters except the three with the four poles! Since Larkar had to be kept lying down, we had put him, Nada, Gaieaa, and Pathak in one of them. I thought having only four people would make it less crowded. When I ducked in to check on them I saw Pathak and Gaieaa arguing over who was going to put fresh poultices of the leaves, ground roots, and herbs on Larkar's wounds. Nada was gnashing her teeth in anger at the arguing and looked like she was ready to kill them!

I quickly said "Good News! We think that we can put up another of the new shelters for you today. "Really? Are you sure?" Nada said with a huge look of relief on her face! Pathak and Gaieaa stopped arguing to look at me with a look that said "You had better not be joking!" I quickly left and found Kaga, Cecina, and the rest and said "We have to build another new shelter quickly! If we don't Pathak and Gaieaa will kill each other if Nada doesn't do it first! Kaga looked like he was thinking hard while Cecina had her hand in front of her mouth to quiet her laughter! Timbu, Garath, and Kika were not as pleased to have to leave the warm shelter and go out in the rain, but I told them "We do not stop taking care of each other because of the rain! What kind of hunters are you?" Shaming them into hurrying out of their shelter to help. With all of us working together it only took minutes to put up a new shelter!

It was big enough for Pathak, Gaieaa, Nada, and Larkar to have plenty of room. We went ahead and put up one more so that the rest of the people in the remaining two smaller shelters could move into the bigger one. We put some of the supplies we did not need with us into the smaller tents using them to give us even more room! The next sun the rains stopped but the clouds were still there, so we packed up and headed across the plateau towards the darker line on the horizon.

Looking at it Samalaa said "It is the beginning of the thick many trees. We will turn once we reach it and go north to reach the place where Elasaa, Paasi, and the rest are waiting." During the sun I noticed that Larkar was staying awake more and asking questions about the things that happened while he was away. Pathak and Gaieaa were glad of the chance to tell him as it made it easier to remember the events to record as part of our history. Larkar seemed to be thinking a lot during this time as he could not do anything for two moons.

I stopped at mid-sun to let everyone rest and eat, while I went with Mearoo and Samalaa ahead to scout. I was watching the dark line ahead which had become clearer and I could see the outlines of some of the largest trees that stood above the rest of the jungle. Suddenly I saw a flight of birds take off from one of those trees and circle several times. When returned I noticed they landed in a different tree. I wondered what caused them to suddenly take flight like that and asked Samalaa as she was closer. She stopped and looked for time at the trees then turned and said "It could be a silent black killer or little screamers. They both will hunt the birds and the eggs." I knew the silent black killer and the little screamer, as my tribe had met them during their travels through jungles like these further south.

The Silent Black Killer was a large hunter like the Tigre, that hunted silently in thick many trees like this one. It was as big as the Sahaat or snow-leaper, sometimes bigger. Its fur was all black, and its favorite way to hunt was to be up in a tree on a limb hidden from sight. When prey went by on the ground below it, it simply jumped off the limb and landed on it with its weight knocking it down. Then it bit the back of its neck to kill it while it was stunned by the impact.

The little screamer was a strange-looking climber with fur, long arms and legs, and a tail. It had a very loud scream that it used to talk to others as they lived in large groups up in the trees. They were known to attack much larger predators to defend their territory or their kills, but they mostly ate fruit, nuts, and leaves from the trees. They did not go down to the ground as it made them easy prey for the Silent Killer, the Two Tusks, Rough Furs, and the snakes. Mearoo was further ahead looking for the driest path to take for the group when I saw something else coming from above the treetops! "Smoke!" I said loudly to get both Mearoo and Samalaa's attention.

They both looked up to see the same thin, gray column of smoke rising up from somewhere in the many trees! *Krieg!* I thought as I ran back to tell the others. By the time I made it back, Mearoo came bounding up and said "I need to go and warn the others on the Plateau! I agreed as it could be a large party of them going through the jungle to attack from where they would not expect to be attacked! Samalaa said "Take the direct path. We will follow you." She nodded then jumped away and was running at top speed disappearing quickly. Samalaa looked at the group thinking then said "I don't know if we can get everyone there safely if they attack." I was thinking the same but we were too small a group to split up and said it. Samalaa replied "I know. I just don't like this at all. We should have run into some of the others by now! We have not. Larkar was nearly killed when a larger party came up. If two parties came up then there are more! The Krieg do not hunt in small groups!" I was upset and worried but I had no ideas on what to do other than to continue as quickly as we could. I did make sure that snow-leaper took over the carriers with people and our people on the ones with the supplies and shelters. I also had everyone get the throwing spears and hollow tubes ready!

I turned and said to Samalaa, "We need to keep together. If they have scouts out and see us we would be tempting prey!" Samalaa said "Yes we would. Let's get moving!" We traveled on the narrow trail left by Mearoo as Samalaa had told her to take the quickest way. We could see it clearly as she had flattened the grass where she jumped or landed and where she ran in between. I still put out scouts in front as I was certain that is where any attack would come from.

We made good time and soon we could make out more details of the thick many trees as we got closer to it. We could see the tangle of tree limbs that made up the top of the thick many trees. Brilliant colored birds took flight occasionally then would settle back down again. I didn't see a pattern that would indicate a large group moving through the jungle toward the grassy area and the great ravine, so I concentrated on getting there! The rains held off giving us a break so we were able to keep going and not stop. We reached the edge of the thick many trees by late afternoon and turned north. Samalaa thought that it was only a few hours to the grass area and then a few more to where our people waited.

I kept us together as now that we were near the thick many trees, the danger was even greater that we would be attacked. I kept watching to see if any more smoke rose but I was too close to see above the tree tops. We were going away from the trees; at an angle now, to find the river that ran down from the cloud stabbers. It started as many streams through the hills, then the thick many trees until it came out in that deep ravine we had crossed. Samalaa said she saw signs of water ahead and we took heart that we were getting closer to it.

Suddenly I heard a high-pitched squealing cry then snorting! "Samalaa! Everyone! Spears!" I yelled as I recognized the sound as a Two Tusk! We stayed in place waiting to see if it charged us as we were not able to see it in the grass. I watched and listened but the sound did not repeat itself making me suspicious. I gave a hand signal for everyone to get down. I didn't know what was waiting for us up ahead, but my instincts said something was wrong! I motioned for Samalaa to scout ahead and she slid through the grass without a sound or a trail. It was several minutes before I heard a scream and saw the grasses several man lengths ahead shake with activity and then stop!

I had to fight the impulse to rush ahead but kept myself and everyone in place to wait and see what happened next. Samalaa made a call I recognized and we stood up to see what she had found. She was standing several man lengths in front of holding up a man! He was not like us but very different! We ran up to see him more clearly as Samalaa held him up with two paws with his feet off the ground. He struggled helplessly in her stronghold. I stopped and saw a small man, no larger than myself, with dark hair and eyes, brown skin, and a face that looked like mine but different. He did not have any of Kaga's or Mahendra's ancient features. He was dressed strangely with a hide clout around his waist, a covering made of grass and bird feathers! He had streaks of brown, gray, green, and black on his exposed face and body! "Who are you! Why do you hide waiting to attack us! He was shaking with fear as Samalaa continued to hold him up off the ground. I said "Are you Krieg? Do you hunt us?" I asked him with some anger as I was ready to kill him if he was! "Yes!"

He finally managed to say "I am Nimi! I am one of The Ones Who Are Lost! I gave him a hard look and realized he looked much different than the others who said they were "The Ones Who Are Lost". I remembered the other set of tracks and the Tigre saying there were 'two' groups. "Put him down," I said to Samalaa.

He looked a little less fearful now so I asked him again. "Who are you?" He looked at me as he said "I am Nimi of the Lost." I shook my head saying "No. We fought with ones that said they were the "The Ones Who Are Lost". They looked different, and were dressed in the furs and claws of predators they killed like the Krieg taught them."

Nimi looked surprised and then said, "We are of the same tribe but followed different paths." "That explains the two sets of tracks on that trail," I said out loud to everyone so they would understand he was not our enemy. "I am Jakool of the Mihakoo and snow-leaper tribe. Samalaa is the one holding you until I am satisfied with the truth of your words. She will rip out your throat with her teeth if you lie." Nimi looked at her and then nodded showing his understanding. "I saw smoke from a fire a few hours ago rising above the treetops. Was that your people?" Nimi nodded and said "Yes. We are hiding there from the others. The ones that joined the Krieg and have done terrible things!" I asked, "How many of you are there?"

Nimi replied "Over twice as many as you have here. Mostly women, children, some young some old. Very few men." "How did you escape being captured by the Krieg?" I asked needing to know that before I decided what to do. "We were not with the main camp when they attacked. My ancestors were always different than most of the others and we were not well thought of by them. So we would camp away from them, hunt separately, and only come together to share skills, stories, and warnings. That is how we heard of the Krieg. One of the young hunters escaped before they were overwhelmed and came to warn us. We fled in a different direction than the others. They ran right for the thick many trees, but we knew the Krieg would go after them there. We went west into the great grass plains then circled back to where they had come from." "I am surprised at such a bold move!" I said in appreciation of their escape. Nimi replied, "We may not be the biggest or strongest, but we think and we plan."

I nodded recognizing myself and others of our tribe in him, so I made a bargain with him. "We have several large groups heading towards the place where the river splits the land in two. There we left warriors and some wounded until we could return. If we take you with us will you speak with your people? Tell them that we mean them no harm, but only to the Krieg and those that follow them." Nimi was surprised as Samalaa let him go and gave him back his spear. He looked at me and said "You speak true? You are not trying to trick us into coming out to kill us all?" I had a good answer for him as I turned and said "Bring Larkar up here. I want Nimi to see why we will keep our word.

Larkar was carried forward by Janai and Farkis and set down. Pathak, Gaieaa, and Nada came too so Nimi could see we were not a hunting party or looking for war. "Larkar lost his family and his entire tribe to the Krieg. Janai, Samalaa, and the others you see that look like animals are people who have lost many to the Krieg. They are the cloud stabber spirits in your stories that came down from their home to fight the Krieg!"

Nimi became excited as he exclaimed "The Spirits of the cloud stabbers? The Leaping Devils? The Ones who walk unseen?" You have returned? You are here to fight the Krieg? Jakool! My people would gladly join your tribe in killing the Krieg! We have prayed to the spirits to help us and you have returned!" Nimi was dancing with joy in a circle and chanting something in his own language showing his joy at having his tribe's prayers answered!

I said "You need to be careful. We believe a large group of Krieg are tracking the different groups coming here." Nimi said "They will not see or hear me! I only made the sound of the Two Tusk to make you go around me, as most will avoid them!" I smiled remembering Mearoo saying the same thing! "Go! Tell your people. Meet us where the river splits the land past the end of the thick many trees. We are going up into the cloud stabbers to safety for our Elders, Women, and Children. We will then gather all of our tribes and come down to kill the Krieg and all their kind!" Nimi gave a whoop of joy, then sped off towards the thick many trees. Samalaa said "I do believe we have answered his prayers. This does explain both the different tracks and the worn trail. They have been hiding by moving around for many years going from the trees to the plateau and down to the endless green grass. Wise of them." "Yes, it was. Now let's get moving!" I said.

I didn't need to urge anyone as everyone wanted to get there quickly after finding Nimi. I felt exposed out there, not knowing if they would come through the jungle or maybe from across the ravine. I kept thinking how to be ready but other than having our weapons ready and watching everything, there was nothing else. I saw the river as we made it up a gentle rise and immediately dropped down at what I saw! "Samalaa! Look!" I said in a whisper to her knowing she would hear me. She very slowly lifted up her head only until she could see over the grass. She let out a string of curses that I remember to this Sun! "Sons of misbegotten dogs! Killers of babies! Spawns of demon bitches! I curse you, your children, and their children until they all die!" There was more but I stopped her to ask How many?" Samalaa hissed then said "At least ten hands!

All are Krieg! They all wear the skins of my brothers!" That explained the curses and the hate I could practically feel coming from her. "We need to go back and warn the others." Samalaa didn't want to leave but I made her by saying "Mearoo would not want you to die fighting ten hands by yourself! She and the others would be mad you didn't let them go with you!" It was the only thing I could think of quickly that might get through to her and it worked!

We backed up slowly and made our way on all fours until we were below the top of the rise and then stood up and ran! We made it to the rest before they made it to the rise and stopped them. "Krieg! At least ten hands! They are using the river to go into the ravine! They will probably climb up the other end to come out and surprise our people!" "Ten Hands!" Kaga said showing some surprise and a little fear. Mearoo quickly said "We cannot keep them safe against that many! "I know! Let me think!" I said sharply trying to find a way to keep our Elders, Women, and Children safe while the rest of us ran to the group waiting for our return to meet the attack from the Krieg! "I wish Merkansoo and the others were here! We could kill all of them!" Farkis said with a snarl. That gave me an idea! Mearoo! Take all the snow-leaper and get to cover inside the edge of the many trees! Get to the other end of the ravine and hide! Wait for them to start to climb up before you attack! Nada! Take everyone else and get all the large nuts we still have! Are there any rocks or small boulders nearby?" I asked them. "Yes! Near the edge of the ravine but out of sight!" "Gather them when you get there! We will rain down the rocks, boulders, nuts, and anything else we have! They will not be able to climb out and they will die trying!

I still do not know how I thought of this but my tribe is grateful to this very sun. We took all the nuts and gave them to Mearoo to give to her people and they ran! We took the carriers and the rest straight for the trees! If we could get them into the edge then they should be safe, while we joined Mearoo and her people to stop the cursed Krieg from ever leaving that ravine! "If only we had more men!" I said cursing that none of the others had made it to the plateau! What had happened? Were they all dead? Killed by these snakes that walked like men! If only one other group made it we would certainly be able to kill them all and keep our people safe! I was panting with the effort to carry one end of the supply carrier loaded with children, while Kaga had the other. Mahendra, Timbu and Kika had Larkar, Garath, Cecina and Prinda had Pathak and Gaieaa. Nada was with Larkar's carrier keeping him in it as he wanted to get up and go after the Krieg!

He was screaming and cursing us for keeping him tied to it so he couldn't get us all killed! We made it to the edge of the jungle and were surprised to find Nimi and all his people waiting for us! "Nimi! Take them and ours back into the trees! The Krieg are coming up into the ravine!" I said to him relieved that at least they would be safe.

"No Jakool. Our Elders and women will look after yours. We come with you to fight them!" Nimi stood with maybe fifteen men, some young some old. They were all like him in size but held their spears proudly and looked ready to fight! "Let's go!" I said turning and then running for the other end of the ravine! I waited until we reached Mearoo and the rest hiding near the end of the ravine with a large pile of rocks and boulders ready! "They came to help!" I told Mearoo as I stopped in front of her gasping for breath. Just then I heard something that sent chills through me! Screams! Coming from the ravine! We all grabbed up rocks and ran to the edge to look down to see where the screams were coming from! We saw Merack and Merkansoo at the front of their group fighting the Krieg! "I yelled and said, "Throw everything, and let's get down there"! Samalaa, Mearoo, Sheena, Farkis, and Girivar threw their rocks and then leaped down into the gorge! They gave blood-curdling screams as they were falling through the air down onto the front of the Krieg! Now the Krieg were screaming as teeth and claws rained down on them with vengeance and blood in their eyes!

The rest of us threw down all the rocks, boulders, and nuts on the ones in the rear so as not to hit our people! The Krieg were falling under the rain from above and the ferocious snow-leaper attack from the front! Merkansoo and Merack rallied their people and charged into the Krieg using spears and knives to stab and slash at them! We had them boxed in the ravine with no way out as we climbed down the shallow end and attacked their rear! They became howling demons once they realized they were trapped between us! They turned to face us as we were the weaker group! They charged into us backing us up against the back of the ravine! We couldn't dodge and maneuver pinned in like that and people were getting wounded and killed! I saw Garath and Timbu get speared and slashed by four while I was fighting two of them! I tried to dodge under one to go help Timbu but it was too late! One had jumped on his back and ripped his throat with the claws it wore on its hands!

Suddenly I heard more yells and screams from above and looked up to see Darshita and six other snow leapers landing on top of the rear of the Krieg! I took out one of the two I was fighting with a sudden thrust to his chin, spearing him up through his head! I didn't try to get the spear free as I would have died trying! I let it go and dodged a slash by the other one jumped high and slashed at his face with my knife! He screamed as I felt it make contact and slice across his nose and one eye! That gave me the opening to stab him in the chest into his heart! I spit on him as I took out my knife and went hunting for another one to kill! I was in a rage at losing Garath, Timbu, and others and only wanted to kill as many as I could!

I didn't think about anything else, as I sliced across the hamstrings of the one that Darshita was fighting! I rolled away and swiped another across his belly as Bamal, Kiraat, and the rest of their group of people arrived and waded into the battle! I was slick with blood from my enemies and my own wounds. I kept going as I saw more of them between me and Mearoo! I saw her fighting four of them and knew she needed my help!

I gave a mighty yell and rushed forward until I reached the edge of the group trying to pin her from all sides with spears! I leaped on the nearest one's back and sliced his throat from ear to ear! I jumped off and landed in front of another and hit him full force in the middle causing him to fall! I fell on top of him with my knife in his chest! By the time I got up the other two were dead from Mearoo's teeth and claws! I grabbed my knife and said, "Kill them all!" I turned and attacked the nearest Krieg until I was standing there facing Merkansoo, Darshita, Merack, Samalaa, Bamal, Kiraat, Farkis, Mahendra, and Kaga as there were no more Krieg left alive!

Kika was going from body to body and spitting on them then stabbing them all in the heart yelling 'This is for Timbu! This is for Garath!' This is for Sheena!" "Sheena!" I managed to say then looked around until I saw her body in a bloody heap by the side of the ravine with several of her people by her. She was not the only snow leaper that lost their life in that sun. When we looked at all the bodies and I counted them, we had lost ten of our men and seven of the snow-leaper! "Timbu, Garath, Lavar, Sheena, and several of Nimi's people! Other names I could not remember at that time of rage, grief, and sorrow, but are remembered and recorded here in this place!

We all had wounds and were slow to climb out of the ravine and when we made it we saw the rest of Nimi's people with ours coming to help. I sat down and gave way to my grief as I held Mearoo and sobbed in her fur. I had killed many that sun! I knew how Larkar felt so well that I wished that there were more Krieg for me to kill!

Mearoo yowled and spit curses as Nada started cleaning the stabs and slashes on her back, arms, and legs, while Pathak did mine. They made us drink a potion to help with the pain and blood loss I was starting to feel; now that my rage had left me from the battle and my wounds.

Larkar was brought over to the edge of the ravine where Merkansoo, Darshita, Kiraat, Bamal, Samalaa, and Merack were standing. When he arrived Merkansoo picked him up off the carrier and held him up to see the dead in the ravine! "Look Larkar! Over ten hands of Krieg dead! None left alive as I promised you! But it is not enough! You were not there because you foolishly tried to fight them by yourself! Jakool killed more of them today than you did by charging into them in a rage! He used his rage at his brothers being killed to kill them! He did not do it alone! Do you understand Larkar? We do this together so we may live! Look well at the bodies of your brothers and sisters who died today for vengeance!" Larkar gave a fierce shout of joy when he first saw the dead Krieg; until Merkansoo told him this!

He looked at how many of our men were dead along with the snow-leapers that had jumped into the ravine to fight! Merkansoo continued speaking to Larkar saying "You could have kept them from dying at all Larkar! 'IF' you followed the plan and the groups as you were told to do! Your people had to come back carrying you to save your life instead of watching for the rest of the Krieg who came after the ones you attacked!" Merkansoo then whirled around and set him down on the carrier. He leaned down and said with his face close to Larkar's "You do this again, you will die. We will not save you from your own need to kill them all by yourself!"

Merkansoo then jumped down into the ravine with Samalaa, Jameeka, and Farkis and started to gather up the bodies of the snow-leaper dead. I wondered why as I looked up and saw large black birds circling high in the air having smelled the blood. I knew that others would be attracted too, as I felt the potion working and I fell back against Pathak. Mearoo said "Rest Jakool." Then she said "I feel so tired!" as she also fell. I closed my eyes to rest and tried to erase what they had seen in that sun.

We slept the rest of the sun and night and woke up early the next morning. The dead were all buried now under rocks that Merkansoo, Merack, and all the rest had piled up to keep them from being food for the scavengers. I asked Merack why they did this and he said "Merkansoo and his people don't leave their dead to be eaten. They put them in special niches carved into the walls of their caves. I think this is a good thing Jakool. So from now on we will no longer leave our dead.

We will bring them back to our new home to be placed in the cave of the dead, to be remembered." I was surprised to hear Merack saying this to me! I slowly said "I think I understand. Have you told the other Elders?" Merack replied "Yes. At least the ones that are here."

I saw Merkansoo coming our way and wondered if we could send out teams now to look for Jarack and Lasaa's group. Merkansoo came up to me and said "I have just spoken with Gaieaa. "She is very concerned about Jarack and Lasaa as am I. I am also concerned about Elasaa, Paasi, and the others. I have already put together a large group of our people to go to them to be sure they are safe. I have come to ask Merack and you if we should send a large group to find them?" Merack looked worried and I knew I was! "Yes! In fact, we should send all the women, children, and Elders with the group you are sending to find Elasaa and Paasi's group. The rest should be ready for a fight like the one we just had here."

Merack showed his surprise at my taking over his role as 'Leader' and turned to ask me "Why? Do you really think they are both in the same danger as we were?" I replied as I saw both Pathak and Gaieaa being carried over to join us. "I know they are! Think everyone! We believed the Krieg would come when they heard about you being in the Great Plains. We both knew just how bloodthirsty they are, and that they hate you more than anything else. Larkar was almost killed by a large group that came up the way we expected them to. But how did this group get here? Merkansoo came up through the hills and part of the jungle to reach the hidden ravine. Nimi's people said they were not in the thick many trees but how do they know? It is so big, how could their small tribe possibly know if the Krieg are using it?"

I turned away and yelled "Nimi! Come here!" I said wanting him to answer that question! Nimi came running over and I told him "How do you know the Krieg are not coming through the thick many trees?" Nimi quickly replied "We know because we know the thick many trees! It tells you if someone is moving through it. We are good climbers! We always have people high up in the trees so they can watch for those signs! Certain birds will fly up making their warning calls as they do! The tree screamers will always scream and you can tell because it will start with a few, then all of them will be screaming!" I asked him "You can see all of the many trees this way? Nimi hesitated before he said "Not all. It goes much further than we can cover but we do not need to worry! They cannot approach us without giving an alarm we can see." I didn't like that answer!

I turned and saw that neither did Merkansoo or Merack! I looked at Nimi for a minute then turned my back on the group and walked over to the deep gorge where the battle had taken place. I went all the way to the end that led right to the edge of the thick many trees. The grass area was only ten man lengths wide there. I then dropped down out of sight and very carefully crawled on my belly until I was at the edge of the trees. I waited to see if Nimi, Merkansoo, Mearoo, or Merack spotted me. After a few minutes, I heard them calling my name. I stayed hidden until I heard them searching for me. I waited until someone came close enough for me to ambush, then I sprang up and yelled! It was Nimi! He almost speared me as he reacted very quickly! I managed to dodge his spear thrust as I was ready for just such a response! I then turned and said to him, "You didn't see me. I was in plain sight, not in the thick many trees, but in the grass! I do not believe your people could know if the Krieg are using trails only they know that go through it!" I turned and said to the rest "We need to leave now! We need to get to all three groups. I know they are in danger!" I said feeling it even more strongly than I did earlier!

Nimi was shaken by both my actions and my words. Merkansoo and Mearoo did not need any convincing as they already knew how dangerous the Krieg were, especially when they could kill and skin snow-leaper people! Merack still seemed troubled by this plan. "What is wrong?" Merack answered "We cannot travel as fast as they can. How will we keep up? How will we not be considered weak?" I chuckled and said "You have forgotten Merack how we arrived in time to save you and the rest of the hunters from the stampeding deer! We rode our snow-leaper allies! Now we are one tribe! Mahendra is much stronger than me. Do not tell me I cannot hunt or fight for my tribe! I swore to Merkansoo that if any refused to join, I would kill them myself! This is no different!"

I turned to Merkansoo and said "Do you feel we are relying on you too much? That we should not join with your people and share in everything?" Merkansoo said "Not using your strengths against an enemy is foolish. We can get all of us there just as quickly as by ourselves. We chose to offer you a joining of our tribes. We do not believe you to be weaker than us. We have seen you hunt and now fight. The Krieg are men not like us but more like you. We are faster and stronger than any one of them, but they killed many of my people! So do not measure yourself or your people by our speed or strength Merack. We do not use such things to measure one's worth to the tribe." Dismissing Merack's fears. Mearoo said "I will carry Jakool where he needs to be! So will all of our people!"

Merkansoo nodded to show his agreement! "We are wasting time! Nimi!" "Yes Jakool?" He replied not sure why I was calling on him. "You said you have people in the trees watching? Are they watching now?" Nimi said "Yes! Of Course!" I said to him "Show Merkansoo and Mearoo where they are! If they can see so much of the jungle from their high perches, then maybe they can see signs of our missing groups?" Merkansoo grinned then called for Samalaa, Janai, Farkis, Girivar, Jameeka, and Saharit to join them as they turned and followed Nimi into the jungle. I turned and said to Merack. We need to send all the women, children, Elders, and carriers with the group to help Paasi and the rest. We take only what we need. I then said, "If we don't arrive in time we will not need any supplies."

I turned and hurried to tell Pathak, Gaieaa, Nada, and Larkar the news while Merack went to tell the group of the change in their mission. Larkar didn't curse, scream yell about being left out this time! He nodded and said "I can help once we get there. I will help Pathak take charge and set up defenses until you return." I smiled at him and said "Don't worry Larkar. There will be plenty of chances to kill more Krieg. I have a feeling that once we reach our new homes, Merkansoo will keep his word to you and all of us." Larkar looked very serious as he said "I hope it does not cost more lives than it is worth." I turned away quickly to hide my shock at hearing Larkar say such words! To even think that his revenge upon the Krieg for killing his family and his tribe was not worth every life lost attempting it was not the Larkar I knew!

I found Kika and the remaining young hunters and sat them down to talk to them. "I want to tell you all that we have a very special thing to do." I could see that Kika had changed overnight, from a young, eager, unsure-of-himself hunter, to a blood-hungry killer because of the loss of his closest friends, Timbu, Garath, and Sheena. He said, "As long as I get to kill more of them, I don't care what I have to do." I shook my head as I knew this would get him and others killed, like Larkar's blind hate and need for revenge had done.

"I need you to go with the group that is going to find Paasi, Elasaa, and the others wounded and waiting for us. You know the other young ones the best Kika, so I need you to go! Larkar will be well enough to help you set up defenses, traps, and ambushes. You need to think of any way they can possibly come and be ready for them! If I am right, They will come and attack with a much larger group this time!" Kika looked at me and I returned his gaze until I saw him understand my orders. He just said, "Yes Jakool." I turned to Mahendra and said, "Were you picked to go too?" He said "No. Merkansoo wants me, Kaga, Samalaa, Janai, and Jameeka to lead the group that will go to find Lasaa and Jarack. They had the shortest and easiest trail. They should have gotten here before us." I felt a little shiver of fear as I realized Mahendra was right! I looked around frantic for a moment; as I didn't see Merkansoo, before I remembered he had gone into the jungle to see if he and the others could spot signs of Lasaa and Jarack's group! I said "Merkansoo has gone with Nimi to put snow-leaper up high in the tall trees that look over the jungle. They may see signs of them for us to use to reach them quickly. We will ride our snow-leaper brothers." This gave Mahendra and the rest some hope as I told them to go and help pack up the women, children, the Elders and injured, and all the supply carriers. I left them and went to find Merack.

He was busy putting together teams of riders with snow leapers for the two groups that would be searching. I approved of his choices and went to find Cecina and Prinda. I found them counting out supplies for those two groups to take with them. I thought they would be and said "Only give us as much as we can each carry tied to our backs. Cecina nodded but Prinda stopped and asked why. "Because we will be riding our snow-leaper brothers and we need to be as light as possible. I am very afraid that we will not arrive in time!" When I said the words 'In Time' I had a sudden feeling of dizziness then I was watching Lasaa and Jarack's group fighting off an attack! I watched as they managed to either kill or run off their attackers but they had dead and injured! I watched as Jarack turned and said to Lasaa "That was the third one! We will not make it to the plateau alive unless we can either lose them or signal for help!" Lasaa gave a grimace as he replied "I will send a signal but I do not know if any will see it."

I watched as he took one of the signaling crystals that all the scouts had and started to climb up a nearby tree. The vision ended with another wave of dizziness, and then I found myself being held by both Prinda and Cecina looking very concerned. "Jakool? What happened to you? You started to fall and we caught you! Your eyes were open but you didn't see us! You didn't hear us when we asked you what was wrong!" I shook my head as I asked for a drink. Once I had taken a long drink of the potion that Prinda handed me, I said "I have to get to Merkansoo! Lasaa and Jarack's group are in trouble!" I ignored their questions as I turned and ran towards the trees. I went in at the spot where Nimi had led Merkansoo and the rest less than an hour before, hoping I could find them!

I yelled out to let anyone know I was there as I ran into the thick many trees. As soon as I entered the sunlight changed to a dimmer, green glow, filtered through the many layers of leaves on the tall trees. Vines were growing up around the trees and crisscrossing from one to the other. I had to keep my eyes on the ground as there were many bushes, roots, rotting limbs, and animals! I saw rats scurrying into deep piles of dead leaves and into rotted stumps and trunks. I caused birds to call out and the screamers to scream to draw attention so I could find someone! Finally, I heard someone call my name from somewhere ahead and turned in that direction.

I found Nimi waiting for me at the base of a giant tree. He shook his head and said "We heard you coming a while ago! Merkansoo saw you when you entered the trees! I felt anger as I shouted "Lasaa and Jarack are in trouble! I saw them being attacked! We need to find them now! Lasaa is trying to signal for help!" Merkansoo responded by climbing to the top of the tree and giving a yell. I hear the rest of the ones in the trees reply. I was feeling so angry and upset as I paced around the tree waiting. Merkansoo suddenly shouted! "Janai sees it! It is coming from the hills east of the jungle and just south of us!" I started running as soon as I heard Merkansoo's words as I knew they would be able to reach the camp faster than I could. Suddenly Mearoo landed in front of me and said "Get On!"

I jumped for her back and grabbed her neck fur as she took off running and jumping out of the trees! I heard the others behind us and I yelled at Mearoo "Don't stop! They will catch up!" Mearoo didn't say anything back but when we reached the end of the trees, she stopped and waited for the others to mount up and meet us. I yelled "I said don't stop!" Mearoo replied "You are an Idiot! Don't be like Larkar!" This got through my anger and fear enough so I kept quiet for the short time it took everyone to get moving towards us. Mearoo didn't wait but turned and jumped again.

I soon relearned the skills of staying on a snow leaper when they are running and then jumping every few seconds!

We were running fast; as we were in the endless green grass, heading east then as we reached the place where the many trees ended and the hills began. There we took advantage of the downhill slopes to make long jumps to make up for the shorter ones on the uphill slopes. Merkansoo was sure he knew where it came from so we trusted his directions as we sped towards where he told us to go. I started to recognize places as we crested more hills as we started to turn south.

I knew we were entering a place where we would go to gather the young leaves of the tea plants that grew in plenty there. It was also one of the most direct trails from the great plains below up into the cloud stabbers! *This is where they are coming up!* I thought grimly as I tightened my grip on Mearoo as she made a flying jump across a stream, followed by more! Soon we came to one of the great rivers that brought water down from the cloud stabbers making this place rich in life! I was not watching for plants, animals, or places I knew now, as I was focused on reaching Jarack and Lasaa's group before another attack took place!

I didn't hear the sounds at first; because of the noise of the wind rushing past me, but Mearoo did! "Fighting!" She yelled and put on a burst of speed as she changed direction slightly to head right for the sounds. We crested a hill and saw them below us trapped against the bottom of the hill and surrounded on three sides! I felt my anger surge as Mearoo didn't slow down but started making the huge jumps that would put us at the bottom in a matter of seconds! I looked at the Krieg attacking and saw someone that looked like they might be the leader! He was wearing magnificent Tigre fur around his shoulders and had claws on his hands. He also had made the skull into a cover over his head and face! I yelled, "Go for the Tigre Skull!" Mearoo headed straight for him and timed her last jump so we landed full on top of him with a mighty crash!

I made sure I had my knife out and dove forward over Mearoo's head at the last second! I landed my knife in his chest! I left it as I knew it would be buried too deep to pull out quickly, but had my thrusting spear out and was using it! Mearoo was snarling and growling as she slashed, bit, and clawed her way to my side! Merkansoo and the rest repeated our last jump and rained down on the Krieg with their war screams as my people jumped from their backs with their spears thrusting! We took out the center of them quickly creating an opening to reach Lasaa and Jarack.

They were both fighting hard and had blood-red eyes as we met up with them! Merkansoo yelled, "Kill them all!"

We turned and rushed them again taking down several before they could react. But the sheer number of Krieg slowed us down and we had to change tactics! There were too many of them for us to attack the middle. Samalaa saw something and yelled "Left side! Left side!" I turned in time to see the Krieg to her left turning to face another attack from their side! I looked up and saw Bamal and Darshita leading a charge by their group into them! "Now! I yelled! And everyone turned and we charged into the front of the left side! They were caught between us and were cut off from the others! We killed them quickly and then we regrouped everyone to face the remaining Krieg!

I heard Darshita yell out a warning and saw Merkansoo turn to see why. There was a small group that had broken off the right side and were running away!

"We can't let them bring more!' I yelled at Mearoo! She gave out a yell then she, Samalaa, Merkansoo, and seven others leaped after them! They jumped over the remaining Krieg, then ran and jumped until they were ahead of the fleeing Krieg! They turned and jumped right at them! I was too busy staying alive to watch them as the middle had charged into us! I was being pushed back by the wave of Krieg until I was pinned against the hill.

But I had learned new ways of fighting from the snow leapers and used one now! I turned and ran uphill with several chasing me! I then turned and jumped at them as high as I could! They were surprised by my sudden attack and fell to each side of the hill to avoid my spear! I managed to spear one in the shoulder as he had not ducked quick enough! I dropped to the ground and tucked my body into a ball and let my momentum carry me downhill away from them! I hit the bottom of the hill and leaped up to use the last of my momentum to attack one in front of me! I didn't have my knife or spear now, so I went for his man parts! He was much taller than me so I just aimed my head at his man parts and crashed into him. He screamed and dropped his spear as he fell to the ground! I straddled him and sliced his throat with the claws on his right hand! I grabbed his spear and used it to fend off another one then another!

Mearoo, Merkansoo, and the rest had finished off the ones that had run and returned! We were determined to not let any remain alive so we kept killing until all we saw were dead Krieg surrounding us, as we met in the middle of them. I was sweating and breathing hard from the effort it took to keep fighting for so long! I felt the stings from the cuts and slashes I had not managed to avoid. I wiped the blood and sweat from my eyes and forehead with my arm as I looked around me. Merkansoo and his people were going through the bodies looking for any of theirs or ours that had fallen. Kiraat, Bamal, Mahendra, Kika, Kaga, and Merack were going to each Krieg and making sure they were dead! It was over and I wanted to sit down and rest, but knew I could not. I wearily said "We need to get back. This was not the only group. I know it." Mearoo, Samalaa, and Darshita heard me and replied "We will leave some here to take care of the dead. The rest of us with return now. I nodded as I threw my left leg over Mearoo's back as she crouched down to make it easier for me to mount. She said, "Are you sure you can hold on to me?" Showing her concern at my weak grip on her neck fur. I gritted my teeth against saying something in anger and instead said: "I trust you to get me there". She nodded then we started back.

We made good time but did not push as hard as we had on the way here. Mearoo was also feeling the strain of carrying me there and back; and the battle, as I could tell she was not jumping as much or as far and was running slower. I did not say anything; for it would only get us killed, to get there quickly but in no shape to fight if we had to! I finally saw the endless green grass appear; when we crested the last of the hills, and was relieved to not see any signs of another group of Krieg. We reached the place where the endless green grass met the thick many trees and swung around it to head for the Plateau and the River Gorge. I felt a great burden lift from me as we reached the place where we had killed the Krieg in the Gorge. Mearoo continued following the trail left by our people; we had sent to join up with Paasi and Elasaa into the highlands that would lead us into the hills at the foot of the great cloud stabbers!

I was starting to have trouble holding on and slipped a few times, but Mearoo always shifted her body to keep me on her when I did. Merkansoo must have seen me do this as he came up beside us with Merack riding him. Samalaa came up on our right with Mahendra and we continued up the trail until we saw the back of the group we had sent ahead of us! I yelled to get their attention and saw them turn and see us! Just then I had a sudden dizziness and fell as I lost my grip on Mearoo! I hit the ground hard and rolled! It was as if I had fallen down a bottomless hole; or off the side of a cloud stabber, as I didn't feel my body hit the ground. I was surrounded by a bright light and I saw the female form of Yuma Samang appear. "Come to my cloud stabber Jakool. Mearoo knows the way." Then I was back, lying on the ground face down in the grass.

Mearoo turned me over looking to see if I had broken any bones in my fall with Merkansoo and Merack helping. I was so tired but I managed to say "I am all right. Yuma Samang says to come to her cloud stabber. She said that you know the way." Mearoo looked startled by this and turned to Merkansoo and said "He has now seen and heard visions several times from Yuma! Why?" Merkansoo dropped his head on his chest as he thought for a moment then turned and said "He must be very special. More than just for becoming your mate and joining our tribes together. We have to go there anyway. I am sure Yuma knows this." She nodded then I felt something being put in my mouth. "Drink this Jakool," a voice I did not know said. I was having trouble seeing clearly as everyone looked blurry to me. I drank as I was very thirsty after two long rides and hours of fighting! I do not know what was in the skin I drank from but it was a dark, liquid that seemed to give me some of my strength back within minutes! I looked around to thank the person but there was no one there with water skin!

I was able to stand with help and soon we were walking instead of riding as we were very near to the meeting place. I heard the shouts of greeting from the front and sighed happily as we had finally reached Paasi, Elasaa and the rest of our tribe. When I finally made it to them, I saw Paasi and Elasaa both looking well! Elasaa looked much better! In fact, she looked fully healed as she bounded around from one person to the next telling them how much she missed them and thanking all that helped to heal her and feed her while she was injured. She made it to me and Mearoo and smiled happily as she gave both of us a hug! "Thank you so much! Paasi told me how much you did for me Jakool! I would be honored to mate with you and bear your children!" I had not expected this especially just then.

Mearoo did not object or act jealous this time but did say "You will have to wait to thank him that way Elasaa. He has ridden and fought hard today." "Oh! No! I didn't mean right now!' Elasaa said laughing at my obvious exhaustion and filthy state. Mearoo said, "We need to bathe!" Elasaa smiled and said "This way! You will like what we found!" She led us back towards the hills at the back of the plateau where the many trees started. They turned and went right following a trail left by others. After a few turns, we were in a small clearing with rocks and boulders surrounding a pool of water. I saw what looked like a mist rising from the surface. I thought of the lake in the large cave where I had my first vision/dream. *"It had mist rising from the water too,"* I thought in my tired mind, unable to remember why.

Mearoo gave a squeal of pleasure as she put a foot in the water and said "It is warm Jakool!" I put a foot in and found it was very warm! "I think I am going to like this!" I said as I undid my loincloth and stepped into the pool! I felt the warm water start relaxing my muscles, soothing my aches and pains immediately as I just let myself sink until I felt the bottom. I shot back up to the surface and returned to the edge of the pool where it was not as deep. I sighed as I slowly washed the ground, blood and sweat from my body then turned to help Mearoo with her fur.

We didn't want to get out but our tiredness; then our hunger, forced us to leave that wonderful, warm pool of water! We returned to the tribe to find that they had set up camp just inside the many trees and had hot food ready and cold water to drink! We sat around the large campfire just eating and drinking with the stories being told by each group of what had happened to them when we had gone our separate ways. I was very tired and wanted to rest as soon as we finished eating. Merack told us to go and sleep as he would stay up and discuss the events with Pathak, Gaieaa, Pathak, Merkansoo, and Darshita. Larkar was also there but was quiet and just listened. I was grateful to Merack as Mearoo said "Come Mate." I turned and grabbed her by her paw and let her lead me a little ways away from the campfire and around a stand of trees surrounded by the thin, tall hollow ones.

We made a bed there in the center and were soon fast asleep. Just as I felt sleep claim me, a soft voice in my head whispered "Rest now. You have much to do yet." Then I knew nothing.

CHAPTER TEN

THE FIVE TREASURES

I woke up the next morning feeling all of my wounds and my aches from yesterday's fighting. I felt Mearoo still there with me, so I woke her up to share my aches and pains! After we 'shared', we got up and left our nest to go back to the warm pool to soak our aches. We both felt much better after we returned to the camp. I said to Mearoo "I want to speak with Gaieaa, Paasi, and Nada about that warm pool. I think the warm water is somehow helping to heal my wounds and ease my sore muscles.

Mearoo showed a little surprise as she looked at me and then said "Me too! I wonder if the ones back home will also feel as good?" "You have these warm pools of water there?" I asked in a surprised voice, wondering how there could be warm anything high up in the cloud stabbers. Just thinking about my one journey following her made me shiver with the memory of the bone-chilling cold! "I will tell them while you get us some food! I am hungry after yesterday!" "And this morning!" I added just to see if she would laugh or swing her paw at me! She did neither as she grinned and then loped off to where several were cooking at the fire. I went over to Gaieaa who saw me coming and greeted me "Good! You're finally awake!" As if I had been lazy and avoiding work! "I worked hard enough killing yesterday. I wanted to know if you have been to the warm pool back in the many trees?" Gaieaa replied "Yes I have. The amazing effect it had on my old joints! Pathak too!" Pathak gave me a smile and a nod while he continued counting the tea plants in front of him. "I noticed this too and it seems to be helping my wounds heal." She looked at my various cuts and scratches. "Hmm. I would say these look better. It has been less than a full sun and they look as if they have been healing for three suns!" She turned to Darshita and asked, "Do your people know anything about healing waters?"

Darshita let her chin drop down and her eyes became focused on a faraway place for several minutes. When she finally refocused on us she replied "Yes and No. Yes, we know that certain springs that feed the lakes and rivers can help ease aches and pains and speed up healing. Some even help with breathing sickness. But not all of them and not for everyone who goes." "I wonder if it has something to do with the fact the water is very warm," I said thinking out loud. Nada spoke up saying "It may be. The joint ailment and sore muscles at least. I know that heat will ease the pain of both. So if you are in a pool of warm water then it must work the same as when we put warm wet hide on someone's joints to ease the joint ail." "It makes sense. We should have all the Elders and the wounded bathe in the pool at least once a sun while we are here." Gaieaa said. We all agreed this was worth trying so we all spent some time telling everyone to bathe in the pool and report back to Gaieaa, Pathak, and Nada. This way they could determine who and what was helped.

Darshita returned to me and Mearoo as we were sitting down to eat. "Yes?" I asked as she looked as if she wanted to say something. "I think we need to leave very soon." I looked at her and saw something I had not seen before. I didn't know what it was but I knew it was not good! Mearoo replied, "We plan to leave in two suns, maybe sooner." I had not been told this, but it made sense not to stay close to where we had killed over twenty hands of Krieg. There would be more once the rest found them.

Darshita nodded then said "Jakool? I would like to speak with you about a private matter. When you are finished?" She then got up and left quickly leaving both of us wondering what 'private' matter she could mean? We finished eating and I got up to go find Darshita as we were both very curious to know what 'private' matter she wanted to discuss. I found her near the edge of the many trees looking ahead to the distant cloud stabbers. I came up beside her and waited for her to speak. She stayed silent as she continued to stare at the distant cloud stabbers seeming to be unaware I was there. I made a noise in my throat to get her attention and she put out a paw and said "No noise. Let me finish." "Finish what?" I wanted to ask, but I stayed silent as she kept staring for a few minutes more. She lowered her head and turned to me and said "I need to tell you some things. Come." She said and led me into the many trees for a way until she could not hear the rest back at the camp. "Here is far enough." She said stopping at a bush I recognized. It was a blackberry bush and had fruit. I was glad to see them but Darshita had not brought me here to pick blackberries!"

"Jakool. Because Mearoo has chosen you as her mate; and is now carrying your children, you have given our people something very hard for us to find." Darshita then took my hands in her paws and said "Our people only exist because of Ooh-mans who for some reason mated with snow-leapers. I do not know why or how this made us. I am more than just a healer and Merkansoo's mate. I am a seeker of knowledge. This is what we call ourselves." I didn't understand what she meant and replied "What is a seeker of knowledge?" Sounding as confused as I am sure I looked just then! "Darshita made me look her directly in the eyes then she explained in a way I was not expecting! She pulled me to her until we were touching. She put her arms around me causing my heart to race as I thought she was going to mate with me right there!

No. But we will eventually I shook my head as I didn't see her lips move or her mouth open, but I heard the the words anyway! *Yes, Jakool. You heard my words in your mind as I did not speak them, I thought them. I can send my thoughts to be heard by others who can hear them. We just found out that you can hear them!* I don't understand! I started to say but Darshita was already answering them! *You think before you speak the words. I heard the thought. One of the differences that occurred in us was this. It seems to follow certain bloodlines but can skip many generations and then appear again. At first, we believed it to be a blessing from Yuma Samang. But she has told us that 'this' is not her doing. She had done other things to help us, but not this! What?* I stopped as I was about to say something then just thought it.

That was very quick! I have not seen someone adapt that fast to thinking instead of speaking! Darshita thought in return. I felt her approval in my head. *So you can hear all my thoughts? No. Only the ones you think of me. If you are thinking about something that you don't want me to hear then I will not hear it.* I tried to not think of her to see if this was true. I thought about Mearoo and how I felt about her. Darshita didn't say or think anything to me at first.

Then I heard her think *You do not have complete control of your thoughts yet, but you have made a good start! I only caught parts of that. She is very lucky to have found you! Not just because you can hear me. Because you really do love her! She loves you too, very much. I know. We have talked about you. We were not sure of her choice at first, but she had the right to choose her mate. But the fact that you can hear me might be one of the reasons she chose you. Why would that matter?* I thought now wondering *why did she choose me?* Darshita caught my thought and replied *You don't believe you are worthy of her? Jakool. No one truly feels worthy when they need to be with someone so bad it hurts to be apart from them.* I was shocked to hear how I felt through Darshita! *I thought no one felt like me. No one in my tribe anyway. Maybe, Maybe not. I cannot hear their thoughts, just yours.*

You are disappointed that I am the only one who can hear you? Yes I am! was the thought

I heard and the sadness too. *This ability of mine and others has saved our entire tribe many times! When it first happened in our tribe we looked at all the mating's trying to find out if there was any connection between the bloodlines and having this!* Darshita didn't have to think the rest, as I thought *hearing thoughts was much clearer and easier than their words. Yes, Jakool it is! We have become very good at improving ourselves by being careful to mate bloodlines together and increase our strengths and our weaknesses! This is a very special strength that gives us something no one else has!*

This is the main way we have kept ourselves secret from the Krieg and others who would hunt, harm, and kill us! All of the scouts have some of this ability. Janai and Lasaa can sense an enemy! They don't have to see them, they can somehow tell one is near! Janai gets flashes of what is about to happen, 'before it happens! Do you mean she sees the future? I thought shocked as this seemed like something only a spirit or god could do!

Darshita replied with some frustration and irritation as she could see my thoughts! *We are not spirits or gods Jakool! You should know that by now! You have seen us bleed and die! You have seen us in battle and in sorrow at the loss of our brothers and sisters. You have seen our kindness to you and your entire tribe and our fair treatment of all. Yes, but seeing what is about to happen? Why didn't she prevent the attacks?"* I thought as I grasped at what I thought was proof that she could not do this! *Janai was with your group remember? Of course!* Then I remembered that it was Janai who had found the trail in the endless green grass with the fresh tracks. She was not with us when we followed the false trail that led to the ambush.

But she must have seen it about to happen because they all returned just in time to prevent our women, Elders, and children from being killed! All of this took only a second or two to remember and think to each other as my own thoughts provided proof that Janai did have this ability! *Remember I said that she works with Lasaa? They seem to boost each other's abilities when together. He senses danger nearby while she receives a vision? Showing what is about to happen. This would be a very powerful ability in keeping yourselves hidden"* I had to admit. *But you said you were 'trying' to find a connection in the bloodlines to these abilities? You have not found one?* Darshita gave me a mental sigh and thought *No. I can tell you the mating of each bloodline that any special ability has appeared in and the year. I can tell you if that ability stayed, disappeared, and reappeared. But I cannot tell you how or why it happens. I can find nothing that we can use to cause this ability to happen more often in our cubs!*

I sensed something and realized it was thoughts Darshita was not sending to me but keeping private. I wondered as I remembered her saying earlier that we would mate in the future. I also remembered Janai telling me the same thing! *Why do I have to mate with you and Janai? There is some reason you are not telling me or thinking to me.*

Darshita showed her surprise in her face but not her thoughts. *I thought I had hidden that well. You just demonstrated another reason that we need to mate with you! You have the same ability as me and it is getting stronger as you use it. 'IF' we mate there is a chance that our abilities will somehow combine and pass on to the cubs. If it does it will be much stronger and might happen more often. The same would be true of Janai and the others who have such abilities.* I thought of Samalaa and Elassa and thought *them too?* Darshita replied "*Elassa no, Samalaa Yes but for a different purpose. While she does not have such abilities as me, Janai, Lasaa, and others, she does have the bloodlines of both the first man and the first snow-leaper female cub of the first that came back and mated with him. We have seen that mating different members of the first bloodlines can be done only so many times before the bloodline starts to weaken. Then an outsider with no blood connections must mate with them to strengthen the bloodlines again.* I saw now what Darshita, Mearoo, Janai, and Merkansoo had been trying to explain to me and my tribe.

You mate with your own parents? Cubs? Sometimes. Not always. We keep very careful records of all matings so we know exactly how much of each bloodline is in each mating and the cubs produced by it. Before we started doing this there were many cubs born dead. Others had health problems or died very young. It took a long time before my ancestors realized that you can only mate with the same bloodline so many times before such problems would happen. So while we mate with members of our own blood, it is done according to the records of our bloodlines. This way we have not only stopped such deaths and health problems, we have greatly improved ourselves and given ourselves abilities that we had no knowledge of before they appeared. I understand much better now why it is so important for me and my tribe to mate with many of you. Darshita appeared grateful for me thinking this but still held me tight to her vibrant body. *Um-mm Darshita?* I thought hesitantly not wanting to refuse her if she did wish to mate with me.

Darshita gave me a slow smile and then just as slowly released me from the embrace. *Touching someone like this makes it much easier to send and receive through Jakool. Though I am honored that you now understand why we need you and others to accept mating with many of us. I do now Darshita, just not while Mearoo is with cubs. This is what Merkansoo and you promised me and her. Yes, and it will be honored for both of you Jakool. We keep our word.* She turned to show the private matter was finished and we returned to the camp. I sought out Mearoo and instead of telling her, I thought about everything that she shared with me! Mearoo was very surprised as it was the most carefully guarded secret they had! *I understand why she did. Since you can receive and read thoughts it is even more important that you mate with her and the others Jakool. Do not worry about me. I will be fine with it. Just think! Our cubs might have this ability too!*

The idea did give both her and me some joy at believing our children might be 'special' in some way. I did not realize until many years later that 'all' parents hope and believe their children are 'special' in some way! I can say that mine have all been special to me and Mearoo! So are my children from all the other snow-leaper women I have mated with!

We went to see Merack, Merkansoo, and the rest of the Elders of both tribes as they had called us to a meeting. We needed to decide when we would be able to leave and where to go. Merkansoo started the meeting by thanking all of us for killing so many of the Krieg. This was met with cheers from everyone including me! He then said we needed to discuss which of their villages we should go to. I had thought we would go to the closest, but that was not what he had in mind! "We have two problems now. The Krieg have been beaten badly by us. They will come out of their hiding places in a rage for revenge! There is no greater insult to them than to be defeated or killed by their sworn enemies! Us! I know this from my own memories of what happened before when we fought. It happened the first time, the second time, and the third! This will be the fourth! I want to make it the last one!" While everyone else was cheering I was trying to understand what made me feel uneasy when he said he wanted to kill all of them! I was not listening as they started discussing the different villages, the trails they would have to take, how long it would take, and what they could expect to find there. The feeling of unease was quickly changing to one of fear! *What is wrong with wanting them all dead?* I thought as I continued to search my mind for the source of my unease and now fear!

I was only barely aware when Merack asked "How many snow-leaper that can fight are there?" It was a good question to ask and have the answer to if you are planning to kill an entire tribe! *That is it!* I suddenly realized what I was afraid of. I had to speak! "Merkansoo? If you were unable to defeat the Krieg three times why do you believe we can defeat them now?" I waited for him to answer me. He looked at me showing a little irritation then said "Because we are much larger and stronger now. As people and as a tribe. We have over two thousand men and women that can fight. They know 'how' to fight!" I quickly said, "How many Krieg are there?" I now had his; and everyone else attention. "This plan to leave all that cannot fight up in the cloud stabber villages sounds good until you think about what could go wrong. We do not know how many fighters the Krieg have, or where they will be coming from! We do not know how many villages they have or where they are!

We cannot just come down out of the cloud stabbers looking for the Krieg! They will be told this by the other tribes that either fear them or agree with them! They are not the only tribe that has made us their enemies and I am sure the same is true for you." This gave everyone something to think about!

It was Merack who said "We should consider his words. They ring true to me." Suddenly I saw Larkar slowly come over and stand beside me facing Merkansoo. "I once made you vow you would help kill all the Krieg. You told me you would. We have killed more Krieg in the last hand and three days than our tribe has ever killed. I do not know how many you have killed this time, but what if they keep coming back just as many and just as strong?" The fact that it was Larkar saying these words was a little frightening. "I went crazy with my loss and my hate. Revenge seemed like the only thing I had left to live for. I was wrong. Now that we have joined our tribes and I almost died blindly chasing them when they appeared, I now see that to do that is not just stupid! OUR ENEMY WILL USE IT AGAINST US!" He spoke the words loudly giving them more weight. Merkansoo said "I am not saying we should blindly come down to hunt them! I am saying that I believe we are now able to defeat them once and for all!" I jumped as I said "By killing all of them? The women, children, and the Elders left in the camps and villages? I will not do this thing! I will attack and kill any who attack, ambush, or try to harm any of us! To try and kill all of them is to be like them! This is why we hate them so much!"

Everyone was silent as they thought about my words! Larkar turned to me and said "Thank you Jakool. I will try to remember this too!" "Yes but will Merkansoo and his people?" I asked him very worried about what might happen if we disagreed on this! I watched Merkansoo as he stood there silently thinking about everything that was said. I saw many things go across his face 'anger' gave way to 'upset' to silent 'thinking'. Suddenly I saw his expression change and he jerked his head up slightly with his eyes opening wider. I wondered what was *happening to him?* as he stayed silent. I noticed that Darshita was standing close to him. She usually was when they were together as they were mates. Then I remembered Darshita telling me that physical contact makes sending and receiving thoughts easier. I looked again and noticed that she had her right paw on his shoulder! *She is speaking to him in his mind!* I realized as the silent talk continued for a few more seconds.

Then Merkansoo looked right at me and said "We will discuss this further another time. Right now we need to get ready to leave. If we go to the village in the west it will take us two weeks of hard travel. Three if too many suffer from the breathing sickness. Gaieaa spoke up saying "We believe we have some treatments that we want all of our tribe to start taking. They consist of plants, roots, herbs, and other things we know to open up the throat and lungs. We know these work as we have used them successfully. I have spoken to all the healers of your people and found out something else. You still lose some young ones to the breathing sickness yes? Why?" This got Merkansoo, Darshita's and everyone's attention! "I do not understand why you are not treating them as soon as you see them having trouble breathing! I am told that you believe it is more important for them to 'learn' to breathe the thinner air? This is wrong. You might as well expect me to suddenly jump up and drag you off to mate!" This got several guffaws and laughs as Gaieaa felt she was much too old to mate with anyone! "I am trying to tell you that if you treat everyone as 'if' they have the breathing sickness there will be fewer that have it!" She stopped speaking and folded her thin arms over her chest waiting for someone to answer her question.

Finally, Darshita said "I can see that we too have to learn new things Gaieaa. I am as much at fault as Merkansoo, as he follows my advice on healing practices. We are willing to give your treatments a try with our newborns and young that show the signs of the breathing sickness to see if it helps." Merkansoo smiled and said, "Thank you Gaieaa for reminding me, us, that you have as much to add to our knowledge as we do to yours." I softly said "I wish we could all read minds. This would be so much easier!" I was startled to see Merkansoo look at me along with Darshita, Janai, and Mearoo. But Mearoo was standing next to me so she probably just heard my words I thought at the time. I stayed quiet as Merkansoo said, "When can we leave?"

He looked at Merack for an answer to this question. Merack said "Tomorrow Early. If we do not have everything done by then, it can be done on the journey." Merkansoo was happy to hear this as was I. Mearoo gave Darshita a strange look and then said "I need to speak with Darshita and Merkansoo. Why don't you help pack?" She turned without our customary touching or kissing! I was a little surprised but was soon busy to think about it. Bamal came and said, "I need you to help me and Larkar with something."

I followed him to where we had been working on the snow foot, spears, and other tools and weapons made of wood. Larkar was there with Kaga and Denali. Larkar greeted me with "Jakool! I am glad you came. I have an idea. He was holding one of the sections of the hollow trees we used to make the poles for the shelters. "I was looking over these when I noticed something. You see how each piece is separated by the solid parts at the joints?" I nodded as he pointed at one. "What if you could drill this out? Make it open at each end?" I was puzzled as I did not see how that would help make it stronger. I said "It would make it weaker. The solid parts give it strength and keep it from bending too much."

Larkar nodded then said, "Watch this." He picked up a different one that did have the solid ends drilled out. He took a sharp sliver of wood that had some small petals from a flower tied to the rounded end and put it in the hollow piece. He drew in his breath and blew through it! I heard a 'thunk' sound and turned to see the sliver sticking into a hidden shelter. I went over to get it and saw that it had gone through the hide and was only stopped by the flower petals! "That is very interesting!" I said as I pulled it out and returned it to Larkar. Kaga said "I drilled out the two ends but we want to find a way to drill out several sections. This would make a longer tube and we think it will give the needle more accuracy and distance." I nodded as I thought about the problem. Larkar said "We tried to use the drills we have but none of them is either long enough or small enough at the same time. "Hmm.." I said as I thought about the problem. I took a piece we used for the pole and looked at it.

It had six to eight sections which were about the same size in length. I remembered that they were bigger around the ground and got thinner at the top as they grew. I asked "Can we burn them out? We do this to make bowls and other wood objects instead of scraping out the wood?" Kaga asked "How would you set fire to only the solid part?? I wondered as I stood up and took it over to the campfire. I kept looking at the long piece of thin tree and then at the fire and the wood in it. I watched the fire burn down as we would be leaving in the morning, so we were going to let the campfire go out. I watched the burning embers become smaller and smaller as they slowly burned out. I had an idea! "Kaga? Is there a way to hold embers?" Surprising all of them! Kaga thought about it and replied, "You think we can burn out the solid parts with embers?"

"Yes. If we can get the embers into the hollow part of the thicker sections, it might burn through the solid part before it burns through the outside." Kaga made a noise in his throat as he considered my idea. He replied "If we get the hollow part wet first, it might help keep it from burning. We can pick up the the smaller embers with a scraping tool, and then put them into the hollow ends. We would drill out the ends first of course." "Of course". I said then added,

Larkar, Bamal, and Denala followed our ideas on how to do this. Bamal grabbed a scrapping tool from the different ones we used to make different shapes. We tried several until we found one that worked. Bamal got the embers, while Larkar brought large wet green leaves he had cut from a nearby bush. He wet them with a water skin first, then wrapped them around the long piece of hollow tube. Once he had done that I put two stones against the sides of the piece to hold it standing with one hollow end pointing up. This way Kaga could pour the embers into it without burning anyone's hands who were trying to hold it. It was not a success the first time. It did burn out the first solid it came to, but it also burned out the inside wall at the second solid. We looked at it after cutting it open to see what happened. "The second one is thicker." "The wall is too." Why did it burn through then?" We commented back and forth to each other as we tried to figure out what to do next. Larkar said "Maybe put it in water? Standing up in the shallow part of the stream sticking in the bottom?" I looked at him then smiled and said: "Let's try that!" We picked up enough embers to stay hot then went to the nearby stream.

We did as Larkar suggested and watched. The embers did burn through more of the sections but not all of them. "Turn it over. Now burn it from the other end!" I finally said after we counted how many it had burned and I saw that it had burned more than half! This time it worked! All the solid parts were burned through, leaving it hollow with blackened burnt sides inside! "Hmm mm," I said as I tried to blow through it. Some air did come out the other end but not all of it. "There must be small pieces of the solid parts left to block the air. Try it again." We did it a second time and it worked better. Larkar held it up and looked through it saying "There are still burnt pieces that make the inside rough. We need to clean it out somehow." Denala smiled and said, "Give it to me!" Larkar handed the tube to him and Denala looked through it. He then took one of the thin spears he made for hunting small prey, like the big ears or even birds! He carefully pushed the fire-hardened tip into the tube while turning it back and forth. We watched as burnt pieces of the wood started coming out of the other end! He cleaned out all the burnt wood from inside, letting all the air go through the tube. We had to use a bigger needle of wood with bigger flower petals or leaves, as the tube was bigger inside than the one Larkar had used. Finally, we were ready and I handed it to Larkar. We returned to where he had demonstrated the short one and did it again. This time the needle went all the way through the hide wall of the shelter and through the next one too!. Larkar turned and walked back four hands steps and blew again! This time it went through the first but stuck in the second. He backed up another four hands of paces and blew again! It stuck in the first wall with the leaves we used still sticking out.

I walked from the shelter to Larkar counting out loud eight hands, nine hands, ten hands! I was very excited by the distance! "This is further than we can throw our spears except when we use the throwing sticks," I said. Larkar grinned and said "It is silent. You don't hear it until it has struck!" I smiled as I realized just how deadly that made it! "You could be hidden up in the trees or behind them or bushes and still stick this out enough to use it to hit someone ten hands away! They would not be able to tell where it came from!" I said excitedly. Bamal added, "Everyone including the children could use this to defend and attack." I nodded as strength was not needed to use it! Anyone who could breathe could use it to deliver a deadly needle into an enemy. We should demonstrate this to the rest." I said and all agreed.

We took it to where Merack, Pathak, Merkansoo, Darshita, Mearoo, Samalaa, Janai, and Lasaa were planning out the trails to take. When Larkar blew the needle over ten hands of paces into a packed carrier they were impressed. When he handed it to Gaieaa and told her to try it, everyone was shocked when the needle went almost as far as Larkar's! Gaieaa said "We need to gather more of the thin trees during the journey and make as many of these as we can. The needles are easy. In fact, we can gather the hard needles from the stick tree." I knew the tree she named. It had long sharp needles growing out of the trunk all around it. They would be the perfect needles for the 'blow tube' as we were calling it. Instead of using flowers or leaves, Nada came up with using the gum from the stick tree to simply stick the feathers from birds we caught onto the needles. This made them even more accurate and flew even further! We experimented with the long, medium, and shot ones and found that the children did better with the short ones, most of the younger hunters, women, and Elders with the Medium, and the rest, and the snow-leapers with the long ones.

Merkansoo finished the meeting on the route to take and came over to us. "I need to ask all of your people something. You must understand 'what' I am asking you to do. I was as curious as everyone else, as we all gathered around the dying campfire to hear what Merkansoo needed to ask us." Now that everyone is here I need to tell you about a different threat. Not to us or to you here or where we are going to take you. Samalaa spotted something very strange about a week ago. It was one of our signals coming from a cloud stabber we do not live on or go to. She wasn't sure so she asked Mearoo and Janai to confirm what she saw. They also saw it moving down the cloud stabber. They thought that it might be Meh Tey carrying one of the crystals we used to signal with. They are fairly common in certain places in the cloud stabbers, but we did not believe they were intelligent enough to use one. We were wrong. A large group of Meh Tey are moving down the cloud stabber. At the foot of that cloud stabber are the villages of a peaceful tribe that came here a very long time ago. Long before you or the Krieg came to this place. They appear to be much like the First in looks and abilities. We met them while exploring the cloud stabbers for safe places to live and resources. We found the Meh Tey living high up in the cloud stabbers. We thought they were another 'Old One; as you call them, that had not mixed with any others. But they were not like any men we had met. They are very big, strong, brutal killers that don't know how to use anything but what they can pick up and use as a club.

They do not use fire or any other tools as far as we have seen. They usually live alone or in small groups in caves high up the cloud stabbers. But when they do come down the cloud stabbers it is to kill! They attack anyone and anything they find. The reason I am telling you this is because there is a tribe at the bottom of the cloud stabber they are coming down. It is helpless to stop them. We are not. My closest people are already moving to stop them. I am telling you this because we are the closest ones to them. They will need help and healing afterward. You have shown us healing we did not know. I am asking that a group of you go with us to help them." *Oh!* I thought in surprise at 'what' he asked us to do!

Merack simply asked, "How far and how many will you need?" I was glad that Merack answered him so quickly! So was Merkansoo as he had a big smile now. "We will carry you and it will take us four suns of hard travel. Paasi? Do you think you could do this?" Paasi looked thoughtful for a moment then nodded. Nada spoke, "Don't forget me!" Merkansoo replied "Thank you! Both of you!" Gaieaa looked troubled by this for some reason. I wondered if she thought she could ride a snow leaper for four suns. Gaieaa seemed to have come to a decision and said loudly "I am coming too". No one was more surprised by this than Pathak! He had such a look of surprise it was funny! I started to laugh and then everyone was laughing and pointing at him. His mouth was as wide open as it could get, showing his yellowed, stained teeth; at least the ones he still had, his eyes were wide open and practically sticking out of his head!

Gaieaa thought everyone was pointing and laughing at her until Nada turned her so she saw Pathak. Gaieaa had to laugh too! I stopped laughing when I realized how serious she was and when I looked at Merkansoo I could see he was considering her offer! "How do you think you would get there?" I said loudly so she would realize it was not a practical offer. But Darshita stepped over to Merkansoo and they had a spirited conversation which I could not hear over the noise around me. By the time I could move closer, it was over and Darshita went over to Gaieaa and said something to her. Gaieaa was grinning as she listened and nodded vigorously to Darshita. Merkansoo then said, "I would like Jakool, Bamal, Kaga, Mahendra, Hanuman, and Jarack to also come with us." I looked at Merkansoo and someone in my mind said *He needs you for something else.* I nodded my answer and turned to Mearoo and said quietly "Do you know why he wants me to go?" Mearoo looked down briefly which meant she didn't want to meet my eyes. "Mearoo?" I asked needing to know what she knew.

Mearoo looked at me and said quietly "You are needed because you can send and receive thought. This is a vital thing on such a dangerous mission. You can save lives Jakool." I heard her words but also heard her give emphasis to 'You'. "Me? You are not coming with us?" I asked her. "No Jakool. I cannot read minds and I should not go on this. It would be very bad for the cubs if anything was to happen." I did see the truth in this and nodded. I realized that it would be the first time we would be apart since our mating for more than a few suns!

I felt my apprehension at this but put it down to my fear for her and the cubs and me not being there with her to help and protect her. *Protect her?* I thought as we went off to find out how Gaieaa was going to make the journey. *She doesn't need my protection!* I thought to myself as I remembered how many times she had already saved my life, us fighting together side by side in the gorge and killing all in our path! We found Gaieaa with Darshita, Samalaa, and Merkansoo in a heated discussion with Pathak. "I don't care! She should not go! It will kill her! She had too much our our wisdom and knowledge to lose on a mission to save others we don't even know!" Pathak said as we reached them. Gaieaa was ready to clobber him with a wooden bowl she used to crush seeds and herbs in for the healing mixtures she made.

Darshita thought It was very funny and was having trouble controlling her laughter! Merack was standing between Pathak and Gaieaa to prevent them from doing more than just yelling at each other. Gaieaa said to him "You old fool! You know as much as I do! Why do you think we have been making all these records? So that when I am dead we do not lose any of it!" I had to admit she was right. Merkansoo looked as if this was a waste of time and was about ready to tell them so. I tried to divert him by asking "How will Gaieaa come with us?" Merkansoo glanced at me and replied "Darshita and Jarack will carry her. Not on there backs but on a carrier that sits between them. This way Gaieaa cannot fall off the sides. They will put her supplies tied down behind her so she can sit against them."

I thought this might work as Gaieaa would need to have something to help her sit upright for that long a journey. I added "You should tie a spear across the carrier in front of her so she can hold onto it. It will help her keep her balance and make the ride easier on her." Merkansoo raised an eyebrow at me then said "Yes. That is a good idea Jakool. Darshita?" I will do it now Merkansoo!" Darshita said giving me a smile as she turned and went to where Samalaa was working on the special carrier for Gaieaa.

I got Merkansoo's attention by saying "Should we take Larkar with us?" Merkansoo looked at me and then slowly said "I am not sure. Come with me and we can talk about this." Merkansoo led me away from the still-arguing Elders to where the many trees started. He turned and said, "I can hear you when you are that close to me." *I thought so!* I thought as this explained much about his words and actions lately. *Why do you really want me to come with you?* I thought as I wanted to know the truth.

Because you can send and receive thoughts. Because you are quick, clever, a good leader, a fighter, and a good healer. We will need all of these things to succeed. I grinned then replied *I was beginning to believe that it was to separate me from Mearoo so Darshita or Samalaa or both would be able to mate with me!* Merkansoo grinned while replying, *I promised Mearoo and you that we would not ask you until after your cubs were born, remember?* Reminding me. *I know. But since then Janai, Darshita, and Elassa have all said they want to mate with me! Darshita told me a lot of things about the bloodlines and how you have improved yourselves and tried to pass on this ability to send and receive thoughts.* Merkansoo repeated *Yes, but not until after your cubs are born. Once they are born you will be glad to get away occasionally, believe me!* I had to as he was thinking about it!

He also let me see his thoughts that contained his memories of not getting enough sleep with five cubs wanting to be fed every few hours, having to hunt for Darshita and the cubs, and having to help her with them when they started to become curious and could leave the cave. He showed me some funny things that they did too. But the one I remember best is the one where he was ambushed by all five cubs while he was sleeping! Cubs were biting and clawing his tail, nose, and back! I had to laugh at his funny way of stopping them! He growled and swatted them off his back then flipped over and started throwing them up in the air and catching them with his paws or mouth! He looked like he was juggling them as they squealed and protested at being kept from attacking him! *But it is worth the loss of sleep and the amount of time and energy it takes to raise Jakool. I am very proud of our cubs. All of them. I can see that. I hope I am as good a father as you Merkansoo.* He smiled but didn't say anything as we returned to the Elders with the argument settled and Gaieaa packing her healing supplies with Nada helping.

Before we were ready to leave we had another matter to decide. Nimi came to us to say that he and a few of the remaining men wanted to join us! "Nimi we thank you for the offer. All of the ones chosen to go have healing skills and some other skills that will be needed. Do you have any of these skills? Nimi looked a little less certain as he answered "I am not a healer, but Esta my mate is! She is the best healer we have! You have seen me fight! You will not be sorry to have us join you!"

I looked at Merkansoo and then felt his thought *I am concerned about so few of his tribe being left. We should make them the same offer as we made yours.* I silently thought *Yes. He and his tribe have already proven their worth.* With both of us in agreement, Merkansoo said "You are welcome to choose any among your people that can heal or fight. But remember we are not going to fight. We are going to help both my tribe and the Ooh-mans after the Meh Tey have been dealt with by them." Nimi squared his shoulders and stood tall as he said "I will choose the best at both immediately!" He turned and went back to his own tribe and we heard the excitement in their voices as Nimi told them he had argued for them to join us on this dangerous mission and we had agreed! I said to Merkansoo and Merack "We might as well make them part of this tribe!" Merack said "Of course! They have proven themselves to all of us!"

We three went over to Nimi. Merkansoo and Merack made the offer as the Leaders of our tribe. Nimi couldn't contain himself when he realized we were 'asking' his whole tribe to join ours! He turned and said loudly to his tribe "Do you hear them? They want 'us' to join them! To be part of their tribe and travel with them into the cloud stabbers! Do we want this?" There was a brief silence in which I later swore I could hear every one of them drawing in breath then a loud shout of "WE DO!" rang out! I had to laugh at the displays of joy and happiness Nimi's people put on until Merack and Merkansoo got them to quiet down as we needed to know how many were coming with the group so there would be enough snow-leaper to carry them! Fortunately, they were so small and light, that one of the snow-leaper could easily carry two of them.

So we spent the rest of that sun making sure both groups were ready to travel as quickly as possible. The group going to the aid of group that went to stop the Meh Tey attack on the human settlement ended up being larger than Merkansoo believed it should be. So he and Merack went over them again and left behind some that would be just as useful to the main tribe. Finally, we were ready to leave the main group as we would be going in a different direction to reach the western cloud stabber quickly.

I said a painful goodbye to Mearoo and realized that she was even more upset than I, was but was resigned to our separation. "I will come back to you Mearoo! I swear this to you before all of the tribe and the spirits!" She smiled away her tears long enough to answer me "You better Jakool! I am counting on you being a father to our cubs!" I swallowed the hard lump in my throat as I turned and mounted Samalaa. She turned to face Mearoo and said "I will keep him safe for you Mearoo. We all will." She nodded and also swallowed hard as we turned then jumped away to take our place in the group. We left them knowing that they would be leaving at first light, taking a direct path to the cloud stabber of the villages that had provided the fighters that went to face the Meh Tey. If things went well, we would be able to meet up with them at these villages later. If not, then she would be safe with her people and mine.

THE END OF BOOK ONE

Printed in the United States
by Baker & Taylor Publisher Services